# HAULER

# Hauler

**ERIC KRUGER**

Space Monkey Press

Cover Illustration - Bryan Vectorartist
Editor - Katherine Kirk

First Printing, 2020

# | one |

Benjamin Drake looked at his reflection in the puddle of oil and water, disfigured and colorful at the same time. The neon lights gave it some extra life, and the trucks made sure the ripples never went away. What the fuck was he going to do now? He had little to no hydrogen left in his vehicle, and his food would soon run out. Tonight's job would have seen him through till at least next month, but that slimy Sammy Sanders had slithered his way in before Drake could and was now halfway down the road already. If only he hadn't stopped at that motel last night, and hadn't gone to that bar, and hadn't spent most of his credits buying drinks for a girl he never met, and hadn't taken her back to his truck, and hadn't missed his alarm in the morning, he would have been on time to get the contract. He was indeed his own worst enemy.

"Where the hell were you?" Bob Turner, the proud owner of this cockroach-infested truck depot, asked Drake.

Drake stared at the enormous man filling the doorway. Best to choose your words carefully, he reminded himself. Many a trucker around here had had a bone or two snapped by Bob Turner if the tone was not to his liking.

"I . . . I just fucked up, Mr. Turner."

"That you did, you fucking idiot," Turner said.

"Would have been a good haul, from what I hear," Drake replied sheepishly.

"Well, that was the last job I had for this week," Turner said, walking back to his desk. If it was any other hauler, the conversation would have been done, but as he sat down, he said: "Come back next week, and I'll see if I have something for you."

For some reason, Mr. Turner always went soft on Drake, and Drake knew better than to bite the hand that fed him and question Turner's motives. Every hauler who dealt with Mr. Turner knew he had a soft spot for Drake, but soft for Turner was still pretty hard.

"Thanks, Mr. Turner. I'll see you next week then," Drake said, hating himself for being so spineless; another body part Mr. Turner had probably broken in the past.

Bob Turner stepped back into his office and slammed the door shut. Assuming that the conversation was over, Drake started to walk back to his truck. The old Hydrostar was sitting alone in the yard since all the other haulers had left by now. Contracts completed or new ones just received. Drake pushed his sleeve back and unlocked the truck with his HIC. It took him two attempts since his Human Interface Console was still a second-generation model and was starting to play up. Unlike his older model, which was implanted under the skin to minimize the intrusiveness of the device and the installation, the newer models required a strip of skin to be cut out and replaced by the HIC itself. They were much brighter and more responsive. Drake knew he needed to upgrade eventually but kept putting it off.

Once inside the Hydrostar's cabin, he got in the driver's seat, flipped the engine switches on, and after hearing the engine whirr into action, drove off, looking for a quiet spot to call home for the night.

The Hydrostar was well equipped, and Drake was happy to spend most of his time inside her cabin. Behind the seats was a small eight-foot aisle, with a single Murphy bed mounted high against the one wall, and a kitchenette underneath it. On the opposite wall were a storage compartment and a small chair and table with an outdated but functioning Data Display Unit. Against the back wall, at the end of the short aisle, was a skinny door that led to the cramped shower and toilet space. Drake spent most of his time inside the Hydrostar, either driving it from one job to the next or sleeping and eating in it. Between contracts, he preferred to find a motel and stretch out a bit, but missing out on this haul meant he'd have to stay put inside the small cabin for a few more days.

Drake drove around for a bit until he found a quiet, dark, and seemingly abandoned alley. He carefully backed the Hydrostar into the spot and flipped the engine off. Drake scrambled to the back and flipped on the DDU. It seemed the unit took longer and longer to load every time he switched it on. Finally, the menu appeared, and he selected the jobs folder on the screen. A new screen appeared with different job listings, from small packages to full truckloads of freight to be taken from one point to another. He scanned the listings but found nothing in his immediate area. If he risked driving to another city, he would use up all his remaining hydrogen and really be screwed if he didn't get a job. The safest would be to wait and hope Mr. Turner came up with something soon. Drake pulled his sleeve back on his arm and swiped his finger over his skin. The green light from his Human Interface Console shone through the skin and became visible. He swiped the screen that was now glowing through his skin and checked his credit level. The number was devastatingly low but was still enough for a couple of drinks at a cheap and nasty bar. Drake decided that was precisely what he was going to do.

***

The first bar he came to seemed to fit his low criteria and expectations. Old beat up hydrocars and some hydrocycles sat in the front. What the facade was missing in upkeep it made up for in neon lights—Live Music, Cold Beer, Girls Girls Girls. Drake stepped through the swing doors, and a familiar smell of spilled beer, missed showers, and fried food greeted him. The counter was placed on the left and seemed to be pretty busy. In front of him were some tables, and to the right, a band was setting up their equipment on a small stage, which he knew from experience doubled up as the stage for the advertised Girls Girls Girls. He went over to the bar counter and grabbed one of the last remaining chairs.

"ID, please," the bartender said automatically.

Drake rolled up his sleeve, and the bartender scanned his HIC. Drake had no outstanding warrants, but even if he had, he was sure the barkeeper would suddenly have a malfunctioning scanner. This didn't seem like the place to follow through on all the laws. Seemingly satisfied, the bartender said, "So, what will it be?"

"Your cheapest and coldest, please," Drake said.

The golden liquid flowed into a glass and left a nice white head of foam on top. The bartender put the glass down in front of Drake and scanned his arm, deducting the credits from Drake's ever-dwindling account.

"Cheers!" Drake said and drank half in one gulp.

A connoisseur or even your average Joe on the street would have gagged and spat the horrendous bile out of their mouths, demanding a refund, but Drake was used to the lesser quality of the unmarked taps that he had been drinking from a young age. Nestem made two varieties of beer, one very expensive and one just expensive. Both tasted precisely the same to Drake. Luckily, most bars also had an unmarked tap that was either brewed in the back somewhere or, most likely, some expired or contaminated Nestem Beer they got cheap on the black market. For the price, very few questions were asked.

"Not the worst I ever had," he said to no one in particular, and no one in particular cared.

Drake swiveled on his chair, propped his elbows on the worn-out bar, and started to scan the faces around him. This was done more out of instinct and survival than hoping to run across a friendly face. Work was scarce; people were desperate, and most of them hung out in dumps like this. Every town he went to was the same. Desperate people drinking their last credits away, just trying to escape. Hell, he was one of them.

A familiar face from across the room locked eyes with Drake.

"Shit," Drake muttered to himself as he recognized the rat-like face of Jimmy Something.

Jimmy's last name was from an unknown heritage and unpronounceable to every single person. His lisp didn't help clarify the matter either, so he became Jimmy Something by default. Jimmy was the opposite of Bob Turner: sneaky, undermining, and never to be trusted. Best avoided at all times. But that was too late now, as he lifted his glass and nodded to Drake.

"Hey dickhead," Drake muttered back, raising his glass.

That was all the invitation that Jimmy needed, as he stood and walked straight to Drake. Drake still had half a glass of beer to drink and was not planning on wasting it, so he stayed put and braced himself.

"I asked myself, 'Isn't that Benjamin Drake, the man himself?' And what do ya know, I was right!" Jimmy sprayed the words out.

Drake had moved his beer out of spitting range the moment Jimmy opened his mouth.

"Hey, Jimmy. What's up?" Drake asked, already dreading not abandoning his beer.

"Not much. Not much. Just killing it, ya know. Actually been really busy, ya know?" Jimmy said, clearly trying to engage Drake.

Drake knew he should keep his mouth shut, so he just started drinking his beer again. It didn't work.

"Yup, got a massive contract lined up, ya know. Just need to get the right kind of people involved. Like-minded folks, ya know?" Jimmy took a sip of his beer, lubricating up a system that was already saturated.

Drake kept his cool, and just nodded, not making eye contact, just staring ahead into space, wishing Jimmy away.

"Just gotta find a hauler, and we're good to go," Jimmy said as he shuffled into Drake's eyeline and took another sip of his beer.

Drake knew precisely what Jimmy was doing. All he had to do was say nothing, finish his beer and find another bar. Jimmy Something was nothing but trouble, and Drake had no intention of getting better acquainted with him.

"Yup, the lucky bastard will get fifty thousand credits just for one haul, ya know. Not bad, huh?" Jimmy said.

Drake was about to take his last sip but stopped, glass mid-air, as if time had been suspended. Fifty thousand credits were what he made in a year if he was lucky. No job paid this much unless it was strictly off the books, no questions asked. Drake was no angel and had done his fair share of no-questions-asked contracts before but nothing even remotely in this pay range. Usually, it involved adding someone else's smaller delivery to another, paid contract, for a direct credit transfer, no contracts. Or turning a blind eye if the cargo was clearly not what was on the paperwork but still legal goods. But this had to involve some people that he made a habit of avoiding. People who made big promises and rarely delivered. People who worked outside the Haulernet. People like Jimmy Something but worse.

*Fifty thousand credits.*

Drake completed the glass's arc to his mouth, finished his drink, and said, "Good luck with that, Jimmy."

He got up and went straight back to his Hydrostar, his evening completely ruined.

# | two |

Benjamin Drake usually had no trouble falling asleep at night. All his sins and indiscretions were quickly forgotten and forgiven by him, and he rarely dwelled on the past. Best to look forward, he always thought—no use in beating yourself up over what's done. But tonight, he had fifty thousand reasons not to go to bed. The Hydrostar could do with a proper service, something he had been putting off for some time. Maybe even an upgrade or two. The Data Display Unit was about to go any day now, and he would be royally screwed if that happened. His old HIC did not have the power or software to run the full Haulernet system, so if his DDU was playing up, he could miss out on jobs. And if he had a truck full of hydrogen, he could grab any job, anywhere, for months. Fucking Jimmy Something. Why did Drake have to be at the same bar as him on the same night he missed a contract? Was it fate, or just the worst damn luck? Once you became associated with Jimmy Something, you were an outcast and had no choice but to slip deeper into the black market hauler world. Not that the usual hauler community was made up of saints and heroes, but at least most jobs had a high chance of being non–life-threatening. Drake decided the best way to get Jimmy Something out of his head was to pay Mr. Turner a visit in the morning and hopefully get a contract to keep him out of Jimmy's reach.

\*\*\*

Drake slept like a baby, a real baby—up every few minutes, going to the bathroom, or just rolling around. He woke up looking worse than when he went to bed. The mirror framed a face that looked forty but was still a few years short of that. His dark brown hair did not show too many gray hairs yet, but the dark circles around his puffy green eyes were not helping today. Drake considered having his weekly, which usually ended up being monthly shave but decided against it. Today was going to be a long one. The Hydrostar was so low on fuel he decided to walk back to Bob Turner's place. The sun was already out, and he could see it burning bright red behind the smog, trying to break through and warm up the planet again. But the smog kept its cool and ignored the sun, depriving the planet its warmth and bathing everything in an eerie yellow-brown glow.

Drake had lived most of his life in New Franco and guessed it was home, but he always looked forward to getting back on the road and leaving this overpopulated, broken down city behind. People flocked here from all over the Penta territories after being lured here by agents with promises of jobs and housing units. Only once they arrived did they find that those jobs were in dark, crowded factories, working side by side with robots, assembling anything and everything to do with killing people. Most of it was cleaning and maintaining the machines and robots on the assembly line. The housing units were hardly any better, with two or three other families usually sharing a one family unit. Everyone in New Franco came from somewhere else and wished they were still there.

Drake pulled his collar up, stuck his hands in his pockets, and started the journey to Bob Turner. The road was quiet, and only a handful of cars whirred past him. They kicked up some dust, and Drake had to cover his face every time they passed. Hopefully, he would be off the highway by the time rush hour started. Half an hour later, Drake turned off onto a smaller road, and within minutes he was standing in front of Bob Turner's door. He could hear noises coming from inside the office. Traffic was still light on the roads. Most people were still at home or using the Hyperloop, but Drake knew Bob Turner would be here, making sure he got a head start on procuring the day's haulage contracts before any of his competitors could. Drake also knew it meant he was busy and hated being held up, but it was worth the risk.

Drake took a deep breath and knocked on the door.

"What?" Bob Turner's voice bellowed.

The door stayed shut.

"Mr. Turner, it's Benjamin Drake. Just thought I'd see if anything came in overnight?" Drake said to the door.

He could still hear busy noises behind the door. He was wise enough to know not to open the door until being told to do so. He just stood there, listening to the noises from inside the office. One minute passed. Then two. Three, four, five minutes passed.

"Should I—" Drake started.

"Check your HIC." Bob Turner replied through the door.

Turner's voice was so loud and deep that he hardly ever had to yell to get his point across. Drake swiped his arm, knowing full well that he had not had a message alert come through since he woke up. He checked his messages anyway, just to make sure. Nothing.

"It looks like nothing has come through yet, Mr. Turner. Did you send me something just now? Could you maybe resend it?" Drake knew he was skating on very thin and fragile ice with a huge and heavy bear.

The office noises resumed. The minutes ticked past again. Drake knew he had just moved down a few notches on the Bob Turner pecking order. Maybe even all the way down. If he wanted to leave intact and in one piece, he had to go right now.

"Okay, then. I'll just check in again tomorrow, shall I?" Drake said. He heard a chair screeching and crashing violently against a wall, followed by stomping footsteps.

Before the door could open, Drake was already gone.

After running for about ten minutes, Drake slowed down. He looked behind him, to confirm he was not being chased down. Cars were now clogging up the roads, but none of them seemed to be heading toward him with ill intent. Drake dusted himself off. You bloody idiot, why can't you control your stupid mouth, he thought, and not for the first time. The same mouth that had gotten him out of countless bar fights, security fines and away from murderous boyfriends had also gotten him into a balanced and equal number of bar fights, increased fines and close to being murdered by jealous boyfriends. It was like his mouth was a perfect keeper of balance; for every tricky situation it gotten him out of, it also got him into an equal amount of trouble. Right now, it had gotten him into as much trouble as he could bear. Being on the wrong side of Bob Turner was suicide. Not real death type suicide, just you'll-never-haul-anything-ever-again suicide.

Drake started walking again, heading toward the Hydrostar and contemplating where to go from here. His best bet would be to go to a smaller town and pick something up, live day-to-day for a few weeks, and then come back again when the dust had settled. Give Mr. Turner some time to cool off. He didn't insult him or screw up a contract but knew it was best to stay clear for a while and make sure he was out of Mr. Turner's head. Surely he would forget this small annoyance in a few days, and then Drake could get back on his good side again. He knew it was best to err on the side of caution when dealing with Bob Turner. Many people had suffered for doing much less than he.

Drake was halfway back to the Hydrostar when the sound of tires crunching the ground behind him, accompanied by the soft whirr of a newer model car, made him stop. A black sedan with dark tinted windows came to a stop beside him. He stared at his dirty reflection in the window, confident it was not Mr. Turner's car but unsure of whose it was. The window slowly slid down, gradually replacing his dirty face with someone else's.

"Need a lift?" Jimmy Something asked.

Wise and successful people like to talk about defining moments in their lives where decisions lead to journeys that sculpt and create the person they became. A life-changing experience or a decision, which these great people then like to regale to an audience of admirers, who are seeking inspiration and guidance. A life lesson they can then use to better themselves and make better or braver choices in life.

Unfortunately, Drake had never heard of these wise people, so he jumped in the car with Jimmy Something, and they sped off.

"So? You in?" Jimmy asked the moment the door closed.

"In what?" Drake asked, annoyed that he leaped without thinking again.

"C'mon Drake. The haul of a lifetime, ya know?" Jimmy said, eyes filled with excitement.

"What exactly is the cargo?" Drake asked, knowing that whatever came out of Jimmy's mouth was most likely going to be a lie anyway.

"Not sure, ya know. I'm just the facilitator between my contact and the hauler. Most likely dodgy beer or something, ya know." Jimmy said, not making eye contact anymore.

Drake swiped his HIC—no new messages, therefore no new contracts. He was stuck between a rock and a hard place. Risk his life by pestering Bob Turner again, or shoot himself in the foot right now and take the contract from Jimmy Something. He knew that working with Jimmy would be a career-ending move. No one from the likes of Bob Turner would ever touch him again. He would be tainted, only good enough for the jobs no one else wanted. It was the wrong move, and he knew it. He also didn't want to starve to death.

Drake was ready to admit defeat, but Jimmy's look infuriated him. His eyes said he had him and that he knew it was a done deal. Drake knew he'd have to stifle his rising ego and get this done with, as quick and hopefully painless as possible. Jimmy smiled.

"Sorry, man, but you have the wrong guy," Drake heard himself say. "You can just drop me off on this corner."

Jimmy's smile faded, and Drake couldn't believe how satisfying it felt. Why did Jimmy bring out the worst in him?

"But, I thought . . ." Jimmy mumbled.

"Yeah, well, I can't risk being shunned by the whole hauler community for accepting a contract for a dodgy operator like you. No offense."

"So, it's about the credits?" Jimmy asked, apparently only hearing some selective words.

"Huh? What? No, it's about association. If I do this, I'm done doing legit work. You get that, right?"

Jimmy stopped the car and turned in his seat. Drake could see the hamster turning the wheel in his head, working overtime to get an idea together. Drake put his hand on the door handle, ready to get out.

"Okay, okay. I hear you, ya know. Guy offers you fifty large out of nowhere, there must be some more where that comes from, right? I'll have to check with my contact, but I'm sure we can bump that up to sixty."

When Jimmy pulled up, Drake had decided to get in the hydrocar, in part to get off the busy road, but also to tell Jimmy to stop bugging him. Mr. Turner always came up with the goods, and Drake knew he would give him a contract within days. Most likely something small to make a point but still enough to keep Drake alive. He just had to be patient and not panic by doing something stupid.

"A hundred and we got a deal," Drake said, knowing that Jimmy could not afford that sort of price and would have to let this go.

"Done!" Jimmy grabbed Drake's hand and shook it.

# | three |

The numbers rolled over, getting bigger and bigger. Filling up the Hydrostar was a costly exercise, but at least the hydrogen lasted a long time. That was one of the reasons Drake loved it so much. He'd bought the Hydrostar from Bob Turner ten years ago. Back then, Mr. Turner had a fleet of them, hauling all over the country. But the competition became stiffer, and Mr. Turner changed his business model and started only using contractors. Most of the fleet went to other companies, except for one. It had a few issues, and no one could bother to spend the credits on it. Drake had made Mr. Turner an offer, and surprisingly he took it. Drake spent six months working on the truck until it was as good as new. It was still outdated and lacked the speed and comforts of the more modern trucks, but it was reliable and very cheap to run. The Hydrostars were known for their fuel economy, which was why fleet owners loved them. Solo operators preferred the newer, faster Hydrocomets which allowed them to get more jobs done but at a higher operating cost.

Finally, the numbers stopped ticking over, and Drake pressed his forearm against the pump's screen. A message popped up, asking for the nine-digit passcode. Drake stared at the screen. He shivered, and his palms became clammy. Once he typed in the code, he would pass the point of no return. After this, he was done completing regular contracts for regular people. He realized he was fooling himself, thinking he still had a choice, especially after just filling up his truck. Drake swiped his arm and opened a message. *Here is the code to use for filling your truck, as agreed. You drive a hard bargain, Drake!* After the message, the code and the sender's name appeared—Jimmy Something. Drake swallowed hard and keyed in the code.

As Drake got back in the cab, he received a call on his HIC—Jimmy Something. He knew he could not ignore it, so he connected via the truck's DDU. Jimmy's face appeared on his windshield.

"Hey, partner! Just saw you used the credit code. Are you heading over to the pick up now?"

"Yes," Drake replied, trying to keep his time with Jimmy short.

"Cool, man! Well, let me know how it goes, ya know, and I'll catch up soon, okay?" Jimmy said.

"Sure," Drake replied, cutting off the connection.

Just because he was now working with Jimmy didn't mean he had to be friends with him. Actually, the less friendly they were, the better.

Drake typed the coordinates that Jimmy had given him into the Hydrostar's DDU. A transparent green line was projected onto the windscreen and appeared to be painted on the road in front of him, guiding the way. At this point, he could easily switch on the Autodrive, but Drake liked to manually drive the first few kilometers of every trip. He enjoyed being in charge of the big machine and feeling connected to it. On shorter trips, like this one, he usually did all the driving. Most people these days didn't even know how to drive, as cars seldom came with manual controls, but Drake liked driving. He only gave up control once he was on the highway and had not much driving to do anyway. That was when he switched the Autodrive on and went back into the cabin to sleep, eat or watch something on the DDU.

Hauling was a pretty mundane job, and the only reason people were still involved at all was thanks to rules requiring all vehicles used as haulers to have at least one human operator. Drake didn't care about politics but knew that without the unions, there would be no humans in the trucks. It was only a matter of time until people would be a burden to the economic monster instead of a crucial part. He loved being on the road, not cooped up in some office or factory or house, but he knew the haulers' days were numbered. The push to only allow autonomous vehicles on the road was growing daily, and Drake wondered if people forgot that autonomy was how they got into this mess in the first place. Machines and computers now did most jobs, and a lot of people had to live on the Basic Citizens Income handed out by the territories' companies. Everyone was sold on the idea of BCI by the companies who told them about the freedom everyone would have to pursue all their dreams and passions. Machines, computers, and robots would do all the mundane jobs no one wanted, and people would be free, but in reality, everyone was just trying to survive. Most people couldn't live on the BCI alone and had to go back to the factories to clean and maintain the machines that had taken their jobs for a fraction of what they used to earn. A win-win for the companies.

Drake shook his head, cleared his mind, and focused on the green line in front of him.

The estimated time of arrival on the windscreen placed the destination only another five minutes away. The road was pretty busy: mostly haulers but a few cars too. Most people used the Hyperloop, and the highways were exclusively used by haulers, unlike in towns where cars were still popular. Drake followed the green line until a big red inverted teardrop appeared ahead—his destination. The red marker was in the middle of a busy shipyard, right in front of a big trailer, ready to be hauled. Drake drove past the trailer and turned slightly away from it. Then he began to slowly back toward the trailer, keeping his eyes on the windscreen, which now showed a picture of the trailer and a crosshair for him to aim his truck at. The crosshair was red, but as he aligned, everything turned green. He kept his line until he heard a loud *thunk*. Drake put the Hydrostar in hold and jumped out. A hauler was solely responsible for the cargo until it was signed off by the recipient, so Drake went through all his safety checks and made sure the load was secure before he started to look around for someone with the paperwork.

Walking around the trailer, Drake was surprised that no one had come over to him already. The shipyard was busy, but no one seemed to have taken any notice of him or to show any interest in getting him and the cargo out of there, which was strange. Most places like these wanted the shipment to turn around as quickly as possible. The faster one trailer load could go, the quicker another one could come in again. Drake stood in the middle of the yard while everyone around him went on as if he wasn't even there. Without the right authorization, he would not be able to program the Hydrostar's DDU with the correct coordinates or the proper travel permissions from the Haulernet to even get started.

Drake found Jimmy's number, and activated his Augmented Reality Projector.

"Hey, partner! It looks like you got the trailer. Everything cool?" Jimmy's face, which appeared to be floating in front of Drake, looked as nervous as ever.

The sight of Jimmy's face made Drake regret switching on his ARP. Seeing the little rat made Drake regret all his decisions leading up to this point. Next time he would send a text. Jimmy gave him a nervous, toothy smile, clearly waiting for him to speak.

"Yes. I'm here, but where is my contact? I need the paperwork." Drake didn't even try to hide his irritation.

"Oh, yes, of course. Actually, ya know, I just received all the details and whatnots for you, so if you give me a second, I'll program it directly into your DDU."

For him to directly program Drake's DDU, he would need access to all of Drake's files and would be able to override anything he wanted. Things like Haulernet travel permissions and travel logs. From here on in, Jimmy could tell Haulernet where Drake was, which could be anywhere he fancied, while Drake could be where Jimmy wished him to go. The moment Drake gave him access, he would have all the control. He could even override Drake's manual inputs and Autodrive the Hydrostar to the location. All Jimmy needed was Drake's password.

"I don't think so, Jimmy. There is no way in hell that I'm giving you control of my truck."

"I hear ya, partner. The thing is, my contact only gave me codes, not actual coordinates, so—"

"So, call them and say we have a problem. No coordinates, no deal."

Drake was getting nervous. Not only was he getting sucked deeper and deeper into the murky swamp water of the hauler underworld, but he was losing any control he had as well. If he gave Jimmy permission, he would be a passenger. He knew he was already over-committed, and there were a lot of credits on the line, but the thought of running away kept popping up in his head.

"What is it going to be, Jimmy?"

Jimmy looked around as if an answer was written on the wall somewhere.

"I can send you the message so you can see for yourself. It's just code, no instructions, or coordinates. I'm in the dark as much as you, ya know?"

Drake studied the weasel in front of him. He was squirming and sweating but not because he was lying. No, he was scared. Maybe Jimmy saw in Drake's eyes that Drake was about to bail and he would most likely lose a lot of credits. Or perhaps Jimmy stood to lose much more.

"Jimmy, if you fuck me over on this, or I even suspect you of doing anything I don't like, I'm out. I'll drop this cargo and you'll never see me again, understood?"

Jimmy was still fidgeting about but looked a bit more relaxed.

"Drake, I would never! We're partners now, ya know? And besides, I wouldn't do anything to jeopardize this contract."

Drake had never been on the receiving end of Jimmy's double-crossing and backstabbing, as he stayed clear of Jimmy and anyone like him, but he knew the stories. He reminded himself never to let his guard down. And he gave Jimmy all the control he wanted.

*** 

Drake got back in the Hydrostar. A new green line was already on the road. Drake put the Hydrostar in Manual Drive mode. The estimated time showed it to be just over 48 hours, which meant 48 nonstop hours of driving. Some jobs paid bonuses for getting there under that time;

some penalized you for going over it. Drake had none of that to worry about, as Jimmy Something had been vague on the details.

"Fuck it," he said to no one at all and started to follow the line.

# | four |

The highway was pretty still, so Drake decided to switch on the Auto-drive and get some lunch in the back. The DDU now showed images of the front, side, and rear of the truck, as well as atmospheric telemetry. He opened his cooler unit and took out one of the uniform white boxes from it, popped it into the cooking and rehydration unit, and waited a few seconds for the beep to tell him his tasteless but nutritious meal was ready. He didn't mind the white box meals, as he had rarely eaten anything else since he was a boy.

Nestem, one of the Big Five companies and territories and the makers of the white box meals, knew what the human body needed, and that's all you were given in a white box meal. Only the essential proteins, fats, and nutrients. If you wanted more flavor, you had to pay a lot more credits to get a white box with a color line on it, and if credits were no issue, and they always were, you got a colored box meal. Drake had tried the line boxes before but thought they were a rip-off and hardly tasted better, but he had yet to eat a colored box meal. Maybe he would spoil himself to one once this was all over.

On one haul, he'd gotten stuck in a sandstorm and had to pull up; he could hardly see out the window, and even the thermal imaging was useless. The Autodrive system was also not engaging due to the adverse conditions. So he just pulled over to what he believed was the side of the road and started to wait it out. He was barely out of the driving seat when he heard a knock on the door. Drake grabbed his pulse pistol, checked it was loaded, and stood next to the door, not in front, in case someone put a bullet through it and him.

"Who is it?" Drake yelled over the howling wind.

No answer, but another knock came. Drake flipped the safety off. He glanced at the little screen next to his shoulder, showing an image of whoever was in front of the door. The sandstorm caused too much interference, and with all the sand blowing around, he could hardly make out the shape. It did look like only one shape, but Drake had been ambushed before and knew others could be waiting just out of the camera's view.

"If you want me to open up this door, you better tell me who you are, or get lost!"

Drake knew if there was a group of them, it would be best to stay inside. The Hydrostar was built like a tank. Drake had been held up before and knew his best chance was to wait it out. They were usually ill-prepared and not the smartest to boot, so he just had to be patient, wait for the storm to subside, and then be on his way.

Another knock came from the door.

"Fuck off!" Drake yelled, walking backward and sitting down in his chair.

He'd wait until the storm cleared a bit and then drive off and hopefully over some of them. These guys would have to try someone else.

Two minutes later, he heard another knock on the door. As Drake stood, ready to shoot at them, he saw a note stuck up to the camera: *Are you okay?* It took him by surprise, as he had never seen hijackers use this tactic before. Unless it wasn't bandits. This stretch of highway was pretty safe, and Drake couldn't recall ever hearing of a hijacking happening in this area. Drake knew that it had to be a sly tactic, but the seed of doubt was now firmly planted. He rechecked his pulse pistol and, ignoring every instinct he had, pressed the button to open the door. Sand rushed into the cabin, and he had to cover his face quickly. Someone bumped into him, and suddenly all the noise and chaos went away as the door slid shut. Drake quickly drew his arm away from his face and aimed at the person in front of him.

"What do you want?" he demanded from the person who looked like a pile of cloths draped over a human shape.

He couldn't even see a face but did make out a set of black goggles buried in the layers of dirt. The pile started to move and removed some sheets from the top to reveal a worn and sun-beaten face.

"Ah, that's better. Name's Norm," he said, looking at Drake's pulse pistol.

Drake kept it pointed at his face.

"Great. Hi, Norm. What do you want?" Drake said, still wondering how this hijack attempt was going to play out.

Norm was at least a foot shorter than Drake, so Drake assumed he was the brains, not the muscle behind this attack. Maybe this was Norm's first rodeo, and Drake felt a pang of sympathy for him: this was not going to work out well for him.

"Under normal circumstances, I could ask you the same, but I guess the storm took you by surprise!" Norm said, sounding too friendly for Drake's liking.

"I need to tell you, Norm, that I have been doing this for a while, and this is not my first hijacking. I am willing and more than capable of shooting you right where you stand, so how—"

Drake did not even see a flinch from Norm, but in a split second, he'd slapped the gun out of Drake's hand, grabbed the pulse pistol, flicked it over, pulled the barrel off, taken the magazine out and presented it back to Drake.

Drake just stared back at Norm's smiling face.

"That's all right, no offense taken. These storms make us do funny things. Let's start again. I'm Norm."

Norm's smile never faded. He still had the dismantled pulse pistol in his outstretched hands, like a peace offering.

"Benjamin Drake," was all Drake could offer.

How did this sand-covered little man do that?

"Hi Benjamin. Would you like to come in for dinner?" the smiling pile of rags asked him.

"Drake. People call me Drake."

"Okay then, Drake, how about it?" he asked, gesturing toward the door.

"So, you're not hijacking me?" Drake asked, feeling like an idiot for even saying it.

"No, Drake," Norm said, shaking his head. "You parked your truck about two steps away from my front door. Gave us all a bit of a fright there!"

Drake stepped over to the DDU. He brought up the outside camera views and zoomed in on the front-facing one. Barely visible through the sand, Drake could make out a dome-like structure. He glanced back at the smiling Norm.

"Your place?" Drake asked him, nodding in the direction of the screen.

"Sure is, and we were just about to sit down for dinner when you almost ran us over. Would you like to join us?" Norm's smile never receded, and Drake started to realize that this was definitely not a hijack.

"Okay." Drake said, but he didn't move.

Norm held the pistol up a little bit higher, reminding Drake that it was his, and he should take it back. Drake sheepishly took it and put it down on a shelf, still in pieces.

"Great. Cover your face as best you can and just follow me." And with that, Norm opened the door and disappeared into the storm.

Drake covered his face and ran after him, immediately bumping into him as they reached his front door.

Inside the small house, a considerable table took center stage in the middle of the room. Because of the dome shape, all the sleeping happened against the sides where height was not an issue. Drake counted four beds, three small and one big—two adults and three children. Behind the table was a roaring fire with various pots hanging over it. Attending to these pots was a female version of Norm, slightly smaller but also wearing rags and the same weather-beaten face. She gave Drake the same friendly smile Norm had when she saw him.

"Nora, this is Benjamin Drake, the man who almost killed us!" Norm said to his wife without a trace of malice.

"Hi Benjamin, welcome to our home. You'll stay until the storm passes?" Nora stated, more than asked.

"People call me Drake. I wasn't really planning on staying. My truck has everything—"

"We have a very special meal tonight," she interrupted, "as it is Norm's birthday. We would be more than happy to have you share it with us." Nora's tone implied that the matter was settled.

Drake became aware of the smells drifting over from the fire. It smelled like nothing he had smelled before. Nora noticed his reaction.

"Norm killed it himself this morning. Pure luck. He came across it while foraging for roots. It seems the Earth is not as dead as they want us to believe!" Nora said.

She opened the big pot, and Drake walked over for a peek. Chunks of what Drake assumed was real animal meat floated in a brown stew that overwhelmed Drake's olfactory system. Nora beamed. Drake close his eyes as he went in for another sniff.

"Now, before you ask the obvious question—what animal it is—I don't know and Norm never tells us. He brings it all gutted, skinned, and quartered to me when he finds something. Just makes it easier to enjoy." She stirred the pot.

Drake found this a bit disconcerting, but the smell was so pleasant, he decided that they might be onto something.

Three children, smaller replicas of Norm and Nora, appeared out of nowhere and started to get the table ready. Drake found himself in the middle of an almighty sandstorm, surrounded by the happiest, most loving people he had met in a very, very long time. He was so overwhelmed by their sincerity that he hardly spoke out of fear of upsetting the balance. Everyone sat down, and Nora brought the big pot over to the table, which she placed right in the center.

Norm, the birthday boy himself, was entitled to the first and choicest portion. But he surprised Drake.

"Please, Drake, as our guest, I insist you go first." Norm gestured to the big pot on the table.

Drake, like most city dwellers, did not have much use for manners or generosity but knew he would offend Norm and Nora more by declining the offer than by accepting it.

"Thanks, Norm. Nora, it looks delicious. I can't remember the last time I had actual meat! In fact, I must have been about your size, I think," Drake said to one of the kids.

The child—could've been a boy or a girl hiding under all the layers of dirty clothes—must have been about eight or nine years old and gave Drake a shy smile back. Nora and Norm smiled at each other, and Drake felt the warm sadness of nostalgia creeping in.

A silence settled over the small hut as everyone devoured their meals. Drake started a bit cautiously, still unable to completely ignore the fact that he didn't even know what animal it was, but after each mouthful, that thought was pushed further and further back. Drake was only a kid the last time he had actual meat and he was amazed at the texture and feeling of it in his mouth. The purpose of white box meals was to provide nutrition and sustenance, not enjoyment, so eating had become something most people did only because they had to. But this meal was something else. Drake relished every bite—the taste, the feel, the smell. Once, he even noticed the kids pointing and laughing at him. Drake just smiled back at them, feeling better than he had in years.

Finally everyone was done, the children disappeared again, Nora started to clean up, and Drake decided not to overstay his welcome.

"Norm, thank you so much for taking me in tonight, but I'm going to head back to my truck now and hopefully be out as soon as I can. I'm losing credits every second I stay put. But again, thank you so much for your generosity. It's a rare commodity these days." Drake said.

"You are welcome, my friend, and next time you see us, just stop next to the house, not on top of it!" Norm said, slapping Drake on the back.

Drake said his goodbyes and braved the storm back to his truck.

Every time Drake passed a small hut, he wondered if it was Norm and Nora's shelter, but he never stopped to check. Some memories are best being just that—memories.

# | five |

The sky was changing from blue to pink; night was falling, and Drake had to decide if he was going to push through, have the Autodrive keep driving, or stop and have a break. Jimmy Something hadn't programmed a time frame into the Hydrostar's DDU, so there was no countdown on the screen urging him on. Yellows and reds now joined the sky and the blues got even darker. The Hydrostar rounded a bend, and the sunset was replaced by an already blackened sky.

Small flickering lights appeared on the horizon. Drake had been on this stretch of highway many times before and knew that the views ahead were Proteus, a small independent settlement. They had a vast underground aquifer, which they extracted and sold. Proteus bottled water was marketed as the purest water on Earth, and the price tag matched the claim. The mayor, who owned the town, was a clever man and managed the resource so that all the residents had work, and the town could stay independent of the local corporations. The Proteus security force was not one to be taken lightly. Unless you were born there, the chances of staying longer than twenty-four hours were slim to deadly.

Drake did not care much for Proteus. Everything was flawless—the lawns were so green and perfectly kept that it looked plastic, the people were all dressed in clean, bright clothes that made outsiders stand out even more, and all the hydrocars were brand new, with no older models to be seen. It felt staged, like they were hiding what was really happening behind closed doors, but Drake never got close enough or stayed long enough to have a peek behind the curtains. The mayor had built a bypass that made sure little traffic came into his town. He'd also erected a small compound out of town for anyone who needed to stop, especially haulers, to ensure they stayed away. The compound was more to Drake's liking anyway, looking and feeling more real, with actual people, dust, and noise. The compound had some official name, but everyone called it Anteus—short for Anti Proteus. Even the hydrogen station, bar, and motel had Anteus in their names. Although Proteus owned them, the people named them. Proteus did not care what happened in Anteus, as long as it kept all the strays there and stopped them from entering beautiful, clean Proteus.

A message appeared on the Hydrostar's windscreen. Every time Drake entered a new corporation's territory, a version of the same waiver appeared, asking him to basically sign away any rights he had and to obey the rules of the territory's corporation. Drake, like every other hauler on the road, had given up reading them a long time ago and just hit the agree button, since the local security force would descend on him and force him to turn around if he said no or did nothing. Haulers really had no choice and just hit yes multiple times each journey, automatically like a machine.

Drake tapped yes and switched off the Autodrive. He smiled as he passed a small unmarked road that veered off to the left—the only route to Proteus. He stayed on the much more prominent, better-looking road, and advertisements promoting all that Anteus had to offer appeared on his windscreen. Proteus spared no expense to keep their little fake haven to themselves. Drake rolled into Anteus and parked the Hydrostar next to the other trucks, behind the only bar in town. No competition needed if everything was already paid and bought for in town. Drake powered down the Hydrostar, switched on the security, and stepped out into the night.

Jimmy Something had not only caved on the fuel but also living expenses, which for Drake included booze. Life on the road was pretty lonely, but haulers tended to frequent the same drinking holes. Stepping into the Anteus bar, Drake recognized most of the faces and furniture. Every bar he had ever stepped into had the same layout—an L-shaped bar to the side, tables in the middle, booths on the far sides, and a small stage opposite the bar. Depending on the bar or the day of the week, the stage would be used for music or usually scantily dressed girls. Some bars even moved the tables out of the way to allow more dancing. Most bars also served food, but no one ever ordered any, as all they served were plated white box meals, and most haulers had stacks of them in their cooling units.

This was a place to socialize, get drunk, forget about the world, and maybe even get lucky.

Drake spotted some friendly faces over at a table and, after grabbing a beer from the bar, went over.

"Drake! Haven't seen you in a while? What's up?" Lyle Miller said, raising his glass as Drake pulled a chair over and made himself at home.

The other two haulers acknowledged Drake, and Drake lifted his glass to them in response.

"Still holding hands across the country?" Drake quipped.

"Only since letting go of your mother's. You should do the same!" Lyle winked at Drake.

The other two haulers laughed but stayed out of it.

"She's always had a soft spot for dickheads. Sorry it didn't work out."

"Fuck you," Lyle surrendered.

"So, what are you guys dragging along?" Drake asked.

Lyle, Burt, Sara and Drake all used to work for Mr. Turner back in the glory days, but after the changes, the others moved on to work for one of the competing companies. They always worked together, and Drake was never sure who was romantically linked to whom at any time.

"Been hauling some minerals. Just silica and crap. Pretty good contract, though. Been going for three months now," Sara replied.

Lyle and Burt gave her a bit of a staredown.

"Relax, boys," Drake reassured them. "I have no intention of crashing your little party. Hauling the same route, weeks on end, in someone else's truck does not appeal to me." He meant it.

Doing the same thing, day in and day out, would kill him. Drake loved being on the road, seeing different places, but mostly he just liked being free. Drake cherished his freedom, above all else. Seeing his dad going to the same job, in the same uniform, in the same old hydro-car every single day of his life, had killed Drake as much as it ended up killing his old man. Well, the car crash killed him, technically, but Drake knew that the job killed him long before that.

"Whatever, the company has not been hiring for months now anyway, so even if you wanted to, you couldn't." Burt said, sounding like a little spoiled child and bringing Drake back to the present.

"Thanks, Burt, although I said I didn't want to, I was secretly hoping you would try to convince me to join you again. But now my dreams are shattered." Burt's bottom lip stuck out, and Drake laughed out loud at seeing him embracing the spoiled child image.

"So, Mr. Big-shot-I-don't-work-for-no-one, what you got on the back of your rust bucket?" Lyle asked.

Drake could kick himself for not thinking ahead. When he'd seen Lyle's group, he just went over and started to chat, as he always did. You see a friendly face in a shark pool, you tend to not feed the sharks but go the safer route. Today the safer route was Lyle and his small group, but Drake knew, as friendly as they were, that telling them he was doing a contract for Jimmy Something would not go down well. Haulers were a tight-knit community, but it was more by natural selection than by choice. Most people avoided haulers, which was usually wise as the majority of them operated in life's gray zone. Haulers knew the laws but tended to be quite picky about which ones they followed. They weren't real criminals, mostly, just plain dodgy. So it wasn't that haulers preferred the company of each other, but rather that it was the only company on offer.

Drake took a sip of his beer, wiped his mouth with the back of his hand, and decided to tell them the truth.

"Decided to take a break from old Bobby Turner and do some independent hauling for a while."

Well, almost the truth; he still had some pride.

"Bullshit!" Lyle called him out immediately. "No way the teacher's pet would walk away. What happened? And don't lie, dipshit!"

"Well, it's mostly true," Drake said, half believing it himself. "Some words were said, and we decided, both of us, to not work together for a few weeks."

"You are full of it, Drake. You screwed up, and now Bob won't touch you. What did you do? He found out you slept with his daughter?"

Drake didn't know how Sara knew that and besides, that happened ages ago, and she was not even living in New Franco anymore.

"Who told you? Doesn't matter. No, he didn't find out, all right, I just screwed up enough to know to lay low for a while, okay?"

Drake finished the last of his beer. He was hoping to relax tonight and get his mind away from Jimmy, but this crowd was not going to let him. It was not every day that they had someone new to pester and help relieve the pain of their dreary lives. He would have one more beer and then call it a night, he decided.

When he returned to the table, Sara asked, "So, if you are not hauling for Mr. Turner, then what is behind your truck?"

"Not sure," Drake said, casually sipping his beer as if that was the end of that.

"What the fuck you mean you're not sure?" Lyle piped in.

"As in, I have no idea what the cargo is."

"Drake, what have you done?" Sara asked, already shaking her head.

"Well, we don't all have lucrative mineral contracts, you know, so I just took a small job from an independent operator," Drake said, starting to doubt the wisdom in disclosing any of this to them.

"Drake?" Sara prompted him.

Lyle and Burt were sitting, beers halfway to their mounts, frozen in anticipation. Vultures, just dying for some good old gossip. Nothing made your dreary life seem better than hearing how bad someone else had it.

"As long as it wasn't with some dipshit like Jimmy Something, you'll be fine, I guess," Sara said and lifted her glass to drink but stopped short when she noticed Drake just sitting and staring at his beer.

Lyle and Burt's eyes were straining to stay in their sockets as they anticipated the bad news that would make their day. Next to them, Sara finally moved her glass away from her face and put it down.

"Drake?" she prompted him again.

"Yes. Yes. I sold my soul to fucking Jimmy Something, all right? What's the big deal, anyway?" Drake slammed his hand on the table and pushed himself back, trying to show he was in charge of his decisions, however bad they might be.

He grabbed the half-full glass in front of him and took a big gulp of the beer. Lyle, Burt, and Sara exchanged looks. When did they become so high and mighty? Like working for a mining company was so ethical. They wished they had his freedom.

"Whatever, I'm out of here. Nice seeing you assholes again." Drake finished his beer and sliding the empty glass across the table, hoping it would crash into one of them.

He was about to get up when Sara spoke.

"You don't know, do you?" she said, and Drake's blank stare answered her question. "Your new boss, Jimmy Something, got a bounty out on his head a week ago. He killed some people and blew up a building. Jimmy Something is a wanted man. Penta Corp is after him, Drake, for murder . . ."

Drake tried to swallow but couldn't. A cold feeling rushed out from his chest to his hands and his head. His whole body felt lighter and then suddenly very heavy. Someone put a beer in front of him and he reached for it automatically.

"What?" was all he could say, his mind running a mile a minute but unable to grab onto any one thought.

"It was all over the Haulernet. I don't know how you could have missed it," Sara stated, matter-of-factly.

Drake got up, legs shaky.

"I didn't . . . I have . . ." He tripped over his chair and made a line for the exit.

# | six |

Back in the Hydrostar, Drake's brain slowly started working again. He stared at the blank DDU screen for ten minutes. Then he switched it on, and after the excruciatingly slow start-up (it was definitely time for an upgrade), he began to search the Haulernet. It took him about five minutes to find the bulletin Sara had mentioned. One drawback in trying to keep one's moral high ground, and not get involved in all the politics and bickering going on, was that sometimes essential things were overlooked. Like a bulletin that says your new partner is a wanted man for murder and arson. And damage to property. And who knows what else. Drake had known he was getting in bed with the wrong people when he took the job, but he never thought things would go sour this fast. He was hoping for more of a gradual slide into the abyss, not a head dive straight into the deep end only a few days in.

He read and reread the bulletin. It was pretty slim on details, but it appeared Jimmy Something had been at a warehouse and that some sort of a meeting or deal was going down. There were no witnesses, but a grainy video clip from a security camera was attached. Drake pressed play.

The camera must have been mounted really high and far away, and half the screen was blocked by a pillar or box or something, but in the middle of the floor, Jimmy Something was clearly talking to someone conveniently behind the blockage. It looked like a deal was made, and Jimmy handed something over, then shook hands, and then turned to leave. There was no sound on the clip, but the man behind the pillar must have said something, because Jimmy spun around, a pulse gun already drawn. Jimmy waved his hand and shouted. Then, to the left of Jimmy, there was a movement and Jimmy fired his pulse gun in that direction. After that, all hell broke loose. Other people came into the frame and then disappeared again, alternating between shooting and taking cover. Jimmy was doing the same, popping his head out, taking a shot, and then retaking cover and moving to a different spot. Jimmy must have gotten lucky or been a better shot than Drake gave him credit for. One after another, his assailants fell. Jimmy came out from behind his cover, pulse gun still pointing at someone, lips moving. The guy behind the pillar moved forward, but Drake did not recognize his face. Jimmy's lips never stopped moving, and he was yelling, not talking, at pillar man. A flash appeared at the end of Jimmy's outstretched arm, and the man collapsed. Jimmy ran over to him and swiped his arm. Drake could not see from this far away what Jimmy was looking for, but he spent a long time going through the dead man's HIC. He must have found what he was looking for, or just gave up, but Jimmy got up and disappeared off-screen. Drake thought that it must be the end of the clip but the little progress bar was only three-quarters full. After about two minutes, Jimmy was back on-screen, setting everything around him on fire. The flames grew bigger and bigger until the screen went black.

Drake sat back in his chair.

"You fucking idiot," he said, either to himself or Jimmy, or both.

Everything on that video pointed to Jimmy being in the wrong. Drake could not imagine what possible explanation Jimmy would have to explain what happened. He knew the only thing to do was to confront him. Drake could not keep hauling unless he knew exactly what was going on and what he'd got himself into. Jimmy would need to have a very, very good reason for what he did to convince Drake from continuing.

Drake called Jimmy. The dots crashed into each other, forming a bigger dot that grew and dissolved to reveal a very nervous Jimmy Something. The projection of Jimmy standing right in front of him was so real that Drake had to fight the urge to punch the air in front of him. Instead, he took a deep breath, trying to calm himself down a bit.

"Jimmy, what the fuck have you done?" Drake yelled, despite his usually foolproof deep breath.

Jimmy's lip wobbled. Drake wished the little rat was in front of him and not just projected. He really wanted to hit something. Or someone, to be precise.

"Hey, Drake . . . partner. So, what's happening?" Jimmy tried.

"Don't even try to play dumb, dipshit. I do know how to read, and I do have a DDU. What have you done?" Drake asked again.

"Oh, yeah, that. I wondered when you would see it. I think we need to talk in person, to be a bit more secure, ya know?"

Drake could not care less about being secure but relished the idea of getting his hands on Jimmy before anyone else did.

"Sure," Drake said, "let's talk, 'cause I'm not going anywhere until you tell me exactly what the hell I have gotten myself into."

"Yes, yes, sure. I mean, you could keep driving, and I could meet up with—"

"Are you fucking serious?" Drake yelled again.

He could not believe how stupid he'd been to get involved with Jimmy. Surely, he could have waited a few days and gone back to Mr. Turner. Why did he always leap before checking first? At least he felt like the power had shifted between him and Jimmy and that he was more in control now. He wished he knew what he was in control of, though. Jimmy was on the back foot, and Drake was planning to keep him there.

"Okay, okay. I'll jump on the Hyperloop and meet you—" Jimmy accessed Drake's position on his HIC, "—at Anteus?"

"I'll be waiting." He disconnected before Jimmy could speak again.

It was already late, so Drake decided to go to sleep until Jimmy showed up. It would take Jimmy only an hour or so to reach him, using the Hyperloop, but Drake wanted to be as sharp and ready as he could be for Jimmy. As Drake climbed into his bunk, he kept thinking of Jimmy, spinning around to something pillar man said. What could the stranger have said to upset Jimmy so much that he went on a killing spree? Granted, he didn't know the other guys were there, and one could argue that killing them was self-defense, but pillar man? After the dust settled, he actually spoke to him before shooting him. Drake knew Jimmy Something had a bad reputation, but most of it was for dodgy deals and crossing people. Never had he heard anyone mention anything violent. Drake knew he would have to allow Jimmy to tell his side of the story but he also knew Jimmy's reputation for bending the truth as far as possible and, most times, beyond. Did it even matter what explanation he had? Drake knew he should unhook the trailer and get the hell out of Anteus. Leave all this crap behind him and crawl back to Mr. Turner. If Jimmy wanted to hunt him down, then good luck to him. He'd never disclosed the full story before getting Drake to agree to the haul, so Jimmy had brought this on himself.

Who was he kidding?

Drake knew he had to be honest with himself and stop blaming Jimmy for everything. He'd taken the contract, fully aware that it was not a Haulernet-approved contract, and that he was dealing with a less than desirable character. Did he really expect it all to go down without a hitch? This was never and would never be one of his regular Bob Turner contracts. This was a black market deal, and he had better get used to it.

***

A knock at the door woke him. He grabbed his pulse pistol from the shelf next to his bed. He made sure the cartridge was loaded and the safety engaged. Safety first, especially if you have a partner who might get accidentally shot in the face. That same face appeared on the little screen right next to the truck's door. Jimmy knocked again. Drake got up and opened the door, forcing himself not to punch Jimmy in the face.

"Hey, Drake. Thought you'd still be in the bar, ya know?" Jimmy laughed nervously and squeezed past Drake into the truck.

Behind Jimmy, the sun was rising. Jimmy had taken his time getting here. Drake decided to stay focused on the issue at hand and not get distracted by Jimmy's tardiness.

"Jimmy, all I want to hear from you is what happened in that warehouse. And make it brief."

Jimmy tried to wiggle out of the way, but there was nowhere else to move to in the cramped space.

"Should we maybe go chat somewhere else? Not a lot of space in here, ya know?" Jimmy pointed out.

Drake knew this but did not want to give Jimmy any more wiggle room.

"I'm good, thanks. Get talking," Drake replied.

"Sure, sure. Nice truck, by the way," Jimmy said, but as Drake inched toward him even more, he cut the small talk. "So, what do you want to know?"

"Who was the other guy, and what exactly went down? I'm going against every instinct I have and giving you the benefit of the doubt here," Drake said through clenched teeth.

"Okay," Jimmy said, "I'll tell you the whole story. No lies or bullshit." And he did, mostly.

Afterward, Drake just looked at him.

"We need to get out of here now."

# | seven |

On the screen, Jimmy Something ran out of the building only to return a few minutes later and to set fire to everything, burning the building to the ground. The screen went black as the flames reached the camera, and Lieutenant Lily Wells saw her reflection in the display.

Tiny lines had started to appear at the corners of her eyes, even though she was still relatively young, by most standards. The dark circles around her eyes also seemed magnified by the bad light and made her look the way she felt: worn-out. At least her auburn hair was full of life, unlike the rest of her. She knew she was being overly harsh on herself.

The last few months had been the complete opposite of the years preceding it. Until recently, Wells was on the right track to becoming captain of a big corporation's security force, her life's ambition. Since she was a little girl, she wanted to be in law enforcement, and she worked hard her whole life at making her dream come true. At school, Wells not only excelled at her academic work but was a star gymnast and athlete too. However, her family did not have the means to send her to a Penta training facility, so she did it the hard way. She worked through the ranks of the smaller corporations, starting at the lowest level and working her way up until she got in with Penta and then worked even harder. Her rise was steady, and the right people started to notice her.

Everything was going to plan until the incident.

She met Jason Bell at a party, and it was a match made in heaven. They hit it off immediately, and in no time at all, they were living together. After a few months, their friends started to hint at them, signing a partnership contract. Everyone knew it was bound to happen someday.

Lt. Lily Wells had never been happier in her life. Her career was on the right track, and she'd finally found a life partner.

Life was perfect, she thought, but it all came crashing down around her the day she responded to a break-and-enter at one of the company's sites. A group of suspected terrorists had broken into a highly secure building and had tried to steal some prototype pulse guns and cannons. Wells' team was the first to arrive at the scene, and within minutes they had control of the situation. In her trademark efficient manner, she guided her team to subdue and capture all the suspects. Once they had them under control, the suspects were lined up against a wall for identification. They all wore masks, presumably so no cameras could identify them, so Wells' team started to unmask them for scanning and processing.

That's when she, and half the team, saw Jason Bell standing shoulder to shoulder with the rest of the terrorists.

Lt. Wells felt every imaginable emotion in that split second, but she was a security officer first, even when it was this close to home. In that instant, Jason became just another suspect to her, and all feelings she had for him disappeared. She treated him the same as every other suspect and left his fate with Penta. In a wink of an eye, Jason Bell was dead to her.

She did her job flawlessly with no loss to life and minimal damage to property, but her superiors still frowned upon the fact that one of the perpetrators were known to her and half her squad. All foreseeable promotions were taken off the table, and Lieutenant Wells' career and personal life came to a crashing halt in the same week.

Getting over Jason was the easy part. Getting over her career getting derailed was the hard part.

That was four months ago and Lieutenant Wells was still stuck on desk duty. Lt. Wells lived for being in the field, getting her hands dirty, getting the job done. Sitting in the small cubicle, connected to five other cubicles, that was part of a grid of over a hundred cubicles, made her feel insignificant and useless. The outside world disappeared every time she sat down behind her DDU. The room was dark, every cubicle illuminated by a small light, and there were no windows in the wall either. The fewer distractions on offer, the more work could be done. It must have been working, as no one ever spoke to anyone, and even after four months, Lt. Wells did not know the names of the people working around her. She was buried deep inside the Penta machine, with no end in sight.

Until the Jimmy Something case came around. It was getting a lot of attention, so she was put on the case as part of the support team. Whatever the lead team needed, she had to get done. She was used to being on the lead team and found it a very bitter pill to now be at their beck and call. But this was not the first setback she had endured in her career. It was definitely one of the biggest hurdles, but she knew that this case presented her with a great chance to prove her worth, yet again. She decided to pull herself out of her slump and get everything back on track. She was secretly thrilled that Jimmy Something, a known person of interest to her for years, finally lived up to what she always knew he would. A security officer could only shine when there were idiots like Jimmy Something to make them look good.

Wells was up against a huge challenge—she was not allowed to do any fieldwork and was bound to her desk, so everything would have to be done on her office Data Display Unit. She could only use the data supplied by the lead team and not get any additional information herself. Her job was to analyze the data from the lead team and file it accordingly. She would have no input or suggestions, but, on the bright side, she had access to all the information that the lead team uncovered.

She would have to be very careful. She could not afford to step on any toes, especially the team leader Captain Raymond Santo, as she was supposed to be a support member and had to remember to stay in the background. She could not risk going rogue, solving the case (which she believed she could), and then making the lead team look bad. She would have to work out a way to do her job but also somehow go beyond that and make sure everyone knew it was her work that got Jimmy Something arrested.

Wells realized she was getting ahead of herself, but that had always been how she did things. She never set herself small goals, only big, hard-to-reach ones. She was going to get Jimmy Something, and she was going to get her job back.

The fire was lit inside Lt. Lily Wells again and it started to burn brighter than ever before.

She pressed the replay button on the DDU screen and watched the warehouse footage again.

# | eight |

"So, what's the plan, big man?" Jimmy finally asked after wisely keeping his mouth shut for the first few minutes after they got on the road.

Drake was still driving, following the green line himself, just staring ahead. When he woke up this morning, he was an idiot who had made some questionable decisions, but now he was a fugitive on the run. By taking Jimmy Something on board, he had moved up the criminal ladder from occasionally dipping his toe in, straight to the Most Wanted list, with no stops in between. In any other field, such a rise to the top would be a remarkable story. In this case, it was the opposite.

"I mean, you do have a plan, don't ya?" Jimmy asked again.

"To keep driving, Jimmy, because that's what I do. I haul things from one place to another, *ya know?* I do not blow up buildings, and I, for fucking sure, do not shoot people. I haul. So right now, that's what I'm gonna do until I decide not to, okay?"

Drake gave him a look to emphasize that the subject was now closed. Jimmy gave him a look to emphasize he didn't know that.

"Okay, but you are still following the line, ya know, so does this mean we are still heading for the destination?" Jimmy persisted.

Drake hadn't even realized he was doing it until Jimmy pointed it out. It was just instinct to get in the truck and start following the line. The highway was busy but mostly only haulers, so Drake switched on the Autodrive, and the telemetry filled the windscreen. He swiveled his chair to face Jimmy.

"I assume the receiver of the goods I'm hauling will not really care two ways of what happened back at the warehouse, correct?"

"I guess . . ." Jimmy muttered.

"So, until I can think of something better, we'll be heading toward the original drop-off," Drake said. "But I think now would be a good time to drop all your bullshit and tell me what is in the back of my truck, and where the hell we are going."

Jimmy had already told Drake what happened at the warehouse, but he'd failed to mention the cargo. His eyes darted back and forth as his brain tried to decide what to do now. Drake tried to help speed up the process by leaning forward, putting his elbows on his knees, his face now uncomfortably close to Jimmy's, his eyes locked on him.

"Bismuth, for making Polonium," Jimmy said, visibly swallowing, just waiting for Drake to lose his cool.

Shuttles leaving for Mars used Polonium to get off Earth and up to speed. Since the shuttles had started using Polonium, the travel time had been cut from six months to two months. The drawback was the number of explosions, with one out of every four shuttles springing leaks, and the Polonium melting everything around it, killing all on board. The companies still found it to be within their acceptable tolerances, considering only convicts and runners used the shuttles. The handful of engineers, medical staff, and guards who went to Mars still used the much slower but much safer older shuttles. Drake knew that making Polonium was a very costly process and somehow involved bombarding Bismuth with neutrons. It was an expensive but not illegal operation. This meant that this load of Bismuth had been on its way somewhere legit before Jimmy got hold of it.

"So, whose was it before?" Drake asked. "Because I'm pretty sure they'll be looking for it."

"I'm not sure. All I was told was that . . ." Jimmy started before Drake cut him off.

"Jimmy, I swear I'll drive you to the nearest security office myself if you start your crap again. Whose shit am I hauling?"

Drake was so close to Jimmy's face that Jimmy could feel the words hitting him.

"Penta," Jimmy said. Drake felt the blood drain from his head and make his limbs go heavy.

Penta Group was one of the Big Five companies, and the biggest supplier of security forces, weapons, armored vehicles, and anything deadly. They had little to no competition in the death industry. If you were going to steal from a company, Penta had better be last on the list of options. Everyone knew this, apart from Jimmy Something, apparently.

"Please tell me you did not know this when you took the contract," Drake said, dropping his head into his hands.

"Firstly, partner, I was as shocked as you when I found out, ya know? Secondly, I was assured that everyone that needed to be paid off was paid in full. So, really, it's not as bad as you think, ya know?"

"Jesus Jimmy, how fucking dumb can you be?" Drake yelled at him.

Jimmy dropped his chin to his chest and stared at the ground, looking like a child being told off, and for a brief moment, Drake knew he had a glimpse into Jimmy's life growing up. Jimmy just sat there, defeated but visibly brewing and mumbling to himself. Jimmy wasn't born a loser; he was a made one. Drake immediately felt terrible for him, which made him even angrier at himself.

"Okay then, we need to start thinking, because I'm pretty sure despite all the stuffed pockets, someone is going to run their mouth off," Drake said, trying his best to sound a bit calmer.

"We could always just complete the contract, get our credits, and become runners," Jimmy suggested.

For ninety years, scientists and engineers had been terraforming Mars, turning it into a habitable planet. They used convicts from Earth as cheap and disposable labor. Smaller companies sold their convicts to the Big Five for a profit, who then used them for whatever purpose they deemed fit. Usually, it involved dangerous, high-risk labor, like digging tunnels for Hyperloops or flying on a time bomb to Mars. As time went on, a small colony was established, and soon people who ran out of options on Earth, usually thanks to to some criminal activity, ran off to Mars, hence the name runners. The companies were always happy to make credits, so none cared when people started to pay to fly to Mars on the shuttles. If the flight didn't kill you, your fellow passengers most likely would. Even if you survived the trip, life on Mars was still far from ideal. A small zone with a breathable atmosphere had been established, but it was still low in oxygen, and most people got sick from it. First-timers usually suffered severe headaches, nausea, and dizziness but after a few weeks, most adjusted. Then there was a shortage of housing and food to deal with. The convicts were not held in prison but lived in small units. They enjoyed more freedom than their earthly counterparts but were still under the watchful eye of the security forces. Crime and violence were high, but as long as the runners showed up for work, the authorities turned a blind eye. If a serious crime was committed—especially a crime against a non-convict—it usually resulted in a swift, on the spot, execution. Life on Mars was no one's first option.

"Become a runner? Are you mad?" Drake said to Jimmy.

"I know what you are thinking, but I've heard that they will soon open up the shuttles to normal folk to start populating the planet with decent people. Mars is going to change soon, ya know," Jimmy was getting the sparkle back in his eyes, "and with all the credits we are going to get, we'll be kings!"

"Been working on that sales pitch for a while?" Drake asked Jimmy. "I'm not going to run anywhere. But, I am interested to hear more about all these riches you are talking about." Drake could see Jimmy's slimy little brain working overtime, trying to cover up the fact he just told him there were still more credits to be made.

"And don't even try to bullshit me, Jimmy. You said we are going to live like kings, so I take it the hundred thousand credits I got was just a tiny piece of the pie." Drake continued.

"The thing—"

"Jimmy, if we are going to make it out of this alive, we'll have to start to treat each other as partners. I'll have to learn to trust you, but you will have to stop the lying and scheming, and be upfront with me. If not, I'm unloading right here, and we're done."

"Okay, okay. Just give me a second," Jimmy said, readying himself to be truthful to someone for the first time in years. "I was offered a million credits to get the Bismuth to a small company called Zuma. I'd never heard of them so I looked them up. They are a gold mining company. That's all I know. Seriously Drake, you now know everything I do." Jimmy's eyes told Drake that he was actually being truthful.

Drake hoped he wasn't making another mistake.

"Okay, partner, I believe you," Drake said.

And he almost did.

# | nine |

After breakfast, just before they set off for the day, Drake asked Jimmy to reprogram the DDU so that it showed the time and distance to the drop-off. Jimmy obliged. The telemetry shuffled around on the screen to accommodate the new data. At their current speed, they would be at their destination in approximately twelve hours.

Usually, Drake would make a twelve-hour trip in one go, but since Zuma had not given them a rigid deadline, he was playing it nice and easy. Penta would expect them just to cut a straight-line to Zuma, as any hauler would, but that was not the smart move. They had to be unpredictable.

If Penta caught up to them, Drake knew they were most likely to shoot first and ask questions later. Drake and Jimmy needed a plan or at least some idea what to do, especially if they did get caught. Would it be best just to surrender? Was there even another choice? The Hydrostar was tough, but if Penta's forces started to engage with the reckless abandon they were known for, it would just be a matter of time before they breached the hull. Hopefully, they would not want to damage the cargo and be a bit more cautious, but who knows. Penta was more a hammer than a scalpel. Eliminating the bad guys was usually a higher priority than retrieving the actual goods. Penta preferred to make examples out of criminals. They reveled in the role of judge, jury, and executioner. If you were going to steal from anyone, Penta should not be on your list.

"Jimmy, now that we know how far away we are, we need to get more organized," Drake said.

"Do you think we can reach the Zuma settlement before Penta figure it all out?"

Drake knew that just gunning it, hoping to outrun the most significant and best-equipped security company, was never going to happen. They had to be smart about this.

Life as a hauler took place in the gray area between what is legal and what is not. Nothing too serious, but deadlines were deadlines, so shortcuts were common. Usually, this attitude spilled into the personal lives of most haulers, and they lived their lives in this gray zone too. Drake was not immune to this. Bending the rules was second nature to him and allowed him to see opportunities where there usually were none.

"First things first," Drake said as he switched the Autodrive off, "let's get off this highway. All Penta has to do is look at the highway camera footage, and they'll find us in hours, if not minutes. You sure there was no time frame from Zuma?"

"No. I mean, yes, there was no time frame. But I think if we take too long, they might get a bit nervous, and who knows what they will do, ya know?" Jimmy said.

"Great, so no hard deadline, but if we take too long, we'll have two groups hunting us down." Drake spotted a smaller exit. He had to drop his speed considerably to get off the highway and get on the smaller road, which made the estimated travel time rise to eighteen.

Drake was making it up as he went along, which was how he preferred to do things anyway. One day at a time, no big picture stuff to worry about. Just look at the task at hand and get it done. He knew that they had a better chance on the smaller back roads than on the highway. Most of the more minor roads had fallen into disrepair as people used the Hyperloops to travel longer distances, and the trucks stuck to the highways, which were easier on their Autodrives. Some companies kept their roads in better shape than others, and Drake was very grateful that they were on such a road. It allowed him to go a bit quicker than he had anticipated, but better roads also meant a higher risk of having cameras monitoring them.

"Voice control active," Drake said.

"Confirm user," a voice replied.

"Benjamin Drake."

By confirming himself as the user, only his voice would be used for input, and Jimmy's or anybody else's voice would not confuse things. A small screen appeared on the display. All Drake had to do now was use a preset word followed by his command, and the DDU would execute it.

"Yolanda, where are we?" Drake asked his DDU.

"We are currently in a Nestem territory with a factory two hours away at current speed," Yolanda replied.

Jimmy had a question written all over his face.

"What?" Drake asked him.

"Yolanda? Someone special?" Jimmy said, eager to bond with Drake.

"Can't remember," Drake lied. "Been using that name since I had my first DDU. Nothing special about it."

Jimmy went quiet, and Drake knew he must be busting to ask him more about the name. Instead, Jimmy just stared ahead at the road, seemingly lost in his thoughts.

"Should be a settlement or even a town near the factory. Should we stop and stretch our legs?" Jimmy asked.

The Hydrostar was well equipped, with all the features and comforts a hauler needed. Drake could spend weeks in it if he needed to and not feel the need to *stretch his legs*. But the cabin had been intended for one person, and besides, Jimmy had most likely never sat still this long in his whole life.

"Yes," Drake said, "but just for a short while. The less contact we have with other people, the better."

He knew that every encounter they had would increase the chance of someone recognizing Jimmy or a camera filming them. They would have to try their best to stay clear of people. A truck traveling on a small back road was not uncommon, but it could raise suspicion and even attract the attention of the local security forces to come and have a look and a chat. Something Drake was hoping to avoid. On the other thand, staying on the highway would guarantee the chance of a shutdown. The moment they passed a camera and were recognized, a local security team would be sent after them and shut down the Hydrostar once they were in range. The back roads were their best option.

"Yolanda, monitor all radio traffic. Keywords: Jimmy Something, Bismuth, Penta Group and Benjamin Drake."

If something came up, the DDU would automatically switch to that channel and play it. Drake knew that Penta and even Zuma would use complicated encrypted channels but thought it was still worthwhile to scan. Drake had a thought.

"Yolanda, background task: monitor Haulernet, same keywords."

Drake knew that haulers loved their gossip, and soon everyone would know what he had done. It was only a matter of time before people would start messaging each other about his whereabouts.

"Benjamin Drake, as I live and breathe, are you running a bridged DDU?" Jimmy asked.

"It's not illegal. I've never claimed to be anything I'm not, Jimmy. But don't read too much into it. We are not alike."

"Sure, sure. It's only a small hack, ya know?" Jimmy winked at him.

Drake could feel his blood pressure rising but decided to let it go. He was no criminal like Jimmy, but he was no saint either. He'd had his DDU bridged when he restored the Hydrostar and used it on occasion to find things that were not allowed to be found. Or places one should not visit. More frowned upon than criminal, Drake always thought.

Jimmy swiped through his Human Interface Console.

"What you looking for?" Drake asked, still not trusting Jimmy as much as he'd said he would.

"Just checking my messages."

Drake noticed, not for the first time and with some regretful jealousy, that Jimmy had the newest version HIC implanted. The first few generations, like Drake's, were implanted under the skin and shone through it. They weren't the best for clarity or sensitivity, but people adapted to the new technology very quickly nonetheless. As people got used to having an implant, Citro (one of the Big Five companies and the makers of most Human Interface Consoles, Data Display Units, and Augmented Reality Projectors) decided to make the HIC's visible by removing the skin covering them. By doing so, they became much brighter and more responsive. The later gen models, like Jimmy's, were installed by removing a rectangular piece of skin and replacing it with the flexible screen of the HIC. Soon almost every human being had a display on their arms.

"And. . .? Anything from Zuma?"

"I think you'd be interested in this one," Jimmy said. "It seems that Nikolatec is releasing a new hauling truck, capable of, wait for it, speeds of . . ."

"What the fuck, man!" Drake yelled at Jimmy. "Penta is chasing us, and most likely Zuma as well, and you are reading the latest news on trucks? Come on, man!"

"Sorry, I just saw the article and thought . . ." Jimmy mumbled, not having a real answer.

Drake once more felt like a parent scolding a child.

"It sounds great, Jimmy, but for now, let's concentrate on staying alive and staying ahead of the people who will kill us on sight."

"Yes, sorry Drake. I'll see if there is anything from Zuma." He started sifting through his messages.

"Are those all real messages, or just junk?"

"Oh, most are just junk, but I can never get myself to block them, ya know? I just like getting messages." Drake realized what a lonely life Jimmy Something had.

He hated that he kept feeling more and more empathy for him. All of this felt easier to swallow the more he distanced himself from Jimmy, yet he kept feeling drifting closer and closer to him. He'd need to keep an eye on it, Drake thought.

"I guess, but let's focus, buddy. Anything from Zuma?"

Jimmy's face lit up whenever Drake talked to him instead of yelling at him.

"Checking, checking, checking . . . yes!"

Drake braced himself for another spam story.

"Mr. Something, it seems there have been some complications. We are tracking the package, and it seems all is still going to plan. Please confirm as soon as possible."

When he gave Jimmy access to his DDU, Drake most likely indirectly gave Zuma access too, at least to the travel log.

Jimmy must have sensed what Drake was pondering.

"All they have is the travel log. That's all. They only have telemetry access, no permissions. I promise, Drake. They can only see us. They can't do anything," Jimmy pleaded.

"That might actually be a good thing," Drake said. "At least they can see we are traveling toward them, and that might keep them off our backs. Reply to them that everything is going to plan."

Jimmy typed away on the HIC in his arm, and when he finished, he pointed to the windscreen.

"Wow, seems like we're quite popular!" he smiled at Drake.

On the screen, the search results were starting to come in.

"Yolanda, Autodrive on." Drake turned his gaze toward the search results. Most of them were just haulers going back and forth, having a dig at Drake for teaming up with Jimmy. Everyone seemed to have written him off since he would surely be in detention soon, yet in true hauler spirit, no one gave away any details as to where they thought he was going or what the cargo was. They all knew that their communications would be monitored, albeit illegally, and kept the details to themselves.

What caught Drake's attention was not what was being discussed but rather the lack of any communication from Penta. No bulletins or any news feeds had gone out about the missing Bismuth. Jimmy Something still had a bulletin out for his warehouse shenanigans, and Drake was mentioned as a person of interest, but it was all related to Jimmy's actions, nothing on the stolen cargo. Were they just embarrassed that someone stole from them? Or had they not noticed yet? Either way,

Drake knew it was only a matter of time before they came looking for their property, guns blazing.

# | ten |

*All going to plan. Don't worry about what's on the news. The package will be delivered as agreed.*

Jacob McKenna had never questioned Jimmy Something's ability to get the Bismuth to him. Jimmy's motivation was greed, and Jacob McKenna had plenty to give a greedy person. As the owner of Zuma, a very profitable gold mining company, McKenna was used to buying whatever he wanted. No was not a word McKenna liked to hear, and he hardly ever had to.

"I want you to find them and track them," McKenna told the mountain of muscle next to him.

McKenna loved to micromanage and did not have room in his operation for independent thinkers. He did most of the thinking and left most, if not all, of the heavy and dirty lifting to everyone else.

"Are we to engage, sir?" the muscle asked.

"No. For now, I want you to keep an eye on them. Make sure no one else is following them or that they are up to anything. If anything looks out of place, contact me. Understand, Anderson?"

"Copy that, sir!" Anderson replied and made a circular motion above his head, which signaled his squad to gather their gear and get in the armored vehicle.

Anderson grabbed his pulse gun and backpack and jumped in the front, next to the driver. "Let's go."

The armored vehicle whirred into life and slowly made its way out of the compound. McKenna watched it disappear into the distance before he returned to his office. Better safe than sorry, he thought.

*\*\*\**

The bar was old, worn-out, and in need of some TLC. The people were in the same condition. Most were haulers and manual labor types, their hands and faces showing the years of abuse and neglect in the elements. Wells stood out like a sore thumb, something that was not in short supply here. Most of the faces that had turned to examine her when she arrived now turned back to their own business of drinking and chatting. A few lingered a bit longer, and Wells knew she had been recognized as a security officer the moment they saw her. No other clean, well-dressed person would enter a place like this with her confidence. She waited for the last person to look away and went straight to them, as they seemed to be sitting alone.

"I'm looking for Jimmy Something. Know where he is?"

Being out of uniform, Wells knew she was putting herself in danger, but she could not risk being seen by another officer and getting pulled off the case. At least if she was spotted now, she had some plausible reason for being here. Having a drink in a dodgy pub was not the norm for security officers, but Wells had had a rough few months and hoped that if someone saw her, they would turn a blind eye and put it down to her lousy decision-making skills of late.

"Jimmy who?" the man tried.

This was usually the opening line of anyone who was asked the whereabouts of a person, and Lt. Wells did not expect anything less. She had done this countless times, always getting the same response.

"Look, I know he comes here regularly, and I know you know what I do for a job. But right now, I'm just a person looking for another person, okay?"

"Sorry, can't help you." The usual follow-up line.

Usually, Wells would grab this guy by his hair, slam his head on the table, and ask him whether his memory was improving. Her team would have her back if things got out of hand, and they would also be scanning the room to see if any other person's vitals were changing abnormally on their ARPs. Increased body temperature, heartrate, and brain activity were usually dead giveaways that they had something invested in what was going down. Sometimes they would grab a random person in a group and start asking them questions, just to monitor the rest of the group.

But right now, Lt. Wells had her HIC switched to personal use, and her ARP turned off. She could not risk Penta security seeing what she was doing. She was all by herself and could not risk getting physical with anyone here. She was well trained in hand-to-hand combat but knew almost any man could outmuscle her in here. One on one, she would back herself to take most assailants down, regardless of their size, but in a bar, it was hardly ever a fair fight, and fighting multiple opponents did not make a lot of sense. Wells knew that confidence and stupidity could very quickly become interchangeable.

Lt. Wells sat down across from her mark and whispered, "Okay, buddy. In a second, I am very loudly going to thank you for telling me where Jimmy is and fake swipe my arm to pay you for your efforts. Then I'll leave and try one of the other joints he frequents. No biggie for me. I'll get the info eventually. But I'm sure your friends here would love to thank you for selling out one of your own. So, what do you say?"

The man sat there, trying his best to come up with an original thought, his eyes fixed on Wells, and his mouth slightly ajar; air just going in and out. He closed his mouth, licked his lips and inhaled deeply through his nose.

"No need to be a dick, okay? Anyway, right now, everyone has seen us talking and would make up things we could have been talking about. I'm fucked already, so how about you just leave?"

Lt. Wells had to admit he had a point. The mouth breather took so long to engage in a conversation that she had been sitting here way longer than planned.

"Fair call. How about I call you a piece of shit, storm out of here, and meet you outside in an hour, and you get yourself a hundred credits for your troubles?" Wells tried.

She hated not having the power of Penta behind her right now. She had wasted too much time on this mark already and would have to leave soon. Too many eyes were on them, and no one else would give her the time of day now.

"Two hundred and you've got a deal."

Wells stood up, grabbed his drink, and threw the whole thing at his head. "You could have just said no, you bastard!" she cried and stormed out.

As she left, she could hear some yelling and hollering from the crowd in the bar, most likely cheering him on. She'd reacted instinctively when he agreed, as she knew her time was up. She hoped she hadn't upset his ego too much by acting so quickly and convincingly. All she could do now was hang around and hope that he would show up before the hour was up.

After about ten minutes, Lt. Wells' mark came out of the pub, scanning the area, obviously looking for someone. She was standing next to her car, in a dark corner of the parking lot. She whistled, and he came running like a good boy. Lt. Wells put her hand on the small of her back to reassure herself that her pulse pistol was at the ready. Set at stun. It was a last resort.

"I thought we said an hour."

"Yeah, well," he said, "You didn't say anything about throwing beer in my face. Anyway, I ran out of credits, so here I am."

No one seemed to have bothered to follow them. "Do you know where Jimmy Something is?"

"Sure. How do I know you'll pay up?"

Now outside and standing, Wells realized the guy was considerably larger than she was. She could also tell that he had been sitting at the bar for quite some time; his words were starting to slur ever so slightly, and he was swaying a bit on his feet. She did not doubt that she could take care of him without needing her pulse gun.

"How about I transfer fifty credits now, in good faith, and the rest when we're done here?" Wells offered.

"Okay, do it." He swiped his HIC and activated the communication portal.

Wells entered the amount to be transferred and held her arm next to his. Each HIC pinged, indicating that the transaction had succeeded.

"I don't know where he is, but I know who he might be with. Benjamin Drake. Usually works for Mr. Turner, but I heard Jimmy had some big contract going on, and Drake joined him."

The guy lifted his arm, ready for the next transfer, apparently happy that the information he'd given her would suffice. Wells had never heard of a Benjamin Drake, which meant he was a new player in town, or someone involved in something they knew nothing about. She doubted that anyone was that stupid, so he had to be a criminal from out of town, using Turner as a cover, or maybe even in on the deal with Turner.

"You know where they are now or what the contract is for?" Wells asked.

"Lady, that's all I know. I'm sure you can take it from here." He waved his arm in front of her face, nodding toward his HIC.

Wells typed in the new amount, and as soon as his HIC pinged, the guy started walking back to the pub, flipping her off as he went.

Wells jumped in her hydrocar and logged into her Penta Group account on the DDU. She opened the search function and typed in *Benjamin Drake.*

# | eleven |

The number on the screen kept ticking over, getting smaller and smaller. Drake felt slightly hopeful. They were now only nine hours away from the drop point. Soon, this would be over. But again, the opposite was also true: the longer they have been traveling, the higher the chance that Penta had closed the gap and might be right behind them. Like a compressing spring, all the parts were drawing together. If Penta brought a pulse cannon with them, Drake and Jimmy would not even know what had happened, as they would be disintegrated within microseconds. That might be the best-case scenario, Drake thought.

Jimmy was up, and already searching his Human Interface Console for any news about the stolen Bismuth.

"Hey Jimmy, how about you warm up some meals for us?" Drake asked him.

"Sure, sounds good. Didn't want to impose, but I am actually starving, ya know?" Jimmy replied.

He must have spent some time in a Hydrostar or equivalent type of truck before, because he seemed to know his way around the cabin. He knew where the cooling unit was located and quickly had two portions in the cooking unit. Within seconds the machine pinged, and Jimmy grabbed the two white boxes.

"Here you go!" Jimmy held one of the white boxes out to Drake.

The roads were pretty good, and Drake switched on the Autodrive again but at a reduced speed.

"Thanks, buddy." Drake started to eat his meal, still facing the windscreen.

Autodrive was one of the best AI systems invented, but Drake always felt nervous when he was on one of the back roads. Some people still drove their old manual input hydrogen-powered cars on these roads, and they were the usual cause of accidents. Either the old vehicles broke down, or the driver made some bad decisions and crashed. Drake was not concerned about his or the Hydrostar's survival rate, as the Hydrostar would most likely just cut straight through a hydrocar, but any accident was automatically reported to the company owning the road they were on. That would spell disaster for them, as Penta would surely be scanning all communications and databases for any mention of a Hydrostar. They would immediately have a lock on their location if anything out of the ordinary happened, especially if it involved another vehicle. So, Drake sat facing the windscreen with all its telemetry, scanning the road to make sure nothing happened.

"Aaah, thanks for that, partner. Really hit the spot, ya know," Jimmy said, wiping his mouth with the back of his hand when he had finished.

"No worries," Drake scanned the road as he ate.

"So, you reckon we are safe now?" Jimmy asked him, all fueled up and full of energy.

"To be honest, Jimmy, I don't think we'll ever be safe again," Drake said, more to himself than Jimmy. As he ate, an undeniable realization dawned on Drake: no matter what they did, they were fucked. If Penta caught up to them, they would most likely shoot-to-kill, even if it meant the cargo was destroyed. Penta was not known to play fair or let justice run its course. They preferred to make examples out of people to ensure things they didn't approve of wouldn't happen again.

If they did evade Penta, then Drake and Jimmy would have Zuma to worry about. What were the chances of Zuma honoring their side of the deal, considering the amount of heat Jimmy and Drake were bringing with them and the fact that Zuma was a company dealing in stolen goods? And even if Zuma turned out to be the fairest and most well-intentioned company there ever was, Drake and Jimmy would still have to leave Zuma territory after they dropped off the cargo. The moment they did, Penta would simply resume the chase. Just because they got rid of the cargo did not mean they'd get rid of their wanted status. They were on Penta's shit list and would stay there until Penta caught them or killed them.

Drake realized that both Zuma and Penta had motive to kill them. Going to Zuma was not the end of this shit show. It would buy them some more time, at best.

"We need to change our plan," Drake said, switching off the Auto-drive and retaking control. "We can't go to the drop-off."

"Whoa! H-hold on!" Jimmy stammered. "We had a plan. A deal. Why? What are you talking about?"

"Jimmy, how well do you know this Zuma Corporation? How did you end up dealing with them?"

He didn't answer, but Drake could see Jimmy's lips moving as he was having a conversation with himself. Drake decided to wait.

"Well, it's not so much Zuma that gave me the contract, ya know? You see, I was sitting in a bar one night, can't even recall which one now. You know how they all look alike after a while, right?"

Jimmy looked at Drake expectantly, and Drake dutifully nodded his head.

"Anyway, in walks this guy. He starts chatting to people at their tables. Spends about five to ten minutes at each one. I assumed he must be some sort of a sales guy. Still, I follow his progress until he reaches me. Introduces himself as Justin and offers to buy me a drink. Obviously, I'm not going to say no, so this guy Justin gets me a drink, and I brace myself for the pitch, ya know?"

Jimmy paused, took a deep breath, and continued.

"Justin starts off with some small talk first, and then he comes out and asks me what I do for a living. I tell him, just some odd jobs, mostly entrepreneurial type stuff, ya know? Then he asks me if I'm looking for an opportunity to get a large sum of credits but strictly off the books. So now I'm wondering, is this guy from security, or is this legit? But also,

I'm really curious, ya know, about what this is all about, so I ask him to tell me more.

Jimmy paused again, either for dramatic effect or to catch his breath.

"He says, unfortunately, due to the nature of the contract, that it would not be safe to keep chatting there. We agree to meet three days later at the warehouse.

Drake realized Jimmy was quiet again and saw him fidgeting with his hands, clearly nervous about the next part of his story.

"So, Justin arrives, by himself, and I'm starting to think that this shit is for real, ya know? He starts with his small talk again, really putting me at ease, ya know, and asks me if I have any connection or know anyone who deals with Bob Turner-"

Drake snapped his head around to Jimmy. "Mr. Turner?"

"Yep, partner, your old boss Bob Turner," Jimmy replied.

Mr. Turner, like anyone in the hauler world, was no angel, but Drake couldn't imagine that Bob Turner would have anything to do with this. Dodgy-look-the-other-way deals, sure, but full-on complicit hauling of stolen goods? No way. Jimmy must have made a mistake or misheard this guy. Jimmy had gone silent and was watching him.

"Go on," Drake said.

"Okay, now, I've known about Bob Turner for years and knew a few people, including you, that worked for him. But I wasn't sure if Justin wanted me to say yes or no, so I played dumb and said I knew who he was but that we moved in different circles. A half-truth, ya know? So Justin mulls things over for a bit and then says to me that Mr. Turner has some cargo that he needs to move, but he needs it done off the books and away from the Haulernet. He tells me that Mr. Turner is willing to pay a million credits on completion. Now, I'm ready to sign whatever to get this contract. I tell him as much, and he says that there is one stipulation: that I get a positioning tracker implanted so that they can keep an eye on me, as this is a lot of credits, and Mr. Turner can get into a lot of trouble if this leaks out.

"So, I agree to get the implant done, and Justin goes to his car to get the machine. Have you ever received an implant? Not an HIC, but a tracker? Well, it fucking hurts. My arm was sore for days after, ya know?" Jimmy rubbed his wrist as if the pain was still there. "So we agreed to meet up again in a few days, and he would give me all the details, coordinates, and whatever to get me going. That's when I found you and, well, you already know the rest."

Drake needed a moment to digest it all. This whole time he'd thought that Zuma Corporation was the sole benefactor, but now he realized that Bob Turner could have been in bed with Zuma this entire time. Zuma was buying something Bob Turner had to sell, and Jimmy just had to organize the delivery boy. Did this mean Mr. Turner stole the Bismuth from Penta, or was he just the conduit to get it from one place to the other? Not that it mattered. Drake had worked with and for Bob Turner for years, and suddenly he felt like he knew nothing about him. How long had he been doing dodgy deals? Why had Drake never caught wind of it? Had he been hauling illegal goods for Mr. Turner all along, without even knowing it? Drake had never once checked the cargo. He just assumed what was on the contract was in the back. Was he just Bob Turner's mule? Turner had a soft spot for Drake and made sure he always had a contract for him. Drake had thought he was just very lucky. Turns out he was just plain stupid.

Drake wished he could unhook the cargo and get out of this nightmare, but he realized he had nothing to go back to. He had been hauling for Bob Turner for over ten years and knew no other life. If Bob Turner was indeed involved in this, then Drake's old life was over anyway. If he walked away now, where would he go?

He had no choice but to see this through, get his credits, and then worry about the future. He had to do what he always did: concentrate on the task ahead and make sure it went down as smoothly as possible.

Then drink.

*****

Anderson activated his ARP and contacted Jacob McKenna. The three circles barely had a chance to dance around before him, before they merged and McKenna's face was in front of him.

"Sir, we have confirmation that the Hydrostar was spotted at Anteus and has since departed," Anderson said. "Sources confirmed that the cargo was still attached. We have replotted our course to intercept them, and we have an estimated time until contact of approximately four hours. It seems they have not blocked or scrambled our DDU access yet, and the information we are receiving is correct. We have been able to confirm all the data by witness accounts. I'll report back in an hour."

"Good," McKenna said. He disconnected the line.

# | twelve |

Sitting at a desk, staring at a DDU all day, was driving Lt. Lily Wells insane. For someone who was used to being in the thick of things, getting her hands dirty, and getting the job done, this was a death sentence. Going through other people's data, interpretations of events, and clues was tedious and frustrating. She had to restrain herself from correcting their reports or adding comments and suggestions. She had to remind herself of the bigger picture and to play her role, and right now, that role was to assist the lead team, not to point out their mistakes.

Benjamin Drake was born and raised in New Franco, the capital of Penta. He must have had a normal upbringing since there were no juvenile records for him, and his medical records were just usual kid stuff, nothing that would be flagged for security follow-up. Between the day he was issued a Penta ID on his birth to the day he got his license to haul, there was no mention of him. But on that day, there were two mentions: his name showed in the system as someone who'd passed the hauler test, but there was also a news article. The article was about Adrian and Yolanda Drake, who were killed in a hydrocar accident, leaving behind one child: Benjamin Drake.

Drake was eighteen when he lost his parents, and it seemed he started hauling straight away: Wells found a traffic violation warning issued to him only days after the accident. Nothing major, but it had been logged in the system nonetheless. Things became a bit busier but more predictable as he got older and spent a few more years on the road. There was the occasional traffic violation, which was one part of being a hauler, as well as quite a few fights, which was another.

By all accounts, Benjamin Drake was a hauler through and through.

Although he was mostly on the road, his Penta ID still showed him to be a New Franco resident, which made sense since he contracted mostly to a Bob Turner, who operated out of the outskirts of the city. Like Drake, Turner was involved with hauling and had the same sketchy but not quite criminal background.

Drake was just a hauler, a nobody, but Lt. Wells had a feeling that there was more to him than the DDU told her. And she always trusted her feelings. She decided to pay Bob Turner a visit on her day off.

The green line guided her hydrocar to a large facility, just off one of the highways. The yard had a high fence, but the gates were wide open as trucks came and went, sending dust into the air that settled on the ground only to be thrown up again by the next vehicle. Through the cloud of dust, there was a hive of activity as the trucks loaded and unloaded cargo. Wells hung back for a while, observing the spectacle, and soon realized that the morning must be the busiest time for business, as, in the blink of an eye, the yard became eerily quiet, and the dust finally found some rest. All the haulers were gone, but cargo still littered the yard. Wells assumed that there must be another busy period later in the day when the whole scene would play out again.

Lt. Wells climbed out of her hydrocar and switched on her ARP. Using voice input, she started to scan the area for human body heat signatures. It was a pretty basic scan, as she was still using her private account, but the yard seemed to be void of any life, except for one red shape. She switched off her ARP and spotted the small building where the red form had been. It was the only permanent structure in the yard. One story high and about six by twelve meters, it was lost among all the cargo. Wells walked through the gates and made her way toward the small building.

The door was closed, so she knocked. She could hear noises inside, but no answer. She knocked again.

"Come back later!" a voice bellowed from somewhere inside.

"I'm looking for a friend. Benjamin Drake. Have you seen him?"

No answer, but the noises inside stopped. Wells didn't know if she should try again, or go around the back to see if the person was making a break for it. Her choice was made for her when the door swung open. A huge man filled the space in front of her. He must have been two feet taller than her and weighed at least three times what she did. Although a layer of fat softened his edges, there was clearly a substantial mass of muscle underneath it. Wells wondered if he'd been a moon miner when he was younger. The mining companies always pumped the miners up with steroids to help them overcome the low gravity conditions, or so they said. Wells suspected it was to get them to work harder and longer. Moon miners were a very tough, violent bunch (most likely from the steroids), and Wells knew she would have to tread lightly from here on.

"Mr. Turner? I'm Lily Wells. I'm a friend of Benjamin Drake. I've lost contact with him and was hoping you could help me find him." She tried her best to be as submissive as possible but feared he would see right through it.

Lt. Lily Wells was a lot of things, but timid and fearful she was not. Even though Turner towered over her, she was willing to go head to head with him if needed. Wells was not stupidly arrogant but rather calculating. Her brain was racing at breakneck speeds to try and anticipate his next move and how she would counter him. Her best tactic with big guys was to defend, stay out of reach, and let them tire themselves out. Then she would use her baton and go to town on them, stopping just short of tiring herself out or killing them. She usually also had her ARP on, and help would be there before she got into too much trouble. That was not something she could count on today.

"Haven't seen him in a while," Turner replied. "Which is strange, really, as he usually hangs around here like a lost puppy."

Wells realized how much she depended on having Penta behind her on a day-to-day basis. If she were logged in to her Penta ARP, she would be able to look at his vitals, pick up on micro-movements in his eyes, rising heart rate, or excess perspiration—data Wells usually took for granted. Today she would have to rely on her instincts.

"Oh. You are my last hope. As I heard it, he works for you all the time. I really have nowhere else to go."

"Sorry, but I really can't help you." Bob Turner closed the door.

It had happened pretty much how Wells had imagined it would.That's why she'd bought a small ARP camera the day before. ARP cameras came in all different sizes and qualities, and the one she bought was a little square about the size of a thumbnail, with tiny cameras on every side and a microphone in the middle. This one was more of a toy, as they had limited range and very low-quality streaming, but it would serve Wells' purposes just fine. Just as Turner had opened the door, she'd quickly flicked the little camera into his office, hoping it would land somewhere he wouldn't notice, but close enough to hear and see him.

As the door clicked shut, Wells turned around and walked toward the gate. She knew that there would be cameras everywhere recording her, but she had to stay as close to the office as possible, to pick up the weak signal from the little camera. If Bob Turner were to contact Drake, he would do it now, not later. She stopped at the nearest cargo unit and sat down, face in her hands, seemingly crying. As she sat huddled over, shoulders bobbing up and down, head in her hands, she switched on her ARP by voice and connected to the camera. Since the ARP projected into her retina via the optic nerve, Wells could shut her eyes and see what looked like a screen floating in a dark space.

The camera connected, and Wells could see Bob Turner looking at her through a window. Still looking at her, he swiped his arm and connected to someone she couldn't see. She could, however, to hear Turner's side of the conversation.

"Have you found them yet? . . . You haven't? . . . Did you tell your goons not to engage? I've invested a lot of time and credits in Drake. I would hate to lose him . . . That's not good enough! I need a guarantee that he will not be harmed . . . Keep me posted."

Bob Turner swiped his HIC to end the call and he went back to his desk. He suddenly stood up and went to the door. Wells knew her time was up, so she got up and wiped her face and started to walk out of the compound slowly. She still had her ARP on. Bob Turner was standing at the door, watching her walk away. As she saw herself leaving the compound and disappearing around the corner, the image started to deteriorate, but not before Turner turned and closed the door.

Wells turned her ARP off and walked back to her car. As soon as she was inside, her brain went to work. The way Turner was talking, it was clear he did not contact Drake, but someone else who appeared to be looking for Drake too. Why would he not call Drake directly? Turner had even called him one of his best. Was he using Drake? Was Benjamin Drake an innocent in all this? That would explain his clean-ish record. But he was still on the run with Jimmy Something, who was not an innocent. Could Drake be a victim, or was he playing everyone? Also, who was on the other end of Turner's call? It sounded like there were some trust issues between the two parties, something that could come in handy later.

Wells knew that the team looking for Jimmy Something would uncover most of this information soon. She hoped that Bob Turner's memory of her would not be something he wished to share with them. Wells logged into her security account on her hydrocar's DDU and pulled up the Jimmy Something murder case. She smiled as she realized she was way ahead of everyone else, as usual. The team was still kicking trees to see what would fall out. According to the reports filled so far, they didn't have much to go on. Benjamin Drake's name was only mentioned once, briefly, but no follow-up had been noted. Wells knew with the information she had so far, she would be able to catch Jimmy Something within days if she was on the lead squad. She knew if she shared her intel now, Captain Santo would use it and claim the victory for himself, which would not help her get back her spot on the team. No, she would have to keep doing this herself, until she could figure out a way to use this information to get what she wanted.

\*\*\*

A small pulse went through Jacob McKenna's arm. Bob Turner's name flashed across his HIC. He took a deep breath and swiped his arm.

"Have you found them yet?"

"Hello, Bob. No, but my team is right behind them." The connection was horrible, and the visual of Bob kept jumping around.

"So, you haven't?"

"No, but as I said, we are right behind them and should make contact within the hour," McKenna said, trying to keep his cool.

"Did you tell your goons not to engage? I've invested a lot of time and credit in Drake. I would hate to lose him."

"I know, Bob. Are you alone?" McKenna replied.

It appeared another ARP was interfering with their signal.

"What? Yes, I'm alone."

"Anyway, they have strict orders not to engage unless they have to defend themselves, of course." McKenna was struggling to focus.

"That's not good enough! I need a guarantee that he will not be harmed."

"I will contact my team and tell them your wishes. But you know if I do not get my cargo, there will be no payment from me, and I'll still need to get that Bismuth, right?"

"Keep me posted," Bob Turner said, ignoring the thinly veiled threat and disconnecting the call.

"And who are you?" McKenna asked rhetorically.

His ARP kept cutting out and showing a low-quality stream of Bob Turner from a different angle during their conversation. And now it showed Turner standing at his door, looking at a woman walking away. As she walked away, the signal got even worse until it disappeared.

"Who are you?" McKenna asked again.

# | thirteen |

Drake's nightmare just kept getting worse. Not only had he become best friends and business partners with a scumbag like Jimmy Something, but he'd also found out that he had been working for a criminal all along. He had always put Bob Turner on a pedestal, compared to the other contract handlers, and had defended him whenever haulers questioned his integrity or dealings. Looking back, Drake realized that maybe Bob had been playing him all along. All the little indiscretions Bob overlooked, the slack he always cut him, the way he made sure Drake had work at all times. He always knew Bob Turner had a soft spot for him but was it just a ruse?

"You look like you are going to lose your lunch there, partner." Jimmy's voice snapped Drake back to the real world.

"This is so much worse than I thought, Jimmy. So much worse." Jimmy just stared at the floor, too nervous to say anything.

"Right now, we're hurtling toward an unknown entity that will most likely rather shoot us than pay us, while at the same time running away from a well-known entity that will most fucking definitely kill us. There is only one thing to do," Drake said. He told Yolanda what he needed.

After a few seconds, Bob Turner's face appeared on the windshield.

"I've been waiting for this call," he said, looking Drake straight in the eye.

Drake tried to bite his tongue, to avoid lashing out at him. His teeth missed.

"You fucking bastard! You played me all along!"

"I did nothing of the sort. I gave you contracts, you hauled them, and then I paid you," Turner replied.

Drake tried the teeth and tongue thing again, this time with success. What Mr. Turner said was correct, but he'd made it very black and white, and nothing in the hauler world was ever that clear cut.

"Yes, but . . ." Drake started, but he realized he had no argument, and maybe he'd acted too quickly in confronting Turner.

"Think of me and our dealings what you will. But right now you need to focus on the job at hand. I have spoken to the guys at Zuma, and they have promised me that they will do everything they can to make this a smooth transaction. Which it is—just another transaction."

"Fine. But why didn't you just make it a normal contract? Why all the fuss?" Drake asked the obvious question.

Bob Turner took a deep breath, his enormous chest expanding and then slowly dropping again. Drake knew that time was running out.

"Because right now you have the whole force of the Penta security group motivating you not to screw up," Bob Turner said, and with that, he disconnected the call.

"That went pretty good, ya know?" Jimmy said, sounding way too cheery.

Drake ignored him. He needed a minute to process it all. Turner had confirmed his fears that Penta was chasing them, but he'd also alleviated his concerns about Zuma. Right now, it seemed safer to hurl ahead as fast as possible, rather than worry about what was behind them.

"I guess so, Jimmy. Let's hope you're right." Drake said.

The estimated time to their destination was now only four hours. Even though the threat ahead had diminished, for the time being, Drake could not risk getting back on the highway to try and make up some time. Penta would be able to use more of their resources on the highway, like cameras, smaller companies' security forces, and tip-offs from their own haulers. Staying on the back roads was slower but still the safer option.

"Any news about us yet?" Drake asked Jimmy, who quickly started typing on the DDU.

After a few minutes, he said, "Nothing much on the news. Actually, nothing about stolen Bismuth at all."

Drake found that very suspicious. Why wouldn't Penta make a big deal about stolen goods?

"But," Jimmy continued, "on the Haulernet, things are heating up."

"Okay, spit it out. What have you found?"

"Well, a lot of talk about us working together. People saying some nasty things about me. . ."

"What else?" Drake barked, not picking up on Jimmy's change in mood.

"Just more stuff, ya know," Jimmy whispered.

Drake was about to knock Jimmy's head against the window when he saw the slumped figure staring at the floor. Drake thought back to what Jimmy'd said and realized his mistake.

Drake was starting to feel like he was in a relationship.

"Hey, buddy, you can't worry about what people say about you. It'll drive you mad," he tried.

"Most people are just speculating as to our chances of survival, ya know," Jimmy said, his mood still gloomy. "There is even some betting going on. It seems most folks reckon we aren't gonna make it."

"Maybe we should put a bet on ourselves, since we know we are going to make it, hey partner?" Drake said and received a small smile from Jimmy.

"Yeah! Show those fuckers who's an idiot," Jimmy said to himself.

The road was clean, straight, and empty. They drove into a new territory, and Drake blindly accepted all the waivers. The truck was still on Autodrive, and all the telemetry looked in order, so Drake turned back to Jimmy.

"So, for the moment, it seems that Zuma won't shoot us, Turner's a lying son of a bitch, and Penta hasn't caught up to us yet."

Jimmy nodded, eagerly waiting for the next sentence.

"But, there's still one thing we need to figure out."

Drake thought it was obvious, but Jimmy still looked like he was waiting for the big reveal.

"You, Jimmy," Drake spelled it out for him. "We need to figure out what happens after we get the credit from Zuma. The fact is, you'll still be wanted for murder and arson."

"Ah, yeah, that. Ya know, you shouldn't be worrying about me. I've been in these spots before, ya know? Nothing Jimmy Something can't handle!" Jimmy said, trying to sound tough but looking terrified.

"Okay, but I haven't, and right now, I'm pretty sure they think I'm an accomplice to all your shenanigans," Drake said.

"I'll just tell them you had nothing to do it with the warehouse!"

Drake took a deep breath.

"If you're talking to the authorities, it'll mean that you've already been captured, Jimmy, and everything, even this little adventure we have now, will be investigated. So maybe we need to make sure neither one of us gets caught."

"I guess you're right."

"Okay, tell me again. What happened at the warehouse?"

***

Anderson zoomed in until the speck became a blob, which became a bigger blurry picture. The image was pixelated but good enough for running analytics.

"Get us another klick closer," Anderson said to the driver next to him.

They sped up until they were a thousand meters closer to the object, then went back to matching its speed. The blurry object became slightly sharper. Although it was two kilometers away, Anderson could see enough on the screen to know it was them. He typed again, and a few seconds later, Jacob McKenna appeared on his side of the windscreen.

"Sir, we have visual confirmation. They are traveling in your direction, and we have not seen any other bogeys," Anderson said.

"Good job, Anderson. Keep your distance and make sure no one else gets close to them." McKenna disconnected the call.

"Yes, sir!" Anderson said to the blank screen. He relayed the orders back to the rest of the team.

***

McKenna turned away from the screen. He wished he'd never agreed to save Turner's little pet's life. It would have been so much easier just to hijack the truck so close to the compound and get rid of them. But he still had plans for Turner, and upsetting him over a trifling thing like two criminals' lives was not worth it. He just had to babysit them now and pay them off when they arrived. A million credits was a considerable amount, even to someone like McKenna, but he knew once his plan was complete, it would seem like a drop in a bucket. McKenna activated his ARP and made a call.

"Sir, didn't expect a call yet," the nervous-looking man in a white lab uniform said. "Everything is going to plan, and we are eagerly awaiting the Bismuth to start production."

"Have shuttles three and four been fully tested?" McKenna asked.

He had already checked the progress earlier with another engineer but needed to make sure everyone stayed on their toes.

"Yes sir, both passed the test, and I sent the report to your HIC. Did you not get it?" The man was starting to sweat.

"I'll check. Keep me posted."

He found the report and read it. Cutting through all the jargon, it said that all four shuttles were now ready for launch as soon as the Polonium was created. McKenna smiled. Building these shuttles had depleted all his funds, but now he was ready to do what only Penta Group had been able to do so far: fly to Mars.

# | fourteen |

Captain Santo's team had some leads on Jimmy Something that led them to Anteus. They had concluded that Jimmy was on the run and getting rides with haulers. He had last been seen with a known hauler named Benjamin Drake. Captain Santo updated the report, and finally, Lt. Lily Wells could investigate Benjamin Drake without raising eyebrows. She was a little disappointed that the team had caught up to her so quickly, but her own investigation had slowed down a bit, and being able to investigate Drake on her Penta DDU would speed things up tremendously.

Now she could really dig into the mysterious Benjamin Drake. She typed his name into her Penta Security DDU and waited as all the information was gathered deep inside the digital vaults of Penta. She was surprised when only a few seconds later, the DDU displayed his data. Usually, the longer it took, the more information there was on the person, which meant that Drake had a pretty small file. She opened his record, and a few photos appeared on the screen.

It showed Benjamin Drake through the years, starting with his first hauler ID at age eighteen, to his most recent Penta security photo, taken after a small altercation outside a hydro station. There were four rows of photos, with six images per row. Twenty-four photos were showing Benjamin Drake go from a fresh-faced youngster to something that annoyed Lt. Wells more than she cared to admit. The last two rows of faces were identical: the same shortish dark hair, an unshaven face with a confident smile that matched mischievous eyes. A few eyes were black or swollen, and in some he sported a busted lip as well. A few must have been ID or license photos as there were no visible injuries. What annoyed Lt. Wells was that the bastard looked better with every frame, even with his injuries, crows' feet, and some salt mixed in with the pepper.

Wells closed the screen an opened another file, one that contained words without any distracting photos.

Benjamin Drake came from a typical, working-class family. He went to a normal school, not some detention center for boys, and after school, he only popped up in the system now and then for assault (bar fights) and some traffic violations. Mostly fines, but he'd done a few overnighters in lockup (drunk and disorderly, and fighting). Lt. Wells had seen cleaner slates before, but in a murder case, this file would hardly get a second glance. She could see now why Capt. Santo had not acted earlier. There wasn't much to go on.

Lt. Wells had to ask herself again whether Drake was caught up in something or if he was indeed a much smarter criminal who had been able to go undetected. And how did he fit in with the warehouse killings? She decided to watch the clip again.

On the screen, Jimmy Something spoke to the guy behind the pillar. Then suddenly, Jimmy turned and started shooting at unseen assailants. More people appeared, and the battle continued. Lt. Wells had watched the clip so many times that she had recurring dreams about it. The bad quality, the awkward angle, and the lack of audio didn't help in getting any real clues from it. The only obvious things were that it was clearly Jimmy Something in the clip and that a bunch of people were killed by him. Although Drake never showed up in the clip, she was sure he had a connection to this. She just had to find out how.

Lt. Wells was still desk-bound, but with Drake in the system now, she could, at last, pursue him the way she wanted to. She cross-referenced his name with all known haulers in the system to see if there were any connections. Most haulers lived pretty rough lives and ended up in the system for things like assault, carrying illegal items, traffic violations, and worse crimes like rape and murder. There were as many haulers building houses on Mars as there were hauling back on Earth. Wells' search brought up a long list of names, and she started to eliminate the ones who were deceased or on Mars. She kept going through the list, looking at the profiles and either keeping or eliminating people based on what she read and her intuition, something she'd used with great success in her past.

She knew which night Drake had been spotted in Anteus, so she used her list to see who else was there. A few names popped up, but two of them had more history with Drake than the others. If he were to talk to someone, she bet it would be with someone he had known longer and had some shared history. Being haulers meant they could be anywhere now, so instead of driving around wasting time finding them, she decided to give them a ring. Doing this was going beyond what her current role at Penta dictated, but she felt it worth the risk. She quickly found their contact details, using Penta's intrusive software, and connected via her desktop DDU.

"This is Lieutenant Wells from Penta security. Please pull over."

The truck's locator indicated it was in a Penta Corporation territory, which gave Lt. Wells all the authority she needed to question them, and if needed, even arrest them by remotely shutting down the truck and locking them in until a local team could pick them up. She hoped it wouldn't come to that, or she would have a lot to explain to Captain Santo. Luckily the hauler chose the path of least resistance and pulled over.

"Thank you. This will only take a few minutes. We are trying to locate two men: Jimmy Something and Benjamin Drake. We have good intel that puts Drake with you only hours ago."

He squirmed in his chair. "Yeah, I saw him, just last night, actually. Why?"

Wells decided to let him stew for a while. She could see sweat starting to build up on his forehead, and his palms must have gotten clammy as well, as he was rubbing them on his thighs. ARP's telemetry readings only worked when the person was standing in front of you, but she didn't need it to see that the man on the screen was not happy to talk about his encounter with Drake.

"We believe that he is traveling with Jimmy Something, who you might know has a warrant out for his arrest," she finally continued.

The guy was nervous but so far cooperative. Before she'd made contact, Wells had programmed her DDU to shut down his truck with a single button, if needed. She hoped she would not have to resort to using it.

"Nah, he was by himself when we saw him."

"We? Who else was with you?"

"Oh, shit, let me think." Lyle Miller realized his mistake and tried to buy himself some time, tossing up if he was going to get Sara and Burt involved. "There were a couple of us, you know, just grabbing a beer at the end of the day."

"I understand, Mr. Miller, but if you could be a bit more specific, please."

Lt. Wells knew he was stalling and trying to protect his hauler friends. Wells appreciated the bond and tribalism that the haulers shared, as she was part of a tribe with her fellow security officers, but right now, she needed less brotherly love and more names.

"As I said, Drake was all by himself when we saw him, and to be honest, he sounded like he was hauling a normal contract, all on his own. Drake's never really been a team player, if you know what I mean."

"So, Jimmy Something was not with him?"

Wells wished she was face-to-face with him so she could get some readings on her ARP, but his body language told her there was more information to be uncovered.

"No, but if I recall correctly, yes, thinking about it, Drake did mention that he got the contract from Jimmy."

Lyle Miller knew he was toeing a fine line between staying out of jail and betraying a fellow hauler. However, he had no loyalties to Jimmy Something and would happily give him up if it would help Drake.

"Wouldn't surprise me if Jimmy duped him into doing something stupid. Drake is not the sharpest tool around," Miller said, smiling.

"Do you know where they are heading?" Wells asked, knowing how he would answer.

"Sorry, he didn't really say much, and I never saw him leave," Miller said, telling the truth. "Drake is not a bad guy, you know. Just stupid."

"Thank you for your time, Mr. Miller, and please contact me if you hear or remember anything else."

Lt. Wells had all the resources of Penta security behind her, and Lyle Miller was still in a Penta Corporation territory, so she typed some commands into her DDU and started to monitor everything that went through Miller's DDU and HIC.

***

Drake was still letting the truck drive itself, and the countdown had just clicked down to three hours when he received a call on the screen. It was Lyle Miller. Drake hadn't spoken to him in months until last night, and now he was calling him? Drake knew this would not be a social call.

"Lyle! Sorry man, if you are looking for your mother, you just missed her." Drake fired the first shot.

"Yeah, yeah. Listen here," Miller jumped right in, not partaking in their usual banter, emphasizing the urgency, "I just got a call from Penta security, and they are hot on your trail, buddy. I assume your DDU is secure?"

"What? Yes, of course. Hacked it ages ago. No way anyone could be listening in. What did they say?" Drake leaned forward in his chair.

Jimmy mimicked his move, putting himself in Miller's view.

"Oh, Jesus, Drake! What the fuck is he doing in your truck?"

Drake gave Jimmy a reassuring look.

"It's okay, Lyle. Things are a bit more complicated than I thought."

"Well, now they are. You need to get away from that dickhead, Drake. Unless you have something to do with all this . . ." Miller let his words trail off, not wanting to state the obvious.

"No. I mean, I am involved with the stolen Bismuth but not the warehouse stuff. They are sort of connected though . . . ." This time Drake just let his words hang there.

Lyle Miller just stared back at him, mouth slightly hanging open. Drake waited for an insult, but it never came.

"Don't worry, Lyle, Drake is as innocent as a . . . as a . . . ." Jimmy tried to think of a smart way to say it, ". . . as a newborn."

Jimmy winked at Drake. *I got your back.* Drake sighed.

"My hands are clean of the warehouse stuff, but I'm afraid I'm knee-deep in the rest. Ever heard of Zuma Corp.?"

"Yes, done tons of work for them. Why? Oh, shit. No no no no. Drake, did you steal this from them?"

"No," Drake replied. "Zuma is the contractor. We are heading there now. Why are you so dramatic?"

"Because Jacob McKenna is a fucking psycho! And everyone knows that. But again, you seem to gravitate toward that sort of character these days," Miller gave a pointed look at Jimmy.

Drake jumped in before Jimmy could get all worked up.

"We have reassurances from Bob Turner that they will not harm us."

"What the hell did you drag *him* into this for?" Miller asked.

"As I said, it has become more complicated."

"Well, I told them nothing they wouldn't know already, but you best lay low, or hurry up, or do whatever you need to do because Penta isn't going to let this go easily," Miller said.

\*\*\*

"Zuma Corporation," Lt. Lily Wells said to herself, as she typed it into her DDU.

The conversation between Lyle Miller and Benjamin Drake was automatically recorded. Drake was connected to the case, and Wells had put a tag on Miller. Although most haulers had their DDUs bridged or hacked, it was still no match for the vast budget that Penta had to counter their every move. Working around their little safety wall took only two seconds.

The file containing the recording between Miller and Drake would sit in limbo until she tagged it with the correct case number and made the appropriate notes. Failing to do so could get you into deep trouble with your team leader, but Lt. Wells had to hide the new information for as long as possible. Some rookie would have the duty of cleaning up all untagged files daily and usually contacted the personnel involved first, as a way to suck up a bit. Wells hoped that would be the case.

The DDU came up with information about Zuma Corporation. It had a lot of small territories, but the region that housed the headquarters was the one Lt. Wells was most interested in. That was the one where Jacob McKenna would be. Assuming that Drake and Jimmy Something were headed there, and knowing they came from Anteus, Lt. Wells plotted all possible routes between the two points. The quickest and easiest way would be the highway, but Wells doubted they were dumb enough to do that. That left a few smaller back roads. There were only a few small settlements and towns on these roads. All Lt. Wells had to do now was to find live footage from these towns and wait for the suspects to show their faces.

# | fifteen |

A message appeared on the Hydrostar's screen, notifying Drake that they had crossed into Zuma Corporation territory. It was accompanied by all the usual waivers. Drake ticked all the necessary boxes without reading any of the print, big or small. Crossing into the Zuma territory gave him a slight sense of relief. Had they done it? Had they actually outrun Penta? Maybe everything was going to be okay. The on-screen map showed their destination to be just under two hours away. Drake turned to Jimmy.

"I think we might have gotten away with this."

"Looks like it, but I'll feel even better when we have our credits and are well on our way, ya know," Jimmy replied.

Drake wondered how things were going to go down. After the drop-off, and once Zuma had transferred the credits, the contract between himself and Jimmy would expire. There'd be no reason to stay together anymore. Except that Drake had grown used to Jimmy. He knew Penta would never give up their hunt for him. Drake imagined Jimmy would spend most of his credits trying to impress people and drawing lots of attention to himself, therefore helping Penta locate him. Drake gave Jimmy three days, tops, before he ran out of credits or got caught.

"So, have you decided where we are going after this?" Jimmy asked him as if reading his mind.

"Oh, well, not really. I mean, you need to make a run for it as soon as we split the credits. I'm sure Penta will still be looking for you," Drake said, trying to disengage himself from Jimmy's future plans.

"You mean us?" Jimmy stated, more than asked. "They will be looking for us, partner. Lyle made it clear that they are looking for us both, ya know?"

Drake knew this, but he also knew he had a better chance of evading Penta on his own. Jimmy was a liability, but Drake knew he couldn't just feed him to the wolves either.

"Okay," Drake said. "Do you know of somewhere we can go that is not Penta friendly? And don't even think of saying Mars."

"Sure, lots of places, but I think you should really reconsider Mars, I mean—" Jimmy was cut off by a loud announcement on the screen.

"This is Major Anderson, chief of Zuma Corporation security. Please stop your vehicle and be prepared to be boarded."

Drake weighed his options but quickly realized that he could not outrun them. He also didn't feel like getting shot at, so he switched the Autodrive off and brought the Hydrostar to a stop.

"Thank you. Please open the door and come out with your hands visible," Major Anderson ordered.

Drake punched the button next to the door and slowly stepped out of the Hydrostar, with Jimmy right behind him.

"Where are they?" Jimmy asked the obvious question as they stepped onto the road. There was no sign of any other vehicle.

They turned around and scanned their surroundings, trying to find the Zuma security team. The landscape was pretty flat, with a few small hills popping up. Short brown grass covered most of the ground, with big rocks and a few leafless trees scattered around. Obviously, this area's riches were not above ground.

An armored vehicle appeared on the horizon, cutting straight through the field, not bothering with the road. It bounced over the small rocks and mounds, its enormous tires making short work of the environment. As it drew closer, Drake could see the gold Zuma security logo displayed all over it. He hoped Mr. Turner had been right about their safety. The vehicle stopped, and six identical men got out. All had half helmets on and heavy armor in black with gold details. Their weapons were lowered but at the ready. Drake could not pick one apart from the other.

"Which one of you pretty boys is Anderson, then?" Drake asked.

"Thank you for your cooperation, Mr. Drake," a guy who looked like all the others said.

"My pleasure. I have something here that your boss wants, so how about you step aside and let us get it to him?" Drake said, hoping he was addressing the guy who had spoken first.

"We have been sent to escort you the rest of the way. If you could please lock your truck onto our vehicle, we can be on our way," the guy who had to be Anderson said.

Locking onto a vehicle was a function of Autodrive. It was used mostly on highways, and when in use, it coupled a train of hydrocars together, all running very close to each other. It was mainly a way of reducing wind resistance but also helped traffic flow on the highways. Any hydrocar could disengage at any time. Once disconnected, the hydrocar would move to the side of the train, and the following hydrocars would fill the void and complete the train again. Since the invention of the Hyperloops, fewer and fewer people used the highways, and hydrocar trains became a rare sight.

The second use of the locking feature was more common. It allowed security forces to lock your car into a mini train with their vehicle, but unlike the civilian version, the front vehicle made all the decisions, and the follower vehicle had no control at all. Only the front vehicle could disengage a lock. Drake dreaded giving up any power he had left.

"Sure, or we can just follow you guys," Drake tried. "I promise we'll keep up."

The one he thought was Anderson did not look amused.

"If you don't mind," he said, and pointed Drake back to his Hydrostar.

"Okay then," Drake said to Jimmy. He led the way back to the truck. "Let's get rolling."

"We have the cargo, sir," Anderson updated McKenna once Drake's Hydrostar was locked in, and they were back on the road.

"Good. Make sure it gets here in one piece," McKenna replied.

Within two hours, he'd have all the Bismuth he needed to create the Polonium for the shuttles.

Everything was going exactly according to schedule.

***

Drake closed the door of the Hydrostar and sat down. Jimmy sat down beside him.

"So, you're just going to lock on, then?" Jimmy asked.

"Well, I don't think we have much choice, really," Drake said as he started to use the DDU to lock onto the vehicle in front of him.

Although Anderson had implied everything was done voluntarily, Drake knew that it would not be a normal lock on, where he would have the power to disengage, but rather a hostile one that gave Anderson all the control. From here on in, they were just passengers in the Hydrostar. A confirmation message appeared on the screen. Drake hated not being in control but was kind of happy for this turn of events.

"Okay, now that we have some time up our sleeves," Drake said to Jimmy, "we need to make a plan."

"But we had time before. Wasn't the truck driving itself anyway?"

A valid point, one Drake chose to ignore.

"Yes, but . . . whatever, Jimmy. Right now, we need to concentrate on a plan," Drake said, trying not to get distracted or irritated.

The big unknown that awaited them post drop-off was getting to Drake. He usually played things on the fly, no plans, just do and see what happens. But then again, he had never been in this big of a mess before.

Drake had to face one massive reality: his life was never going to be the same again. When he took the deal with Jimmy, he thought that he might have had to lay low for a while after the cargo was delivered, but now that Bob Turner was involved as well, Drake realized his previous life was over. He was about to make a lot of credits, but he still had a lot of heat on him. Even if he could distance himself from Jimmy and the warehouse thing, he was still involved in hauling stolen goods. One way or another, he had some bad news coming his way.

Drake only had an hour to figure out a plan and decide if Jimmy was part of it.

# | sixteen |

Jimmy Something's childhood was less than idyllic. It was the kind of upbringing that would lead most people to pity him. And most people did, with their looks and sad head shakes. Jimmy hated that. He hated people thinking their lives were so much better than his miserable one. The only thing Jimmy hated more than his own life was pity. So, from a very young age, he decided to hide his problems and bruises from the world and be his own man. Jimmy spent as little time as possible at home and soon started to hang out with fellow house avoiders—the kind of kids who would eventually end up on Mars one day. Jimmy was smaller than most of the kids, and he had to learn how to defend himself. But he quickly realized he was better at avoiding getting into that sort of situation altogether. Clearly not by his quick wit and thinking but by his sheer will to survive; Jimmy could improvise and double-cross and burn bridges faster than anyone around, and somehow he always came out more or less unscathed.

Jimmy spend less and less time at home until he just stopped going back at all. He fell in with some gangs and lived wherever he could squeeze in. It was not a glamorous or stable life, but Jimmy had never felt so at home. With his happy-go-lucky attitude and lack of any foresight, Jimmy made plenty of friends but also some enemies. Most people in town, of a particular disposition, heard the name or crossed paths with Jimmy Something at one time or another. So it was no surprise that Bob Turner made sure Justin joined that group.

When Justin Lake saw Jimmy Something at the bar, he knew it would be a cinch to convince him to transport the Bismuth. Jimmy was moving from table to table, trying to be friendly with people and getting the brush off, but he never gave up. The moment one table told him off, he made his way to the next, trying his luck there. Some tables tolerated him longer than others, but he always seemed to be moving around, never settling down.

Justin went around pitching his deal to a few people half-heartedly, keeping an eye on Jimmy. He had to make sure it looked like he was trying his luck with everyone. Jimmy looked over a few times and Justin knew Jimmy was aware of him. He kept doing the rounds until he saw Jimmy settle at a table alone. He made his way over.

"Hi there. Justin Lake," he said, extending his hand.

"Jimmy. What ya selling?" Jimmy asked, ignoring Justin's outstretched hand.

Justin dropped his hand onto the back of the chair in front of him.

"Very perceptive there, Jimmy. You from here, or just passing through?" Justin pulled the chair out and sat down.

"Born and raised, ya know," Jimmy replied.

"Ah, a local! Great. Is it always this warm here?" Justin asked with a big insecure smile.

Jimmy seemed to relax a bit, and Justin knew he had a foot in the door.

"Yip, that's why we call it summer," Jimmy said.

Justin laughed harder than Jimmy's reply deserved.

"And a sense of humor. Guess I walked into that one. Can I grab you a beer?" Justin asked, already getting up and walking to the bar.

Jimmy looked a bit confused by Justin's question. Justin knew he had the upper hand and had control of the conversation.

"Sure, but nothing fancy, okay?" Jimmy finally replied.

Justin returned with two beers, and Jimmy quickly drank half. Justin made sure it wasn't the most expensive stuff but also not the unmarked beer either. Jimmy seemed to liked it.

"Pretty good, eh? So, what do you do with yourself in the daytime?" Justin asked.

"None of your damn business," Jimmy replied defensively

"I mean, what sort of job do you do?" Justin tried again.

"Oh, sorry, misunderstood you there, ya know. Well, I'm a bit of an entrepreneur," Jimmy said. "Nothing too specific, ya know. Just a little bit of this and a little bit of that."

Jimmy took another big swig from the beer.

"Sounds like the sort of partner I'm looking for," Justin said, nodding.

Jimmy finished his beer and put the empty glass close to Justin.

"Well, looks like I'm done for the night, so unless you can wrap this up very quickly . . ." Jimmy was clearly not a card player.

"How about I get us another round, and we keep talking?" Justin got up before Jimmy could fake protest.

When he got back, Justin said, "So, as I was saying. My client is looking for someone who operates independently and discreetly. The payment reflects this."

Justin took a slow sip of his beer, waiting for Jimmy to bite.

It didn't take long.

"Say I'm interested. How much does it pay?"

"Well, here's the thing, Jimmy. This contract is a strictly off-the-books deal, so at this stage, I can only tell you that it is well over six figures."

Justin did his slow, sipping thing again. Jimmy struggled to keep a straight face, and Justin could see the excitement washing over his face. Playing cards against him would be like shooting fish in a barrel.

"So, how do we do this?" Jimmy asked, failing to hide his enthusiasm.

Justin told him to meet him at a warehouse the next day and that he would divulge all the information he needed. He gave Jimmy the address, got him another beer, and excused himself.

\*\*\*

Jimmy could hardly sleep that night and was already well on his way, spending all his newfound riches. He imagined all the new clothes and gadgets he could buy. Finally, people would show him some more respect. First, he would get a new hydrocar. The latest model from Nikolatec so that everyone would see him coming. Definitely a new hydrocar first. Then he would upgrade to the newest HIC and ARP from Citro. And new clothes. Lots of new clothes. He couldn't wait to see Justin again and get this contract done, and his credits transferred.

He was so eager that he woke up way too early and arrived two hours before the agreed time at the warehouse. He couldn't find a chair, so he sat on the bare floor to wait, his excitement never fading. Every few minutes, there was a false alarm, as something made a noise, and he thought it was Justin, but eventually, he showed up.

"Jimmy! Great to see you. Been waiting long?" Justin asked as he came walking over.

Jimmy got up and almost fell again, as both his legs had gone to sleep. He decided to stand on the spot and wait for the blood to flow again and not risk a wobbly walk toward Justin.

"Nah, just got here myself, ya know," Jimmy said, feeling the pins and needles in his legs spreading.

"Great. Man, you guys sure love it warm up here!" Justin said as he wiped his brow.

"I guess," Jimmy said, "never been anywhere else, so—"

"Trust me, this is warm," Justin replied, smiling.

"So, ya know, what's the deal, man?" Jimmy asked, not wanting to rush Justin but also struggling to contain himself.

"Straight to the point, I like it. The deal, my man, is that my client has some Bismuth that he needs to haul. That easy."

"So why all the secrecy and stuff? Is Bismuth illegal or something?" Jimmy asked, not ever heard of Bismuth before.

"Not illegal, just very hard to find!" Justin smiled at him.

Jimmy knew there had to be more to it.

"So, why not just haul it out?"

"Okay, so there is a bit more to it," Justin conceded. "Have you ever heard of Bob Turner?"

Jimmy knew the name well but had never met the man himself. Bob Turner was the owner of one of the last independent hauling companies in New Franco. Jimmy had nothing to do with him but had heard some stories about him. Scary stories, most of them about broken bones.

"Everyone knows Mr. Turner, why?"

"Well, he is the client looking to haul the Bismuth. As it is off the books, he would prefer not to use his own people. That is where you come in. Mr. Turner is willing to pay one million credits to ensure the cargo reaches its destination undetected."

For the first time in his life, Jimmy was lost for words. A million credits for a simple job like this! Was this guy for real? Jimmy wondered what the catch was, as this was definitely too good to be true.

"There is one small catch, though," Justin said, reading Jimmy like an elementary school book. "The Bismuth was not obtained through the normal channels, and the original owner might try to get it back."

"Oh, so it's stolen. Figured as much," Jimmy lied. "Who was it stolen from?"

"I'm not going to lie to you, Jimmy, as I believe we have already gotten to some verbal agreement," Justin paused long enough for Jimmy to ponder his words, "so I'll be frank. The Bismuth came from a Penta Corp facility."

Being one of the Big Five corporations, who between them controlled most of the territories on Earth, Penta was also the largest manufacturer of weapons and had the strongest security forces on the planet. If you were to steal anything from anyone, it best not be from anyone remotely connected to Penta, much less directly from them. Justin knew this, as would anyone else, but Jimmy's face implied he didn't.

"So we might get some heat. No biggie. It might shock you, ya know, but old Jimmy is no stranger to the wrong side of the law." This time Jimmy paused for effect.

"I just wanted to be clear with you, lay all my cards on the table before we signed off on this."

"Well, your cards are on the table, and I am ready to sign!" Jimmy said.

"All right then," Justin said and rolled his shirt sleeve up to access his HIC.

Jimmy noticed that it was the latest model and promised himself to get the exact same one as soon as he got paid. Justin moved over to Jimmy, typed something on the screen, and swiped it toward Jimmy's HIC. The file contained pages and pages of writing. Every time Jimmy swiped down, another bunch of pages appeared. It seemed to be a never-ending loop of words.

"That is the contract detailing everything we've discussed. Feel free to read it, but as I said, this is off the books, so the file will disappear within thirty minutes or when you close it. Take your time," Justin said and turned around to give Jimmy some privacy.

As he did, his HIC pinged.

"All done. So, where is the Bismoot?" Jimmy asked.

"Bismuth. You sure read that quickly. Did you even look at when you'll get paid, or about the tracking device?" Justin asked him back.

"Sure, I mean, as you said, we already talked about everything, ya know?" Jimmy said. "But just to make sure, when exactly do I get paid, and what is this about a tracking device?"

"As per the contract you signed," Justin said, sounding way too formal suddenly for Jimmy's liking, "the full amount will be paid upon delivery of the Bismuth. A small amount can be paid upfront to cover any expenses needed to get going. And as for the tracking device, it's just a standard little implant that will sit under your skin, so Mr. Turner and I can keep track of you and the cargo without the need to hack your HIC. See it as a security device."

"And where do I get this implant thing?" Jimmy asked.

"One minute," Justin said and walked over to his hydrocar.

When he came back, he had a small, black case with him. There was a silver, surgical-looking instrument inside. Justin took it out and held his other hand out to Jimmy.

"Your arm please," he said.

Justin pressed the tip of the instrument against Jimmy's wrist, and, just as he was about to press the button, he said, "This might hurt a bit."

He was right. Jimmy let out a yell as fire shot up his arm.

"What the fuck, man?" he screamed at Justin.

He walked in circles, rubbing his arm where Justin had implanted the device. The burning sensation crawled back down his arm and now centered on the implant area. Jimmy kept rubbing and walking, but it failed to help.

"Sorry. But most people get too nervous and move too much if I tell them it's going to hurt," Justin replied.

Jimmy could feel the stinging starting to subside but still felt the need to do one more lap of rubbing and walking.

When Jimmy finally stopped walking, they agreed to meet up again in two days to finalize the logistics. Justin packed up his torture device and left Jimmy still standing and holding his wrist.

Jimmy had some work to do in the next 48 hours: he had to find someone willing to haul stolen goods from Penta, and he had to try and get it done as cheaply as possible. The less he paid the hauler, the more he would keep for himself.

No problem, Jimmy told himself.

# | seventeen |

Lieutenant Lily Wells was hours away from the Zuma Headquarters. Even on a Hyperloop, it would take her too long to get there. Captain Santo's team was closer, but if she told them where to go to right now, they would just swoop in and take all the credit. She would get a pat on the back and be sent back to her desk. She had to figure a way out to keep track of Drake and Something after the cargo was delivered, so she could then catch them herself. Or, Wells had to face it, she could tell Captain Santo now and hope for the best. If they got away, she would find herself chained to her desk forever.

Her plan to monitor the live feeds from the back roads worked. A small town had picked up a Hydrostar only a few minutes ago, and Wells verified it to be Drake's. She plotted the route on the DDU's screen. They would be in Zuma territory within minutes. Penta and Zuma had no working agreements, and Wells had no way to tap into their surveillance. Her options were running out. She had to come up with something fast. She was staring at her DDU, hoping for something to come to her, when the screen went dark and three circles started dancing around. They came together, formed one circle, and spread out to fill the screen with a face.

"Lieutenant," Captain Santo said as he appeared on the screen.

"Captain. How can I help?" Lt. Wells asked, made slightly paranoid by the timing of his call.

"We have followed up on a few leads and updated all the files," Santo said. "But we are still missing something. Somehow we are overlooking something."

Wells had known Captain Santo for years, and looking at him on her DDU told her one thing: he was not happy. He didn't look angry, but she could tell something was happening that made him very uncomfortable. She was used to his intense eye contact, something he used to great effect, but today his eyes were anywhere but on hers.

"I need someone," Santo paused, searching for the words, "with your skills."

And there it was. The admission that he had made a mistake. It was, after all, Captain Santo's idea to put her behind a desk when the whole Jason Bell incident took place. He was embarrassed that one of his best could be so compromised. He had tried to hide his mistake in an office filled with mediocrity.

But now he needed her.

"Yes, sir. Whatever you need, you know I can do it, sir."

Wells' heart pounded in her chest. Was he about to lift her suspension? Was this nightmare about to end?

"I know. You have always been one of our best, but that whole fiasco was really embarrassing to Penta. And to me, personally."

Captain Santo paused, and Wells didn't know if he was going somewhere with this or wanting another apology from her. She decided to stay strong and wait him out.

"Since we have not been making the sort of progress that HQ was expecting, they have allowed me," Santo forced the words out, "to bring you back onto the lead team."

Wells immediately knew what had happened. Someone higher than Captain Santo was getting heat for Santo not getting results, so they'd told him to bring her back in. They wanted to protect themselves and did not care how Santo felt about it. He was trying to make it seem like his idea, but she knew he was trying to save face and hated this. This was perfect. She could get the team up to speed and maybe get to Drake and Something before they slipped through the cracks. Since it would be evident that the breakthrough came when she returned to the team, she would not need to worry about getting any credit. This way, if she played her cards right, she could get her job back. She would have to be sure not to step on Santo's toes or make him look incompetent in any way.

"Whatever the team needs, sir. Not to push my luck here, but does this mean full reinstatement?" Wells asked, trying to hide her excitement.

"Yes."

"Thank you, sir. If it's okay with you, would you mind if I catch up here on some of the details before I meet up with the team?"

Wells didn't need to catch up on anything; she was ahead of everyone else. But she knew to show up knowing more than everyone else would raise suspicion. She had to play this cool. Take an hour or so, make it look like she was the one catching up.

Santo agreed and gave her the team's location before disconnecting. They were still camped at Anteus, obviously not making any progress since she last checked.

Wells immediately went to pack her bag, smiling all the way home.

*** 

The number on the screen that showed their time to the destination dipped under an hour.

"So it's settled. Once we get the credits transferred, we dump the truck, get a hydrocar, and go to the nearest Shangcorp territory. Yeah?" Jimmy asked.

"Yes."

Drake hated that he'd have to get rid of his Hydrostar. For years he had been driving and living in it. All his earthly possessions were in the truck. He knew it sounded silly, but it was a part of him. When he'd bought it from Bob Turner, it was about to be scrapped, but he got it for a steal and spent all his free time and credits bringing it back to life. It was pretty rough, but it was mechanically flawless. Drake was not attached to many things in life, but his truck was one. He had never had to think about getting rid of it before and now that he did, he realized just how much he would miss it. He also knew that to keep driving it, with Penta surely tracking it by now, would be suicide.

Shangcorp was estimated to be the largest company, owning the most territories on Earth. Finding a Shangcorp territory nearby would be easy, but getting in would be tricky. Shangcorp and Penta Corporation had a frosty relationship. That was the main reason Drake and Jimmy had decided to go there. This tension between the two companies also meant that Shangcorp was very strict about who they allowed in. With Drake and Jimmy having warrants out on them from Penta, it would be impossible to gain entry. Impossible, except if your name was Jimmy Something. Jimmy had made plenty of dodgy deals in the past with Shangcorp officials, which allowed him to make up a list of names of people who should be open to the odd bribe.

All Drake and Jimmy had to do was find a border post that had someone working there who was on Jimmy's dodgy Shangcorp officials list, and then bribe their way in.

"Jimmy, this is your play, buddy," Drake said. "How do you want to do this?"

The only way they would be able to get through a border without raising a red flag, would be for them to know where a Jimmy-friendly official would be. If they went to the wrong crossing and got caught, Shangcorp would refuse them entry and practically hand them back to Penta. If they tried to bribe the wrong official, they would end up in a Shangcorp prison mine, which would be much worse than getting caught by Penta. They had to make sure that the crossing they went to was big enough to warrant having personnel there, and that said personnel included a bribable official. If they went through a small unguarded crossing, the automated systems would pick up the Hydrostar's registration, which would alert the authorities to the warrant, and summon the security forces.

"I got this." Jimmy was in his element. "I'll make some calls."

He got up and went into the small bathroom cubicle, closing the door behind him.

"I'll just wait here then," Drake mumbled to himself.

\*\*\*

Lieutenant Lily Wells always had a tactical bag packed and ready to go, stored at her house. Even though she had been desk-bound for the last few months, she'd kept herself tactical ready. In the bag, she had a knife, LED light, rope, two pulse pistols with extra charges, a telescopic baton, protein bars, three water bottles, a raincoat, first aid kit, plastic cuffs, and a few more items she might need. Next to the bag, her field uniform and armor were hanging, ready to go. The team would have the heavy rifles and anything else she would need. Most of the things in her bag would not be required, but she was always over-prepared.

Lt. Wells decided to jump on the Hyperloop. It would get her to Anteus in just under an hour. She had planned on stalling a bit, for appearance's sake, to make it seem she had just found out some of the information she had. Instead, she decided to get there as fast as possible and try to trickle out her intel.

The Hyperloop was empty, which made sense as it stopped at Proteus, not Anteus, and everyone knew that Proteus hated tourists. For a short period, people had liked going there as it was so clean and beautiful. As soon as it became a bit too busy, the Protean powers-that-be had stopped serving outsiders at cafes and restaurants, and soon people stopped going there altogether. Lt. Wells had never been there herself and was looking forward to seeing if it was worth all the hype.

As the Hyperloop pulled into the station, Wells caught a glimpse of Proteus. She was not disappointed. The houses had lush green lawns, and gardens with beautiful colors. The streets were clean and sealed. That glimpse was enough to tell her the hype was real. It was the most beautiful town that she had ever seen. Everything looked new, staged.

The station had no windows, and she figured the glimpse she had seen was a small oversight in the design of the structure. The station gleamed in all its white cleanliness. There was no litter or any sign that humans had ever trespassed here. The sense of awe and wonderment Lt. Wells had felt only moments before was replaced by an eerie sense of isolation. There was no human touch here, no vitality. She realized there was no warmth here either, despite the high temperature.

"Can I help you?" A huge man in a security uniform appeared from nowhere.

Two more security personnel stood a few meters back, watching. They scanned all the incoming passengers as they disembarked, letting a few past that must have been residents. The same three-team was set up talking to another person a short distance from her. He must not have been up to Protean standards as the guards ushered him back into the Hyperloop, not very gently either.

Wells turned back to the man in front of her.

"I am from Penta security. Just passing on through to Anteus," she said, holding her ground.

The man inched forward a bit.

"So, why did you come here first? Where is your team?"

The legendary Proteus hospitality seemed to be no myth.

"Logistical reasons. My team should be here to pick me up soon." Wells stood toe to toe with the guard.

He nodded to the other two. One disappeared around a corner, and when he came back two minutes later, he whispered something into his ear.

"Your team is waiting just outside of town. We told them to wait there. We'll take you there now."

A heavily armored hydrocar came around the corner and stopped in front of them. Unlike the cars she was used to, this one was clean and straight. It looked like it had just rolled off a Nikolatec assembly line. In fact, the guards and their equipment looked brand new as well.

"Ever used that thing?" Lt. Wells nodded toward the guard's pulse gun.

"Get in," was all she got back.

Lt. Wells climbed into the armored car and sat beside another guard, also in an immaculate uniform. The car took off, and Wells got a second, longer look at the town. The more she saw, the less she liked it. Everything was perfect and new. The cars, houses, and even the people seemed too good to be true, and Wells was sure it was. Something strange was going on here, but she had too much on her plate to worry about a quirky town that hated outsiders.

The car reached the city limits and pulled over. Lt. Wells could see a familiar dusty and well used Penta armored vehicle waiting for them. The complete opposite of the one she was sitting in.

"Thanks for the ride, boys. Make sure to give your car a good wash when you get back. Looks like shit."

And with that, Lt. Wells jumped out and walked over to her team.

# | eighteen |

Drake waited patiently for Jimmy to finish his business in the small bathroom. He knew they only had minutes now until they reached the location and assumed that things would happen quickly once they got there. If it went down like a standard hauling contract, this nightmare should be over fairly quickly.

Usually, he would have the coordinates for where to deliver the cargo and would drive straight to them. He would park the Hydrostar, inspect the shipment and unhook it. Some places were automated, and all he had to do was sign off on the contract on his HIC. Others still used humans, and once they were happy that the cargo was intact, he could sign off on his HIC. So, if this was going to go down like normal, al he had to do was unhook the cargo and, instead of signing off on the contract, leave it to Jimmy to get the credits transferred. Quick and easy.

That was the easy part. The part Drake had done many times before. What would happen after that was the problem.

The nearest town was about an hour's drive, and they would need to take the Hydrostar there, dump it and then quickly buy a hydrocar and get moving. It would have to be from a less-than-reputable place that would not mind skipping the paperwork in favor of some extra credits. As time was not on their side, they would most likely leave the Hydrostar parked on the road where they bought the hydrocar. Selling a truck was not an easy task, and the market for it was pretty small.

They would have no choice but to abandon it right there and flee in the hydrocar. If they could have sold the Hydrostar, Drake might have felt a bit better about it, but just abandoning it . . . Drake tried not to see it for more than it was—an old Hydrostar. But that proved to be impossible. This was his home, not just a truck. He might have been able to convince Jimmy that he was okay with dumping it, but his stomach was aching just thinking about it. It had been years since he had felt this sense of loss. He hated Jimmy for getting him into this mess but himself more for allowing it to happen.

The bathroom door opened, and Jimmy came out, wiping his hands on his pants.

"Did you just—" Drake started, but he realized time was running out. "How did it go?"

"Okay, so I'm just gonna be straight with you." Jimmy had, what Drake guessed to be, his serious face on. "I found a guy, but it's going to cost us fifty thousand credits, and he is about six hours away."

"But—"

"I got him down to a more reasonable amount of twenty thousand credits."

Drake wondered if the original amount included Jimmy's cut, but he said nothing and decided to give Jimmy the benefit of the doubt for now.

"Good job, buddy," Drake said. He opened a map on the DDU. "I think our best bet would be to drop the Hydrostar here." Drake pointed to a town on the map. "We can get an overpriced off-the-books hydrocar as well."

"But it's not on the way to the border post."

"Precisely. Penta's not going to give up, so if we drop the truck there, it would seem like we are traveling in that direction, but we'd really be going here." Drake pointed to a new place on the map, in the opposite direction.

"Cool, cool. Make sense, ya know. Keep 'em off our backs as long as possible. Yeah, makes sense now."

"Now, we need to make a hundred percent sure—" The truck came to an abrupt stop.

They had been so involved in their chat that neither of them saw the gate across the road appear. Flanking the entrance was a nine-foot-high metal fence that stretched as far as the eye could see. On top of the fence was a pulse beam that was interrupted every hundred meters by a box that had to be a signal amplifier of sorts. Another pulse beam surrounded the amplifier box. On top of the box was a black dome—a 360-degree camera. There was no way in or out except for the gate, which was operated by four security guards in heavy armor.

"Shit. We're here." Drake's heart suddenly pounded in his chest.

A yellow message filled the screen, informing them that the lock was about to be disengaged. Drake knew it would not do so until Yolanda sensed his hands on the wheel, so he dutifully grabbed it. The message disappeared, and the armored car rolled through the gate.

Jimmy seemed as calm as could be. Drake realized yet again how deep in over his head he was. This was Jimmy's life. Dodgy deals and life-threatening situations were what he did best—or so Drake hoped.

One of the guards came over to Drake's side of the Hydrostar.

"Name and appointment number," he barked.

"Hey, buddy. I'm Benjamin Drake, and this is Jimmy Something, and we are with those guys," Drake said, pointing to the armored vehicle, assuming that the gates would part for them.

They did not.

Instead, the remaining three guards raised their pulse rifles to their shoulders, ready to engage.

"Appointment number," the guard repeated.

Drake turned to Jimmy. "I hope you have a fucking appointment number for this gentleman here, or else we might be stuck here for a while."

"Shit, yeah, ya know, I recall seeing something," Jimmy said as he tapped and swiped away on his HIC.

Drake gave the guard a sheepish grin. "You guys really should communicate a bit better. Your friends over there have been pulling us along for quite a while now, so I'm sure we are cleared to go in."

The guard was staring at Drake, apparently not allowed to go off-script, when Jimmy yelled, "Yes! Got it!"

Drake felt his arm vibrate. He quickly gave the number to the guard, who typed it into his own HIC.

"So, are we on the party list?" Drake asked.

The guard ignored him. He turned back toward the other guards and they all lowered their weapons. When he rejoined them, they got in formation on either side the road, and the gate slowly opened. The guard that came over waved them on. Drake put the truck into drive.

"Shit, buddy, here we go," he said to Jimmy. They slowly crawled through the gate before increasing their speed.

Beyond the gate, a reasonably large hill came into view. The road made a big sweep, and on the side of the hill, Drake could see an entrance. It was open, and Drake, following the armored vehicle, drove straight through, coming to a stop in what appeared to be a vast warehouse.

Drake powered down the Hydrostar and opened the door. Their chaperones disembarked and grouped up. One guy, who still looked exactly like the others, stood in front of them and barked orders. Orders received, they broke ranks and formed a perimeter around the vehicles. The one who did the barking (and had to be Anderson) came over to Drake. Drake heard Jimmy jump out of the truck but kept his eyes on Anderson.

"Mr. McKenna will be here momentarily," the guard said.

"Shall we just wait here then?" Drake said to a face made out of stone. "Oh, and thanks for having our backs out there."

The complete silence he received as an answer told him that they should wait there. The walls and ceiling were made up of uncarved rock. They were inside a huge cavern. The floor was paved over, and there were small temporary buildings scattered around. Both sides of the cave had large sliding doors: the open one they had come through, and a closed one on the opposite side.

"So this is it? Do you guys actually work out of a cave? I hope you have enough credits to pay us," Drake said to Anderson.

"I assure you, Mr. Drake," a voice behind Drake said, startling him, "I have more than enough credits to pay you and your colleague."

"Jesus! Where the hell did you come from?" Drake asked the new guy.

"Jacob McKenna. Please to meet you." McKenna offered a hand to Drake.

Drake accepted and shook hands with him. McKenna took his time letting go of Drake's hand, and said, "I am glad you delivered this cargo to me in such good time and condition, Mr. Drake. It is good to know who one can rely on."

"Jimmy Something. The actual contractor and organizer of this endeavor," Jimmy said, grabbing McKenna's hand from his side and shaking it vigorously before dropping it like a hot potato.

McKenna wiped his hand on his jacket.

"Nice to meet you too, Mr. Something," McKenna said. "Now, if you don't mind, I'll have one of my engineers verify the cargo, and then we can get on with business." He waved a man in a white lab coat over.

Where did these people appear from? Drake wondered. The warehouse appeared deserted, yet people kept popping up.

"How long will this take?" Drake asked.

"Shouldn't be too long, Mr. Drake. About an hour."

Drake did not like that time frame. Penta was surely hot on their heels by now, and every minute counted. They had to get out and gone, fast. Jimmy winked.

"Sure, knock yourself out. Can't be too careful, ya know?" Jimmy said. "Say, how about you keep that old piece of junk? No need for us to even unload it, and you just get one of your clones to give us a lift to Spirig."

McKenna considered it, giving nothing away.

"I assume this vehicle would be too easy to find out on the road," McKenna replied. "As I said before, it is good to know who one can trust and rely on. So in the spirit of our continued efforts, I will gladly help you."

A hollow feeling settled in Drake's stomach. He was getting into debt with a person who he should not owe anything.

"Great," Jimmy piped in from the side. "Just great. Let's get that nerd of yours on those crystals and us on the road."

***

Lt. Lily Wells got out of the armored car and walked over to the group of men and women, all dressed in Penta security uniforms. Egos were about to take a pounding, and she knew she had to play it cool.

"So, whose idea was it to pull me out of my cozy office?" she said to the group. "I was just getting used to the good life."

"Bullshit. You hated it!" a guy yelled back.

"It sure looks like life treated you good. Carrying a few extra kilos there, huh?" another one chirped while patting his belly.

"Just trying to fit in, Hayman." Wells already felt back at home.

"That's enough. Welcome back, Lieutenant." Captain Santo dramatically walked through the group, dividing it into two. As if incapable of functioning alone, the two groups melted back together once Santo stood in front of them.

"Thank you, Captain. Very happy to see all these sad sacks again, sir."

A few rumblings came from the group.

"Well, I had to pull some strings to get you back here, Wells, so you'd better not disappoint the team, or me," Captain Santo said.

Wells knew the only strings that had been pulled were the ones controlling Santo.

"I know, sir. And I won't," Wells played along.

"We will regroup in ten minutes, and you can debrief us with anything you might have learned while sitting at your desk."

"Yes, sir," Wells said. Captain Santo walked off.

Wells opened the back door of the armored vehicle. The Mongoose could carry ten passengers, their weapons, and some extra gear. It was capable of going off-road and had armor that could withstand most light pulse weapons. The back door of the Mongoose swung open sideways and had a big DDU built in, which the team used for debriefs and intel sharing. Wells connected her Human Interface Console to the Mongoose's DDU and transferred all her files on the case over. She used her HIC to organize all the data remotely and got her presentation ready. By the time she had finished, the team had already assembled next to the Mongoose. Captain Santo, standing at the back, gave her a nod to proceed.

"Okay, so unlike you guys, I had the luxury of sitting on my ass and go through all the evidence and leads you all collected on the road. There was plenty and it sure gave me plenty to do," she embellished, making sure she was not taking any credit but rather dishing it out.

"I made some calls, connected a few dots, and came up with this." Wells opened a file on the DDU. A picture of Benjamin Drake filled the screen.

"This is Benjamin Drake, no aliases. I believe he is the key. I have confirmation that Jimmy Something is currently traveling with him."

Wells paused to read the faces staring back at her. And stare they did. She loved this team and would take a pulse in the chest for them, but they were followers and doers, not thinkers or leaders. They needed a leader to shine. That was her role. It had always been her role. Lt. Lily Wells could feel that old familiar feeling inside her rise again. Time for the whammy.

"And I know exactly where they are going."

# | nineteen |

Jacob McKenna had agreed to transport Drake and Jimmy to a settlement called Spirig. McKenna would also get rid of the Hydrostar for them. While waiting for the engineer to do whatever it was he was doing, Drake pulled Jimmy back into the cabin of the Hydrostar.

"Everything I own is in this truck, Jimmy, so I'm just going to take a few minutes to grab some stuff, okay?"

"Sure, sure. Of course. You really like this truck, eh?" Jimmy asked.

"It has been my home and livelihood for years. Not sure what I'm going to do without it, to be honest."

"I'm sure you'll be able to buy yourself the best model Hydrocomet when the dust settles," Jimmy said, trying to cheer him up.

Drake knew that was true, but he had restored this truck with his own hands and felt a real connection to it. He had never thought of himself as a sentimental type, but he was having a hard time letting go.

"You're right. Pass me that backpack behind you."

"Sure. Here ya go. Don't you think it's strange that Penta never caught up to us?"

"Well, we haven't gotten away yet, buddy," Drake said as he stuffed things into the backpack.

He had thought about it a lot and did think it was strange that a corporation the size of Penta could not track down two amateurs like them. All the results Yolanda was able to pull up on Drake and Jimmy were still focused on Jimmy's warehouse killings and Drake's possible involvement. A few mentioned that Jimmy might have kidnapped him, but mostly Drake was considered an accomplice. All the focus was on the killings; there was nothing on the missing Bismuth, at all. Either they didn't know the Bismuth was gone, or they didn't care. Drake had a feeling it had to be the first option.

"Penta is so big; maybe they just haven't noticed it's missing yet?"

"I don't know. Sure, they're big, but isn't this Bisma-whatever stuff tricky to get? Wouldn't they want it back, ya know?"

Bismuth was not that rare, but massive quantities were needed to make Polonium, and most of the Bismuth deposits and mines were Penta-owned. When Polonium propulsion was invented, Penta had bought up all the smaller companies that had territories with Bismuth. Some of the companies thought they had leverage on the mighty Penta and tried to hold out for more credits, but the Penta steamroller just crushed them, and soon Penta was the only company making Polonium and using it for their new, faster shuttles.

"I guess. All I know is we need to get out of here fast, and make sure your friend comes through," Drake said.

"He will. What sort of hydrocar should we get? I was thinking a—"

"I don't care," Drake cut him off. "As long as it gets us to the border post, I don't care."

"So, I'm in charge of choosing one then?"

"Sure, Jimmy, you can pick our new disposable ride."

Drake wondered if he should grab anything else to put in the bag. There was a knock at the door.

"Mr. McKenna is ready for you now."

The guard at the door looked indistinguishable from all the others. Drake followed him out.

Outside, Mr. McKenna was talking to the engineer in the white coat. The guard stopped short of them and turned around to face Drake and Jimmy, clearly implying that they should wait right there.

"Would you like for us to wait here then?" Drake asked the block of a man in front of him.

He answered with a silent stare over Drake's head.

"Looks like we're waiting, then, Jimmy."

Drake wondered if the guard would actually chase him if he ran around him.

"Gentlemen," McKenna said. The guard moved ever so slightly to let them by. Drake and Jimmy walked over to McKenna. The engineer had already left.

"It seems everything is in order," McKenna stated. "As per the contract, full payment will be made upon satisfactory delivery. As that is the case, Mr. Something, I will transfer the credits to you." McKenna waved his open palm at Jimmy's HIC.

Jimmy pulled up his sleeve, swiped his arm, and held it up in front of him. McKenna swiped his arm in the direction of Jimmy, and a small tone emitted from Jimmy's HIC that was only audible to him. He looked down at his arm, and a huge grin spread across his face.

"Never seen so many zeros in my life, ya know."

"Jimmy, if you're happy, I think we should get going," Drake said, hoping to pull him out of his trance.

"I have a vehicle and driver ready to take you to Spirig." McKenna motioned to a hydrocar at the inner door. "As you can understand, I have a lot of work to do, so again, very glad to have done business with you." And with that, McKenna turned around and walked toward one of the small offices.

"This way," the guard that blocked them said.

"Please tell me you are the one who is going to drive us?" Drake said to him.

"I am."

"Yippee!" Drake replied but still got no reaction.

Jimmy was looking at his HIC again, slowly shaking his head, still grinning.

"Jimmy, buddy, we got to hustle," Drake edged him on.

His hopes of Jimmy taking charge of the situation got shattered. Except for getting them a lift, Jimmy was pretty useless. But then again, maybe that was his charm, just getting things done on the sly. After all, they have survived this far and had a plan to try and get out alive.

"Yes, yes, I'm coming. Have you seen this?" Jimmy said, pointing to his forearm.

"I will, as soon as we're in that car. Let's go!"

Jimmy snapped out of it and ran to catch up with the guard who was already walking toward the car. Drake threw his backpack on and followed them. The guard got in the front, and Jimmy and Drake spilled into the back. The hydrocar had no logos or insignias on it and was a pretty standard, run-of-the-mill model. Inside, no modifications had been made at all to adapt it to be a security vehicle. Drake wondered if this was the guard's personal car but knew asking him would be futile, as he would not get an answer out of him anyway. The guard put the vehicle in manual drive and slowly approached the big doors. As they drew closer, the doors slid open to reveal a wide open expanse. Drake had expected the door to lead to an even more elaborate cave system with who knows what inside but realized the cavern they were in was just a tunnel: the gateway to the rest of the Zuma territory. The guard punched something into the DDU and sat back as the Autodrive took over, aiming for Spirig.

***

These people were loyal and very good at their job, but they had no desire to think for themselves. They needed someone to come up with the plan, tell them what to do, and then manage them through it. With good leadership, they were flawless and would excel, but right now, they had too much information and not enough orders.

Lt. Wells caught Captain Santo's eyes and did not like what she saw. He looked like someone who had better places to be.

She had just finished debriefing the team on Jimmy Something and Benjamin Drake. She had told them how she tracked Jimmy down and found out he was hitching a ride with Drake. At first, she thought that Drake was just a chump who gave the wrong guy a lift, but the more she dug, the more she realized they had to be in it together. Once she'd figured that out, she realized that it would be much easier for them to use a hydrocar to flee than Drake's truck. This meant the truck was part of their plan, somehow. The surveillance footage she found showed they had cargo on board, so she set out to find out what it was. She had contacted Lyle Miller again, and before long, she knew what they were hauling and where they got it. She immediately searched the Penta security network to see which team was tracking the stolen Bismuth so she could access their files. Every search she did came up empty. No one in the whole Penta Corporation had reported the Bismuth missing or stolen. At that point, Captain Santo had brought her back on the team, and her investigation into the Bismuth had come to a halt.

"So," she continued the debrief, "we are chasing a murder suspect, his accomplice, and a truck full of stolen Bismuth that no one at Penta bothered to report. My only conclusion, at this stage, is that they had inside help, and someone is covering it up."

The team shifted uncomfortably. No one wanted to chase after one of their own, but they would do whatever she told them to. All they needed was their orders, and Wells was willing to give them.

"Get your gear and be ready to deploy in fifteen minutes."

Everyone scattered, except for Captain Santo.

"Good work, Lieutenant. I should have brought you back on earlier."

"Thank you, sir. Appreciate the compliment, but I'm just doing what I was trained to do."

"Still, you're one of the best. With you here, there's no reason for me to stay. I'll get transport back to headquarters, and you'll have the lead here."

Santo seemed very keen to get out and Wells couldn't blame him.

She hated being micromanaged and could not have hoped for a better outcome. Only a few hours ago, she had been chained to a desk, plotting her return, and now she was back leading the team. What she'd thought would take weeks, if not months, had only taken a few days.

She was just lucky that the world had idiots like Jimmy Something and Benjamin Drake in it to make her look good.

And corrupt officials like Captain Raymond Santo.

# | twenty |

Spirig was a Nestem-owned town and had a big factory manufacturing the actual white boxes that white box meals came in. Most people in town worked at the factory, and the town included a thriving retail sector. All in all, Spirig had a lot going for it, and Drake really liked the place.

"What a shithole," Jimmy offered his view.

"What? This place is heaven compared to most places I've seen."

Jimmy just shrugged.

They were standing in front of a big gray building with *Nestem* written in big blue letters on it. As they arrived in town, the driver took over from the Autodrive, went straight to the most prominent building in town, and stopped. He didn't say anything, but Drake and Jimmy knew that the ride was over. They had barely got out before the car whirred off. It seemed the guard had dropped them off in the commercial part of town, but what they needed was somewhere less busy. Jimmy looked out of place here, among people who showered more than once a week, and Drake could sense that his internal compass was already pointing them in the right direction.

"Lead the way, buddy," was all Drake had to say, and Jimmy was off.

Jimmy's nose for unsavory places—and people—led them to precisely the kind of dive Drake had in mind. Behind a broken and rusty fence sat a small single-story building, which was in dire need of paint or a quick mercy demolishing. Drake had trouble reading the worn-out sign above the gate, but in the end, he settled on Joe's Hydro Shop, Repairs, and Salvage. Joe sounded like just the guy they needed. The small building was set right in the front of the yard, but Drake spied a few more or less intact hydrocars hiding in the back.

The office was small and overflowing with magazines, brochures, parts in and out of boxes, and a massive conical shape behind a DDU. On top of the shape was a mop of curly yellow hair. Symmetrical straight lines went down on both sides from the mop, forming a head, a neck, shoulders, and a body that disappeared beneath a desk. There were no contours or distinguishable body parts, just one seamless human pyramid, but at a guess, it appeared to be female. She peered up from her DDU at Drake and Jimmy, waiting for them to speak.

"Hey, love, Jimmy Something," he said, leaning up on the counter and flashing his pearly whites. "Who do I see about buying an old junker?"

The woman just sat there, looking at Jimmy.

"We are in a bit of a rush, so we were hoping to get something cheap for not so cheap." Jimmy winked at her.

She continued to stare. Drake nudged Jimmy and gestured with his head for them to get going; this was going nowhere fast.

"Okay then, your loss." Jimmy turned around to leave.

As he grabbed the handle and opened the door, he paused to give her one last chance. She had already gone back to work on her DDU.

"All right, so that didn't work," Jimmy said. "On to the next one."

And without any debriefing or overanalyzing what had just happened, Jimmy shrugged off the experience and moved on to the next one. Drake had to admire him for this quality and wished he could do that more often.

A few minutes later, they came across a very similar looking and sounding shop, but this one had a few hydrocars parked in the front with prices on them. Very cheap prices, indicating that what-you-see-is-what-you-get deals could be made here. Precisely what they were after. This time it was a huge man who approached them. The salvage game seemed to favor a particular body type.

"You fellas looking at buying or stealing?" the big man asked, wiping his hands on an oily rag.

He was about twice the size of Drake and smelled twice as bad as Jimmy.

"A bit of both," Drake said. A pulse gun jutted from the guy's hip pocket.

"I see. Come with me." The man walked around the office building to the back, still trying to get his hands clean.

Drake knew that following the big guy would put them in a compromised position, but he had a feeling that this was the place they were looking for, so he gestured to Jimmy, and they followed.

The big guy stopped in front of an old but clean hydrocar. He sat down on the nose of the vehicle, and the whole thing sank to the ground. He worked the rag in his hands.

"I'm Jimmy Some—"

"—thing, and this is Benjamin Drake. Both wanted for murder. With quite a nice bounty as well."

"Ah, I see our reputations precede us," Drake said. "So, how is this going to go down?"

The big guy shifted his weight around, trying to get comfortable, the hydrocar creaking and protesting underneath him. The pulse gun slipped out a bit, and he repositioned it back into his pocket, making no effort to hide it. Then he started back on the oily rag again.

"Well, it's all math, isn't it? The bounty is a hundred thousand credits. Each. So, let's say a hundred for both of ya, and that way, we all walk away happy."

Jimmy started to protest, but Drake's scowl shut him up. The only way the big guy could claim the bounty was to call the security forces, and Drake reckoned he did not want them snooping around his place or to be known as the kind of guy who calls the authorities.

"Seventy-five and a clean car," Drake countered.

A car with no outstanding notices would not attract any attention from patrol units or set off any alarms at border crossings. Drake knew he had little leverage, but the fact that they were still talking gave him hope. Something told him if he just rolled over and accepted the guy's offer, they would come off as weak, and the guy would most likely turn them in anyway. If Drake showed some backbone, the guy might see them more as equals and maybe even treat them as such.

The guy grunted and finally put away the rag.

"You can take this one." He pointed to the one he was using as a chair. "It's clean."

Drake took a minute to mull it over. More for the sake of pretenses then anything else. They needed to get on the road, and this was as good a deal as they would find.

"Jimmy." Drake nudged him. Jimmy walked over, and within seconds it was done.

Once they had exchanged the credits and some barely legal paperwork, the big guy patted Drake on the back.

"Good luck, boys." He headed back to the office, hands already busy with the oily rag again.

"What a reasonable guy," Jimmy said as he got in the car.

"Just the best," Drake said. He put the hydrocar in manual drive.

***

As they left Spirig behind, Jimmy entered coordinates into the DDU. The interface was old and clunky, and it took him several attempts and multiple swear words to get the job done. Finally, the familiar green line appeared on the screen and was superimposed on the road in front of them. Drake took a deep breath of relief. Maybe, just maybe, they could do this. He was not at all surprised to see that Jimmy was fast asleep. Drake decided not to engage Autodrive and settled into a comfortable position. It was nice to have the road in front of him and not think about the mess they were in. Drake had always felt the most at peace when he was on the open road.

Jimmy was snoring now, and Drake smiled. How did a ratbag like Jimmy Something get him into so much trouble, make him rich, cost him his beloved Hydrostar, and still manage to get under his skin? Jimmy was becoming more like a little brother to him, although he guessed them to be the same age. He wanted to kill him more often than not but always felt sorry for him at the last moment. He was going to miss him.

The landscape was changing from flat, dry grassland to hills and then some trees. The road had been pretty dull and straight until now, but the hills forced the road to bend and snake, and Drake loved the drive. He had to force himself not to go too quick and attract unwanted attention. It had been a few years since he had driven anything but his Hydrostar and he was not used to being so nimble and quick on the road. The Hydrostar was many things but maneuvrable it was not. This old junker was most likely a dog by anyone else's standards, but Drake was already getting attached to it. A bit of work, and it might actually be worth keeping.

A waiver appeared on the screen as they crossed an unguarded crossing. Drake's heart jumped into his throat. They were about to find out how good the paperwork, for which they had paid way too much, was. He pressed the accept icon on the screen, and a new message appeared:

*Welcome to an incorporated Penta territory.*

*Please obey all laws and rules and enjoy your stay.*

No alarm went off, and there was no triggering of an automatic shutdown of the hydrocar, which meant the paperwork must have held up. Being cautious, Drake stayed well below the speed limit and kept an eye out for any fast approaching security vehicles. After a while, he started to relax a bit more and eventually settled back into his driving.

"Fuck yeah," he said, mentally punching the air.

If they could get through a Penta crossing, they would have no problems getting to the Shangcorp crossing undetected.

For the first time, Drake felt like they might actually get out of this alive.

***

Nestem was one of the Big Five corporations and had strong trade relations with Penta. Since Nestem made most of the white box meals in the world, Penta did not have to worry about manufacturing their own; they just got them cheap from Nestem. And since Penta made most of the weapons and trained the people who used them, Nestem did not have to worry about security, as they got all they needed from Penta. The two companies had a long and peaceful history together. Something Lt. Lily Wells was planning on using to her advantage.

Once Something and Drake's Hydrostar entered the Zuma territory, they'd had to give up the chase. Penta had no agreements with Zuma, so security forces at their borders would raise hundreds of red flags and questions. Penta had grown so big that it could easily take over a small company like Zuma Corporation, who would be defenseless against Penta's sheer might and power. The only thing stopping Penta from taking over the world was Shangcorp, who would join the race to take over the world the moment they caught wind of Penta doing so. The two would go to war, and soon they would be back to the days before corporations had bought out all the governments of the world. A time of chaos with battles being fought all over the planet. Things weren't perfect, but the last war had ended six decades ago, and these days most people lived in peace and safety.

Lt. Lily Wells decided to go around the small Zuma territory and use all the surveillance available to her to see where the Hydrostar would pop out again. Her research showed that there were a few mines in this territory but no significant towns or settlements. This meant that they would not be able to get rid of the truck and get another vehicle while inside the borders. Unless, of course, they stole one, in which case she would be back to square one.

"Make sure all the surveillance includes face recognition and make them search all vehicles, not just trucks," Wells told the guard sitting next to her, who tapped her commands into the DDU.

"The amount of traffic is too high to give us a live update, ma'am," he said.

Lt. Wells had to come up with a new plan. The more she thought about it, the more she realized that she should not underestimate Drake. He had been very cunning so far and he'd been able to stay ahead. But she was sure he would make a mistake very soon. They always did. Probably that idiot Jimmy Something would get something wrong. She just had to make sure she was close enough to capitalize on his mistake.

"That's fine, keep the search as instructed," Wells replied.

# | twenty-one |

The big white shuttle towered over Jacob McKenna. He was standing right underneath shuttle two, with two more to his right and one to his left—four identical works of art. The engineers had indeed outdone themselves, he thought. There were few straight lines to them, or any sharp corners, except for the flaps that would fold away with the landing gear and disappear. The shuttles had no windows and relied only on display units, so the outside of the crafts were one continuous surface. The loading hatch was located at the bottom and was barely noticeable when closed. The whole craft looked fluid; even the propulsion units at the back, which was just a hole, seemed to flow back into the body. The thing looked like a teardrop with its tail pushed back into itself.

McKenna could marvel at them all day long. Compared to his shuttles, the Penta Polonium-powered shuttles were ancient. Those were designed two decades ago and were just evolutions from the regular shuttles before them. They still had the classic design, a tubular body with wings attached—a model that had been in use for centuries. McKenna's shuttles were in a class of their own.

He was in the hangar admiring his fleet because he'd just got word from the lead engineer that they had completed all the testing and simulation work. His shuttles were ready. All they were waiting for now was the production of the Polonium, using the Bismuth.

"How far along is the Polonium manufacturing?" McKenna asked the nervous-looking woman in the lab coat beside him.

"I checked before coming down here, sir, and they estimate roughly forty-seven hours," she replied.

"Excellent. Keep me posted." McKenna returned to admiring his new fleet of shuttles.

\*\*\*

"Yes, they are ready and on standby," Captain Santo said to the man who was only visible to him via his ARP.

"You've done well, Raymond. I was a bit nervous when you told me that Lt. Wells was back on the team, but removing yourself was smart. She's very clever, that one, and the more distance between the two of you, the better."

"Don't worry about me, or how I run things, okay? I'll control my side, as long as you uphold yours."

"Raymond, we are on the cusp of achieving immortality. Once we have taken control, we will have done what no man has ever achieved."

"I'll see you in two days."

\*\*\*

The night was falling, and Drake was still behind the controls of the hydrocar. Most people would have turned on Autodrive and sat back, but Drake always found that driving relaxed him more than sitting around idly. The downside to manually driving the car was high fuel consumption. The hydrocar had turned out to be somewhat inefficient on hydrogen in manual mode, so Drake decided to pull into a roadside station for fuel, food, and, hopefully, a nap. They were still deep inside the Penta territory, but so far, there was no indication or reason to believe that someone was following them. Drake assumed that they were merely leading the race and that it was far from over. There was no way Penta was letting this slide. He was enjoying the jump they had on Penta. But he knew it would not last.

"Hungry, buddy?" Drake woke Jimmy, who had been happily sleeping for most of the day.

"Huh? Yeah, sure. Food'd be great, ya know," Jimmy replied, still between the world of the dreaming and this one.

"Well, you'd better wake up then. C'mon!" Drake got out of the hydrocar and hooked it up to the hydrogen pump.

Jimmy got out of the car and stretched himself out.

"Wow, that was a bit of a ride," he yawned.

"What the fuck are you talking about? All you've been doing is sleeping and snoring my ears off!" Drake protested.

"You haulers are used to this life, but we normal folk find it quite taxing, ya know?"

"I'm so sorry if I hurt your feelings or sensitive backside. I had no idea how difficult sleeping in a car was to you normal folks."

"All good, partner. We're still figuring this out, ya know?"

The menu was pretty standard for a roadside cafeteria. It had five different flavors of white box meals and one or two drink options. Most of them tasted the same to Drake, so he left it up to Jimmy to order and pay for the meals, while he grabbed them a table.

The roadside station was a pretty run-of-the-mill affair: first were the hydrogen pumps, lined up in three rows, then the cafeteria building. Behind the cafeteria was space for the trucks with fewer hydrogen pumps spread out further apart. Drake usually used the back entrance to the cafeterias when he stopped to use the pumps. Some places had some non-white box meals if there was something specific that grew or lived in the area, but those were the exception to the rule. Most just served the standard white box meals.

Drake sat down at a table and watched Jimmy order the meals and some drinks. The cashier grabbed the white boxes from a heating unit behind him and the drinks from a cooling unit next to it. Jimmy pressed his arm against the scanner and returned to Drake with the meals.

"Here ya go, partner!" Jimmy said, handing Drake his share of the feast.

"Thanks."

"Are these places always so bright? I can hardly keep my eyes open."

Drake had noticed, through his years on the road, that the higher the quality of a cafeteria was, the brighter the inside. It was like they were trying to show off how clean it was and that they had nothing to hide. The opposite also held, and Drake had eaten plenty of questionable meals in dark, musty joints.

"I guess most places you go to only have a single light dangling from the ceiling," Drake said as he started on his meal.

"I'll tell ya, one light is much better than this."

"So, not to jinx us, but so far, so good, huh?" Drake said as he took another bite.

Being in a familiar setting, doing a familiar thing, was having a soothing effect on Drake.

Jimmy took another bite.

"Good? It's fucking delicious!" Jimmy replied with a mouth full of food.

"Great, buddy, but I meant the trip. You know, us not getting caught or killed."

"Oh, yeah, silly me. Of course. Yep, reckon we are scot-free, partner."

Jimmy was done with his meal. He had barely chewed it, just shoveling it in, one bite after another. Drake had never seen anyone devour a white box meal so fast.

"I know it looks like it, but we are far from free, Jimmy. We are now in the most dangerous part of this adventure of ours. We are sitting in the heart of a Penta territory. If they are going to catch us, now is the time."

"So we better get going then, ya know?" Jimmy got up.

Drake was only halfway done with his meal. It was not particularly memorable, but it did feel good to have something warm in his stomach.

"How about you go and check if the hydrogen is full, and I can finish up here?" Drake suggested. Jimmy agreed and went out to the car.

Drake sat in the glare of the light and kept eating. Jimmy tried to figure out how to work the pump, pulling and pressing things, until he figured it out. He swiped his arm over the pump's screen and walked back to the cafeteria, smiling at Drake. All Drake had been thinking about was when to ditch Jimmy, but Jimmy never had any thoughts remotely like that. He was in this for the long haul. Partners, *ya know?*

"All done, partner. You want me to take the wheel for a bit? It's been a while, but I reckon I can figure it out," Jimmy said, standing next to him, hands on his hips and feet apart, looking way too confident.

Drake was dead tired and could have done with a rest, but haulers rarely trusted anyone else's driving skills.

"The moment we get on the road, you switch to Autodrive." It was a command, not a suggestion.

"Well, obviously. Who the hell would want to actually drive that?" Jimmy grimaced and turned to leave. Drake took one last bite and followed him.

*\*\*\**

"Ma'am, Jimmy Something just purchased some meals and hydrogen, about three hours away from our position."

Lt. Lily Wells sat up. She'd taken a nap, with clear instructions to be woken if anything, even the smallest event, popped up on the searches. And this was not a little thing.

"Good work. Plot a direct route to the location and also possible destinations."

Suddenly it felt like they were right on top of them. Three hours meant they were getting within striking distance. Wells had two vital missions ahead of her now. She would focus on capturing these two first.

Then she would deal with Captain Santo.

"Is there any visual data from the location?" Wells asked the DDU operator.

"Yes ma'am, downloading it now."

The file included different angles and feeds. One clearly showed Jimmy microseconds after he'd paid for the food and triggered the camera. That set a domino effect in motion, and cameras started to follow him. The DDU quickly identified Benjamin Drake as the two men left the cafeteria and got into an old hydrocar. The DDU operator zoomed in on the hydrocar, got the details, and flagged the vehicle. By doing so, all Penta security vehicles in the area would be on the lookout for the vehicle.

"No, don't flag it," Lt. Wells said. "Let's get them ourselves."

# | twenty-two |

Fine red-brown dust covered everything in sight. Even the man, sitting still for too long, was now covered. There was no blue to the sky, just a bright, eyeball-searing white glare. He had sun protectors on, but they offered very little help. The building propping him up was right at the end of the habitable zone, and beyond it was nothing but sure death. It said so on the building in big red letters, telling anyone who read it to turn back. Out here, the landscape and climate conspired at all times to kill you. The only chance of survival was to stick close to the others inside the compounds and townships.

But this was tricky, considering most people here normally tried to avoid other people or kill them. Now they had to live and work together like it was the most natural thing for them to do. They had to let go of all their instincts to lie, steal or kill and instead hold hands and skip along. But he couldn't do it. It was not in him, never was. So he decided to kill the guard at the gate and get out of there. He had heard about his ancestors and how they used to live in caves. If they could do it with their primitive brains, it would be a breeze for him with all his modern knowledge. All he had to do was head to the mountains, and he'd be a free man. Everyone knew the habitable zone was expanding every day, even though the guards denied it. Since he had killed the guard, he had no choice, anyway. He was as good as dead already.

He picked a spot on a hill that looked like it was slightly darker, maybe even green, and hoped it meant that it had some vegetation on it. If there were plants, there would be water and oxygen. With a destination set, he started his trek. He had never had to walk very far or gauge a distance, but he was confident he would reach the hill before nightfall.

As he got further and further away from the last building he'd seen, breathing became more and more difficult. Night was approaching, and he pushed harder, toward the mountains. But the mountains kept their distance and refused to get any closer.

His tongue was swelling up from a lack of water, and he was struggling to swallow. Things were getting worse much quicker than he'd anticipated. He had imagined it would be a hard journey to the mountains, but now he realized how much he had underestimated it.

Swallowing was now impossible, as was breathing. He turned around, and his heart sank into his empty stomach when he saw the building he'd left earlier. It felt like he had been walking for hours, but the building was only a few hundred meters away.

His thoughts were struggling to stay in his head. The moment he had one, it disappeared, and a new one floated in, only to go as well. He understood then that he had made a big mistake, even though he couldn't put it into words.

That's when he saw the footprint.

Just to the side of him and heading toward the mountains, was a set of footprints leading toward it. He was on the right path, after all! Knowing this gave him the motivation he needed and re-energized his body. He started to follow them, dragging his feet but moving.

Soon the footprints disappeared and were replaced by lines in the sand. Two lines, running parallel to each other. Drag marks. They led to something lying in the sand, covered in the ever-present red dust. He froze, looked around. There were maybe ten or twenty more.

He fell to his knees, nothing left in him to keep him up or alive anymore. He understood then that he was about to die. He felt his body go limp. Everything shut down, enveloping him in a warm blackness, just like falling asleep.

His body fell forward, sending up a puff of the hated dust, taking its place among the other bodies strewn around the desolate Martian landscape.

***

Drake woke up in a sweat. Night had fallen, and the road was empty in front of them. Jimmy was reading something on his HIC.

"You always struggle to breathe like that when you sleep? It sounded like someone was choking you, ya know."

Drake was still waking up and not listening to what Jimmy was saying. He was happy to see Jimmy awake behind the controls. He had assumed he would wake up with Jimmy fast asleep and the car parked on the side of the road. Autodrive had an auto-park function built in which was activated if the system could not detect the user's retinas for a prolonged period. This function had been mandated after hundreds of people had died in the early days of Autodrive.

"Where are we?" Drake started to look at the information on the screen.

"Less than an hour away from the border crossing," Jimmy replied.

"Wow, must have been asleep for at least two hours." Drake tried to stretch out but found it impossible within the confines of the small hydrocar. This was never an issue in the Hydrostar. He forced himself not to dwell on it.

"Uh-huh." Jimmy was back on his HIC again.

Drake turned his attention back to the windscreen and all the telemetry, which, compared to a truck's, was minimal. From the little information available, everything seemed to be working fine. Most of the numbers were hovering below optimal, but still above the red warning lines. Overlaying the numbers, three circles started floating around and then joined to reveal a face. Jimmy and Drake shot each other a quick look, but neither showed any trace of recognition.

"Ah, we finally meet."

Drake knew that the feces were about to hit the propulsion unit.

"Let me introduce myself: I am Lieutenant Lily Wells, and I'm the one who is going to ruin your little party."

Jimmy mumbled some obscenities, but Drake was not concentrating on him. Right now, all his attention was on Lt. Wells. The fact that they were still driving meant that Wells was close but not close enough to override their DDU and bring their car to a halt. They were still in the game and, with less than an hour to go, might even have a chance. All he had to do was stall for a few minutes, and they would be home free.

"Nice to meet you, Lieutenant. Just so there is no confusion when the pulse guns start firing, I am Benjamin Drake, and *that* is Jimmy Something."

Jimmy gave him one of his hurt looks.

"It does not matter to me who is who. You are both wanted for murder and will both be arrested or shot if you resist."

Drake went cold when she said this. Murderers? He'd never killed anyone. And why hadn't she mentioned the stolen Bismuth? Nothing was connecting him to Jimmy's murders, except Jimmy himself. Who was sitting right next to him. In the getaway car. Fuck.

"I prefer the term 'accomplice,' if I had to choose one." Drake tried to keep his cool and wished the border was closer.

"Whatever, Drake," Lt. Wells said, no more fake sincerity left in her voice. "Your ass is mine. We know where you are and where you are heading, so why prolong the inevitable? Just hand yourself over now and plead your case later. Who knows, I might even put in a good word for you if you make my job a bit easier."

That was music to Drake's ears. Not that she would put in a good word, as that was clearly a lie, but if she wanted them to surrender, it meant the lieutenant and her team were still further away from Drake and Jimmy than the two of them were to the border. This whole communication was a bluff. If Penta had been anywhere near them, they would have taken over the hydrocar's DDU, brought it to a stop, and most likely opened fire first and asked questions later. If there was anyone left. It was a desperate move from Penta, and Drake knew that put them back in the lead.

"Mmmm, never even thought about surrender, until now."

Jimmy perked up at Drake's confidence.

"But now that it is an option, I will have to discuss it with my partner first, obviously."

"I would suggest—"

"Talk soon." Drake disconnected the call and turned toward Jimmy. "Stop this shit bucket and swap places with me. We need to get to that border as soon as fucking possible."

"I thought you told the lieutenant we were going to think of surrendering, ya know?" Jimmy said, completely confused now.

"Jimmy! Stop this fucking car right now!"

Jimmy immediately slammed on the decelerator, which in turn switched the Autodrive off, giving him full control. The tires protested and lost grip, sending the car into a slide. Drake watched as Jimmy closed his eyes and grimaced. He was in safe hands. Luckily the slide only lasted a few meters, and the hydrocar came to a complete stop in the middle of the road.

"That'll do." Drake jumped out, making sure there was no other traffic coming their way.

Back in the driver's seat, he put the car in manual mode and floored the pedal—no point in being subtle now and worrying about speed limits. Penta already had them in their sights and was definitely tracking them. They might not be within firing range, but by contacting them, Penta had proved to be on their trail. And most likely not too far behind.

The old rust bucket didn't like getting up to speed. Drake had the accelerator set to maximum, and everything inside the cabin was shaking and rattling. Jimmy sat, arms crossed over his chest, eyes closed. Drake had to work hard to keep them on the road. His hands were getting numb from all the vibrations going through the steering controls and into his arms. He started to doubt the merits of pushing the hydrocar so hard when all the shaking and rattling settled down, and she began to purr along. Once she was up to speed, the old girl was much happier.

\*\*\*

"Okay, it seems we are being hunted down for murder, not theft."

"Well, that's one thing less to worry about, then."

"I guess, Jimmy, but I did not fucking kill anyone, remember? And I know what you did was not completely your fault, but it is still your mess to clean up, not mine. Our partnership starts and ends with the Bismuth."

Jimmy mulled this over.

He had forgotten that he was alone when the shootings happened. He had been having so much fun with Drake that he forgot Drake wasn't there when it happened. They were working together so well that Jimmy felt like they had been partners from the start.

"Yes, of course. Maybe I can explain it to the lady lieutenant? Ya know, set her straight."

"If you think it will help."

"Anything for you, partner," Jimmy said with the biggest, sincerest smile. He felt like he could be Drake's little brother.

"I guess it doesn't matter. We're not getting caught anyway, are we?" Drake said.

"Hell, no!" Jimmy yelled back.

"Hell no," Drake said, with less conviction.

*\*\**

"Damnit!" Lieutenant Wells said as the circle on the screen dissolved.

There was no way they could catch up to them in time and prevent them from entering the Shangcorp territory. Each territory controlled the incoming traffic, not the outgoing traffic, which meant she would have no authority at the crossing. If it were any other territory, one that was in alliance with Penta, she would have some leverage, but Shangcorp was as close to an enemy as a corporation could get. They would be more inclined to harbor these clowns if Penta requested help, rather than actually help. Her only hope was to get close enough to shut them down, since her little scare tactic hadn't worked.

"Do we have any patrols in the area? Anyone who can cut them off?" she asked out loud. Everyone got busy with their HICs or DDUs.

"Ma'am, there is a patrol stationed right about where they are now. It's the last post before the border."

Having a frosty relationship with Shangcorp meant that both sides tried to be overcautious with security measures and gave each other a wide berth. No security stations were placed too close to the borders.

"Flag the car and tell them to intercept," she hissed.

The DDU operator next to her made the necessary keystrokes, and a message appeared on the screen, showing the vehicle's current position, photos of the vehicle as well as its occupants. Any Penta security vehicle in their vicinity would see it pop up on their screen and act on it. Wells hated getting other teams involved but Drake and Jimmy had forced her hand. Time was running out fast. Rather share the credit than face the humiliation of failure.

"Ma'am, the patrol units have responded and already have visuals on them. They will be in shutdown range within ten minutes."

# | twenty-three |

The guy at the bar, sitting in the middle of a group of similarly dressed men and women, was clearly the leader. They all looked the same: dusty black clothes, big black boots, and long hair that was a mess from blowing behind them on their hydro cycles. What made him different wasn't physical but something more subtle. Everyone around him appeared immersed entirely in their conversations, but every time his beer ran out, someone would run over to the barkeeper and make sure he got a fresh drink. It just happened automatically; no words were needed. Everyone was talking and laughing their heads off, but he was the eye of the storm, quiet and calm.

A large mirror ran the length of the bar, and in it, the leader locked eyes with a man, sitting by himself, blatantly checking him out. After staring at each other for a few seconds, the leader said something very quietly and quickly and the four guys flanking him got up and walked over to the man who had been observing them.

"Boss wants to have a word, perv," one of the unwashed grumbled.

The man got up and walked over to the boss, leaving the guys to catch up. He stopped in front of the boss, who had by now turned around, and had his elbows on the counter behind him. The boss was sizing him up, but the man just stood there waiting for him to speak. The four meatheads had regrouped and stood next to the man, avoiding eye contact with their leader. Their job was to intimidate, not play catch up.

The boss was becoming irritated with his silence. He got up from his chair.

"You like what you see, boy?" he said to the man who was at least his age, if not older.

"Yes, but not the way you think." The man did not budge an inch and was holding his own. The boss was not used to this.

"So . . . that still makes you some sort of a pervert, but my boys will happily cure you of that."

The boss gave his men a slight wink, and they closed in on the man.

"Or, you can call your goons off, and we can talk business."

The boss lifted a hand, and everyone paused. "What sort of business?"

"The kind where you scare a guy, maybe kill him by accident, and get a hundred thousand credits for your efforts."

The boss waved his men off and turned back to the man.

He was standing so close to him that he had to pick one eye to look at. Every man and woman was holding their breath, waiting for the first punch or order to attack. Everyone was ready for the inevitable.

"Get my friend over here a beer," the boss yelled to the barkeep, and all the tension in the room faded away.

***

Justin got into the hydrocar, which he had stolen earlier, and sat next to Captain Santo. After his new friend had bought him a beer, he gave him the details of where to be and transferred some images of Jimmy Something and ten thousand credits as an advance.

"Did you find the mark easy enough?" Santo asked.

"Yes, he was at the bar and matched the picture you gave me." The picture came from the Penta security system and was of a known gang leader suspected of multiple murders, robberies, and such.

"Good. And they agreed to all the terms?"

"Yes," Justin replied. "The credits were a good amount, enough to get their interest, but not enough to seem suspect."

"I know. That's why I picked it. What did you tell them? Do not spare any details."

"Of course. After the initial banter and the number of credits had been discussed, I spoke to the leader. I think that most of the gang was out of earshot. I explained that all they had to do was to go to the meeting point, tell Jimmy to hand the contract over to them, and if he refused, to shoot him. Hell, even if he did hand it over, shoot him. I also told them about the crate with untraceable pulse guns I would leave there for the job and that they could keep them as a bonus."

What Justin did not tell them, since he didn't know it himself, was that these guns were high spec security guns and that they could be programmed. These were set to always miss the set target. In this case, Jimmy Something. Jimmy Something was quite a good shot, so given the faulty guns and his excellent aim, Jimmy should walk out of there unharmed but as a marked and wanted man.

Santo would appoint himself team leader and spearhead the search for Jimmy Something. This way, he would be able to keep an eye on him to ensure all goes to plan. And if it didn't, or Jimmy started to get any silly ideas, he had the best leverage possible—a warrant for multiple murders.

If Jimmy pulled through and made the delivery, Santo would swoop in and arrest him shortly after. With Jimmy Something's history of criminal behavior and his tendency toward violence, a shoot-first-ask-questions-later policy would seem appropriate. The death of a murder suspect saves everyone a lot of paperwork, and no one would question Santo's motives.

A foolproof plan.

*** 

Jimmy knew something was wrong. He was a pretty good shot, but being outnumbered ten to one, it made no sense that no shots had come close to hitting him. He was taking whoever this was out one by one, and they kept missing him. Was this just the most incompetent crew ever? If so, he surely would have heard of them by now. A few seconds of silence went by, and Jimmy risked popping his head out, but no pulse fire came his way. Cautiously he surveyed the massacre. At least seven or eight bodies were spread out on the ground. Fuck! This contract was already way more than he'd bargained for, and he hadn't even started yet.

A movement behind a pillar caught his attention.

"Just you and me now, pal." The guy who did all the talking came out from his hiding spot, pointing a large pulse rifle at Jimmy.

"Sorry, I killed all your men, but they sucked anyway!" Jimmy said, keeping his gun squarely on the guy's chest.

"Doesn't matter, 'cause I have already contacted the rest of my crew, and soon you'll be in a world of pain!" he yelled at Jimmy. "So how about you just lower that little gun of yours and maybe we can work something out."

Although every single pulse round had missed him so far, Jimmy was taking no chances and kept his eyes fixed on the guy. He didn't believe that any more people were coming but couldn't risk finding out. Who knows, maybe the B team knew how to shoot. He knew that in the next few seconds, someone's pulse gun was going to go off first, and that person would be leaving here, alive. The tendon on the back of the guy's hand popped up and Jimmy knew he was about to move his index finger, which was resting on the trigger. Jimmy pulled his trigger first, and the guy dropped on the spot. The first one to shoot leaves.

"Fuck fuck fuck fuck fuck," Jimmy kept muttering.

He had to get out, and fast, but he knew that if he left all the bodies there, they would surely be discovered, and then the security forces would find him within days, if not hours. But if he could delay their progress, get the cargo out, and get paid, he would have enough credits to escape.

That's when the light bulb went on.

***

"Here goes nothing," Drake said as the three circles danced on the screen, became one, and a face appeared.

"Don't ever cut me off again!" Lt. Wells greeted them.

"Sorry about that. My finger must have slipped," Drake replied. "I'll be more careful next time."

"So, I take it you are ready to surrender, then?"

"Hardly, Sugartits. We have something much better, ya know."

Drake shot Jimmy one of his disapproving looks.

"What my, um, partner here meant was, we have something to discuss."

"The moment you surrender, I'll listen to all your wonderful stories. So be a good boy and do the right thing."

"Well," Drake countered, "I really want to be good boy, but I think what we have to tell you—what Jimmy has to tell you—might change things a bit."

"Sure. I have footage of him killing multiple people and then burning a building down, but please, tell me how you are going to change my mind." Lt. Wells didn't mind playing these silly games. They were still a few minutes out of reach of shutting down and commandeering the vehicle remotely, so the more time they wanted to waste, the better. "Entertain me."

Jimmy took a deep breath and told his story, starting with the man approaching him in the bar, the gang trying to kill him, and how he had panicked and burned the place down.

"I believe you, Jimmy," she said, "I really do. And so will a jury."

Jimmy's face lit up, and Drake could see the relief wash over him. The opposite was true for Drake. As he had listened to Jimmy telling the story, he realized it sounded more like a confession than an explanation. Drake was too close to it all, so when Jimmy had told him the first time, it seemed like self-defense and very logical. Listening to it now, it sounded less rosy—a criminal getting caught in a bad situation, killing nine people, *maybe* in self-defense, and then committing arson. Best-case, Jimmy had still broken a bunch of laws, and since he destroyed most of the evidence, it was just his word that it was self-defense.

Drake slowly turned back toward the DDU and Lt. Wells.

Her smug look confirmed his fears.

# | twenty-four |

Lt. Wells was smug but not for the reasons Drake thought. Once she made Jimmy the center of her investigation, she had put all her focus on him, and while she was still desk-bound, she kept searching and digging. Wells found it implausible that one man could outshoot so many foes and not even get a scratch, so she decided to look at what little evidence had been tagged and filed at the scene. Not much had survived the fire, but between the rubble and ashes, they found the remains of nine guns. The guns were completely destroyed, and their CPUs had melted away. Even their silhouettes were difficult to distinguish but not impossible. It took Wells a few days, but eventually, she found out the makes and models of the guns. The case files showed that Santo's team had dismissed it as a dead end. Considering that nine known criminals were off the streets, nobody pushed it further. They knew who had done it, so it was an easy case to close.

If they had kept looking though, they would have found that it was the same guns they, and every other security force, used. Penta Corp manufactured these pulse rifles, but they weren't available to the public. These guns were for security companies only. So Wells kept on digging. The fire had destroyed any serial numbers that would have been on them, so she started looking for any company reporting guns missing or stolen. It took her a while, as losing arms as a security company was embarrassing, to say the least, but finally, she found some.

She was quite surprised at the high number of guns lost by security forces, and it took her longer than expected, but finally, she found what she was after. Two weeks prior, a batch of guns had been checked out of a Penta armory for training and never returned. Instead, they were sent back and destroyed as they were deemed defective. The file showed all the correct paperwork indicating that they had been adequately and securely destroyed—no red flags there and no reason for anyone to recheck it. But Lt. Wells had a feeling, something she had trusted her whole career, that these were the guns she was chasing.

So she kept following the leads until a name popped up that should not have been involved in something this mundane. According to the files from the armory, the guns were checked out by a Sergeant Gunderson, but a low ranking officer named Harper had done all the follow-up work. Usually, a supervisor, a sergeant or lieutenant, had to issue an order to destroy any company assets, especially weapons. Somehow everything had been approved, and all the boxes ticked, and the guns had been crushed under the watchful eye of Officer Harper. A week later, Harper got into trouble for being drunk and attacking a superior officer and was dismissed. The paperwork had been done by his lieutenant and signed off by Captain Raymond Santo.

Again, this was routine stuff and would have seemed reasonable to any observer, but Wells' gut told her to look further into these guns. Something was still not right. She decided to have a word with Harper. However, he'd committed suicide shortly after his dismissal. The trail was getting cold. So she decided to have a chat with Harper's lieutenant.

Lt. Wells was Lieutenant Davis's peer and equal, but one would never have guessed it listening to him. Every question she had, he dismissed, insinuating that she was out of her depth. She gave up and turned around to walk away, when he muttered under his breath, "Santo was right about you, bitch." She kept on walking, but the words echoed in her head. The insult was nothing to her, and not even the worst she had received working in security, but the thing that stuck with her was that Santo would discuss her with Davis. Santo had never worked in the same group or team as this guy. Wells knew this, as Santo had been her superior since she started working at Penta, and she had never even seen Davis until today. The fact that he'd signed off on some paperwork for the dismissal from his team was not unheard of, as it was more of a check to see all the paperwork had been done correctly and nothing to do with the dismissal at all. Captains usually signed off on each other's paperwork to ensure there was no corruption or discrepancies.

For Santo to discuss her with Davis meant they had to have had some connection, either socially or somehow professionally. Back at her desk, Wells decided to look more into Lt. Davis. She pulled up his file on her DDU and got to work. Lt. Davis had been in the company much longer than Wells but had plateaued at Lieutenant. Although he had a personnel file riddled with disciplinary hearings and allegations of corruption, nothing ever stuck. All it did was halt his climb up the ranks. There was plenty to imply he was dirty, and some more digging would undoubtedly uncover more wrongdoings, but Wells had neither the clout nor the time, so she decided trust her instincts, and followed him home.

Lily Wells was single, hardworking, and a lieutenant in the most prominent and best paying security force on the planet. This meant that she could barely afford a small but admittedly nice apartment in town. Dirty Davis was a washed-up, certainly corrupt officer, with the same rank and position as Wells. Yet he lived in a two-story house, and although he left work in an ordinary hydrocar, a brand new Nikolatec Roadster stood in his driveway. Wells knew her gut was right.

"What do you want?" Davis spat out the words as he opened the front door.

"I already got most of what I was looking for, but you could confirm something for me," Wells said, standing well inside his personal space. Sweat was starting to appear on his brow, and Davis took a little step back.

"If you have anything to say to me, say it at work."

Davis stretched his arm out to press the door closure button on the wall, but Wells had inched her way into the doorway. The safety feature built into the door would not allow it close with someone standing there.

"No. We are going to talk now," Wells said, "and you are going to start by telling me who is paying for all of this."

"You are out of your mind, woman. I inherited this place, okay? If you have to know, I got this because someone I loved died."

Wells was not buying his little show.

"Could be. I'll check it out in the morning. It should all be in the public records, right? But I still think that you are a dirty little rat, so I am giving you one more chance to come clean. Who is paying for this?"

Davis puffed his chest out as best he could over his soft belly.

"You got nothing, sweetheart. Bigger, scarier men than you have tried to take me down before, and yet, here I stand."

"I believe that, but did they have evidence showing Captain Santo as your benefactor?" Wells decided to go all out, put everything on the line, and see how he reacted.

It was tiny, most people would have missed it, but Wells saw the twitch in his eye. The moment she said Santo's name, it happened. If Wells had had her ARP on, she would have seen his entire body telemetry spike. But she wanted to do this her way. Go with her instincts. And she was right. Captain Santo was as dirty as this weasel before her and somehow behind the whole Jimmy Something case.

"Thanks for confirming my hunch," she said and left a mumbling Davis behind.

***

"So, what now? Are we clear?" Jimmy asked Lt. Wells.

"Well, Jimmy, you have just confessed to murder and arson, to a Penta security officer. So, what do you think?"

"Yes, yes, but I told you, it was a setup, self-defense, ya know?" Jimmy hoped Drake would jump in and say something. He didn't.

"Team B is five minutes from effective range," someone yelled in the background behind Wells.

Drake checked the DDU. The border was still another ten minutes away.

They were toast.

"I take it you have run out of time?"

"Not quite, Lieutenant," Drake replied.

He knew that the lieutenant was still at least forty minutes behind them, so if they stopped now, jumped out, and started to run, they might just make it. If they waited too long, Penta would come within range and override their hydrocar and lock it down, trapping them inside.

"I can see you are thinking, Mr. Drake, but let me assure you, we have shoot-to-kill orders, so don't do anything silly."

And Wells meant it.

***

The last thing she wanted was for Jimmy Something to get killed. He was a crucial piece in bringing Santo down, and she needed him in a talkable state, not dead. Her team could not know this yet, as she had only just been allowed back in the fold, and they would rather side with Santo than her. No, she would have to capture Jimmy alive and then explain to them what was going on. Drake's face told her that he was not going to go down without a fight. Wells was happy to lose him but feared Jimmy might go down guns blazing if they shot Drake.

Wells had less than two minutes left to decide before everything could come down like a pile of bricks.

# | twenty-five |

"Okay, gents, I have one last offer. There is something that might help you decide—"

"Get out now!" Drake yelled at Jimmy as he cut the transmission short. "She was trying to buy more time. Ten more seconds and they would have had us."

Drake jumped out of the hydrocar and ran around to Jimmy's side and flung the door open. Jimmy sat there, making his preference between fight or flight clear by choosing Option C: freeze. Drake grabbed Jimmy's arm, pulled him out of the hydrocar, and started running, pulling him along.

"Let's go, buddy! Time to make a run for it!"

Jimmy looked bewildered but picked up the pace and followed Drake nonetheless.

"I thought she was about to make a deal!"

"Nah, buddy . . . far from it . . . she was just . . . buying more time . . . they almost . . . had us!" Drake said, still running and breathing hard now.

The terrain was pretty flat, but rocks and grass popped up everywhere, which they had to avoid or jump over. Drake knew one fall could mean the end for them. He was in no state to do math, but he reckoned they were twenty minutes away from the border by foot, and Penta was a little bit more than that behind them. It was going to be a race to the finish line.

Drake had to concentrate on where he was stepping. A small building appeared on the horizon, and he hoped that it was the border post as he aimed right for it. He dared a quick look behind him, stumbling, but could not see anyone approaching.

"C'mon Jimmy . . . don't slow down . . . buddy!"

Drake was in better shape than most haulers, due in part to a strict daily calisthenics routine, but he was still no athlete. Jimmy, on the other hand, was just skin and bone and was starting to lag behind Drake, struggling to breathe.

"I . . . all good . . . just . . . damn," Jimmy forced the words out.

Drake turned and did a quick scan again. Still nothing. He waited for Jimmy to catch up, still scanning the horizon. Jimmy was walking now and stopped next to Drake, breathing hard.

"Buddy, we are running out of time here. I'm not sure we can make it walking," Drake said, eyes peeled on the horizon behind them.

"I know . . . just . . . need . . . to . . . fuck . . . catch my . . . breath."

"Okay, okay. Keep walking, take five deep breaths, and then we try again."

"Okay."

Drake heard Jimmy taking deep breaths while he walked next to him, head turned back, looking for Penta. He heard Jimmy take one last deep, slow breath.

"Here we go!" Drake said as he started running again, pulling Jimmy along by his sleeve.

Jimmy's pace barely increased, but at least he was moving quicker again. And he needed to; as Drake peered back over his shoulder again, he caught the first glimpse of a dust cloud. He snapped his head back to find the small border building again, but it was still some distance away. He knew he would make it if he ditched Jimmy.

"Jimmy, if you don't start running quicker, I swear I'm leaving you behind, you hear me?"

The dust cloud was getting bigger. A second one appeared, coming at them from a different angle. Drake could just make out tiny black shapes in front of the dust clouds.

"Shit. Jimmy, they're here. C'mon!" He yanked Jimmy forward.

Drake could now make out people standing in front of the small building and started to wave his arms.

"Hey! Over here! Don't shoot!" he yelled as he ran.

Drake sneaked a quick look back and almost stumbled over his feet when he saw how close the first Penta armored vehicle was. He could see the headlights and make out shapes behind the windscreen. Drake and Jimmy were about fifty meters from the building now and Penta about four hundred behind them, coming at them from two sides.

Drake forced himself to move faster, still pulling Jimmy along. Freedom or death was only meters away now.

"Slow down! What's going on here?" one of the guards yelled to Drake, gun at the ready but still pointing down.

As Drake opened his mouth to reply, he heard the Penta vehicle's tires locking up and sliding on the dirt. He looked back, just as the vehicle finally stopped. The doors opened.

"We seek asylum!" Drake yelled, not even sure if that was what they were after.

"Freeze, don't move!" someone yelled behind them. "We have shoot-to-kill orders. Surrender now!"

One Penta vehicle, doors open, with two personnel in front of it, pulse guns aimed right at them. Behind it, another bigger Penta armored vehicle was coming to a stop.

Drake was still holding onto Jimmy's arm. He started to move toward the building, pulling him along.

"Drake! Don't do it! If you step over that line, I can't help you anymore," Lt. Wells cried out behind him, as she jumped out of the second vehicle.

Drake turned around to face her. There was no way she was here to help them. All she wanted was to catch them and throw them in jail or ship them off to Mars.

"Thanks, but so far, your help has been quite sucky," Drake said. He stepped back onto the paved area and to within a few feet of the painted line on the ground. If he crossed that line, he was officially in Shang-corp.

"Please, you need to trust me. Do not step over that line," Lt. Wells pleaded.

What was her angle? She was begging him, but Drake knew she was just being a sly security officer, doing her best to get her target. Her voice had lost some of its hard-ass edge, but surely that was part of the ruse? Pretty transparent, really.

"Sorry," Drake said, and suddenly all the Penta Security officers drew their weapons and aimed at him and Jimmy.

The two Shangcorp officers immediately drew their weapons, and one called in reinforcements via his ARP, never taking his eyes of the targets. Things escalated quickly, with both sides yelling at each other, and at Drake and Jimmy. They were standing in the middle of two firing squads, and both sides seemed happy to pull the trigger and take everyone out. Conflicting instructions were shouted out to Jimmy and Drake from the opposite sides, and threats were flung between the two security groups.

No one was budging, forcing a stalemate.

"Stand down! Stand down!" Lt. Wells yelled at her team.

They held their ground, eyes still fixed on their targets, but dropped their guns ever so slightly. The two Shangcorp officials held their weapons aimed at the Penta team but stopped their yelling. An eerie calmness settled over the adrenaline-fueled scene. Drake felt a cramp in his hand and realized he was still gripping Jimmy's arm quite tightly. Jimmy just looked at him sheepishly, waiting to be pulled in his chosen direction. Drake relaxed his hand and dropped Jimmy's arm back to his side.

"Drake, Jimmy, please listen. If you hand yourself over right now, we can work something out. Things are not as dire as you think. But, if you cross that line, I cannot help you. Just think for a second."

"I like this reasonable side of yours, Lieutenant, but I find it a bit hard to believe," Drake replied, his heart thumping in his chest.

Sirens became audible in the distance, which meant back up was almost there. Drake hoped it was from Shangcorp and not Penta.

"Jimmy, I believe you acted in self-defense, but if you cross that line, it does not matter. You will be a fugitive until we get you. And we will."

Jimmy looked at Drake for guidance but his partner was just as confused.

"Fuck you," Jimmy spat out at Lt. Wells. He took the final step over the line.

One of the Shangcorp guards quickly stepped in front of him and backed him up toward the building. The Penta team raised their guns again, each one tracking their target, awaiting orders.

Sirens and screeching tires announced the arrival of more Shangcorp personnel. Drake was still frozen in place as the Shangcorp forces grew to about ten.

"Please lower your weapons. Who is in charge?" one of the new Shangcorp personnel demanded.

"I am," Wells replied, "and we need to take these men into custody." Her team did not lower their weapons, although they were now slightly outnumbered.

"Well, this man has already crossed into the sovereign territory of Shangcorp. As for that man, he is standing in the neutral zone, as agreed upon by our two companies. So, I suggest you turn around and go back to your superiors and let them figure it out," Lt. Wells' opposite number said.

Wells knew that she was outgunned and outdone. She had no plan or idea how to get Drake to come over to them willingly. As long as he stood in the neutral zone, no one would touch him, but in theory, she could grab him and not break any rules. There would be a lot of political backlash but nothing that couldn't be resolved. The problem was the man she needed was already across the line and in the hands of Shangcorp. No point in causing an incident if she only got half the prize she was chasing.

"Drake, you win for now. But surely, you must know that Penta will not let this slide?"

"The thought never crossed my mind, Lieutenant. But I'd rather run as a free man for the rest of my life than give up and rot in jail." Drake turned around to take the final step and cross the line.

Drake turned his back to her, one step away from crossing into Shangcorp and most likely to disappear forever. Shangcorp was three times the size of Penta Corporation and ten times as corrupt. The perfect place for people on the run.

Drake gave Lt. Wells one last glance over his shoulder as he shifted his weight on his front foot to make that final step. Her eyes were pleading him, and it looked like she was mouthing the words, *Don't do it*, to him. What was her deal? Why was she suddenly so desperate? Surely Penta had the resources and contacts to easily keep tabs on them and strike as soon as an opportunity arose? This could not possibly be it. And yet.

The whole Penta team dropped their weapons and relaxed as Drake stepped over the line. He was now out of their hands, at least while he was in a Shangcorp territory, and they knew it. Lt. Wells' shoulders drooped as she stared at Drake and Jimmy Something.

"C'mon Lieutenant, let's go home," one of the Penta team yelled at her as they got ready to board the armored vehicle. The Shangcorp security team hustled Drake and Jimmy Something into their armored vehicle and sped off, leaving the two guards alone again. She watched the Shangcorp vehicle disappear around a corner and turned back toward her team.

# | twenty-six |

Jacob McKenna woke up and started to read his messages on his Human Interface Console even before he got out of bed. Doing this was not unusual for him, but this morning there was an urgency about it. He had a feeling that there was a message in there that could not wait until after he had his morning caffeine pill. And he was right. About ten messages in, he found one from his chief engineer. Production of the Polonium had been going better than expected, and the first batches were ready to be used. Everything was going to plan. He swiped his arm to close the messages and tapped another part of the screen. The familiar three dots started to dance and merge in front of him.

"Raymond. Did I wake you up?"

"I was up. Why are you calling?" Captain Santo did not sound like a morning person.

"Good. Well, my team informed me this morning that the first batch of Polonium is ready to go. So I suggest you get your men over here!" Jacob McKenna was as giddy as a kid on Christmas morning and struggled to contain himself.

"They are ready and prepped. I will assemble the team and give them orders to dispatch within the hour. I'll see you soon, Jacob."

The face in front of him faded. Jacob McKenna got up, dressed, and left for the hangars.

A hive of activity greeted him when he arrived. Everyone knew what the expectations were and what to do, and more importantly, the obscene credit bonuses that awaited them on completion of this project. The lure of obscene numbers of credits, more than anything else, made them work harder and more precisely than any workforce around.

One of the lead engineers came running over.

"Mr. McKenna, we didn't expect you so early."

"It is a big day for all of us. Will we be ready to launch tonight?" McKenna asked the engineer, who suddenly looked a bit sick.

"The . . . the deadline was for completion tonight and launching to-morrow night, sir."

"You, over there," McKenna yelled to a nearby worker. "Grab me whoever is next in charge to this man."

"No, no, no! As you were! Keep going," the engineer yelled at the worker and immediately turned back to McKenna. "Sir, I was just con-firming that we are moving things ahead a day, that's all."

McKenna ignored the engineer and surveyed the activities in front of him. The four teardrop-shaped shuttles were facing each other in a cross pattern, and people in white coveralls were moving about loading things, checking things, and generally just getting on with their jobs. Everything was just right.

"Good," McKenna said, still facing the shuttles. "The passengers will be here soon. When they arrive, make sure they board immediately."

"Of course, sir," the engineer replied. McKenna was already walking away.

***

Captain Raymond Santo walked over to the washbasin and looked at the face in the mirror. He had never been a very moral or ethical per-son, so the need to reflect on where his life had taken a turn for the worse was not going to happen. Neither did Santo have any sense of being in over his head or losing control. Instead, he just looked at his own face. He splashed some water onto it to help him wake up, popped a caffeine pill, and went back into the room to get dressed.

The men and women he had selected for this mission shared a bar-rack, under the auspices of a major training exercise, which was true, to some degree. Everyone had been handpicked by Santo, as they had shown themselves to be excellent marksmen and team players. All these officers knew that after today, they were no longer Penta employees, and the lucrative contracts they signed meant they also didn't care who their new employer would be. Captain Santo knew how to manipulate the system, so he had set up a special unit, comprising of his newly selected crew, and started training them in advanced combat. Day and night, they trained. Santo believed that they represented one of the best fighting forces credits could buy. Exactly what Jacob McKenna ordered.

Captain Santo walked into the barracks, and immediately, everyone jumped to attention. He could feel his chest swell.

"At ease. Mission Pandora is a go. Teams are to be packed and ready to leave in fifteen minutes. Drivers get the carriers ready."

With a nod, they were dismissed, and everyone sped off to get themselves ready for the mission they had been training for. They were all prepared to go on short notice, so within five minutes, most were lining up at the doors, waiting for the personnel carriers to arrive. As they came, people started pilling in. Each carrier held twenty people and one driver. Santo's team consisted of fifty officers, so he'd had three carriers disappear off the records, which showed them as having been decommissioned, shipped out and destroyed. But the vehicles never reached the scrap yard. Instead, Santo'd had them sent to Bob Turner, where they were resprayed, and their DDUs were replaced with generic ones, so Penta could no longer locate or hack them.

When everyone had boarded the newly refurbished vehicles, Santo got into the last one. It had only eight officers in it and was the least cramped.

"Move out." The convoy departed.

***

The engineers usually anticipated a change in the schedule and worked within a time frame that would allow them to speed things up at any moment. So when Jacob McKenna had told them to be ready within a few hours instead of another day or two, they were more than capable of doing so. McKenna paid well to have the best minds, and that's what he got, including their heightened sense of self-preservation.

The shuttles were ready to go, but Karen Giles, one of the lead engineers, decided to do one more round of checks to ensure absolutely no failures or complications. McKenna's narcissistic self-importance meant that the Zuma Corp hierarchy consisted of McKenna at the top and everyone else below him. So the different teams and disciplines organized themselves into a natural pecking order to ensure that things ran smoothly.

A group of five engineers, called the Brains by the other workers, were the de facto leaders, like a group of elders, and made all the significant decisions on the project as a group. Karen Giles was one of the Brains and had the responsibility of testing and quality assurance. Although McKenna was only sending security personnel on the first voyage, the second trip would include some of the workers and most of the engineers. They'd all had the option of staying behind, but McKenna always made sure he paid enough to entice people to follow him. Also, once the shuttles reached Mars, most people associated with Zuma Corp would be better off leaving rather than staying behind to deal with the fallout.

Karen Giles walked through the last shuttle, scanner in one hand, eyes glued to her HIC, making sure that she didn't miss anything and that all the scans and test results were perfect. She released a deep sigh of relief when the last scan came back positive. Giles lowered the scanner and started back toward the exit of the shuttle. She walked back from the cockpit, that was at the furthest end of the shuttle and which would be seating two operators during lift-off and landing. At other times the operators, three per shuttle and working in shifts, would be running tests and keeping an eye on all the telemetry throughout the month-and-a-half-long journey. No one had ever traveled this quickly to Mars. McKenna's engineers had designed these shuttles to be twice as fast as the Polonium shuttles used by Penta.

Behind the cockpit, Giles walked past the food preparation area, then the communal area, and finally the twenty small two-meters-by-four living cubicles. Each cubicle had a sleeping bunk and a DDU. Spartan, but adequate. Last, she walked past the four shower and toilet modules. She climbed down the ladder into the cargo area underneath. It was only a third full at the moment, predominantly with food, but once the officers embarked with all their luggage and weapons, it would be full. She opened the only external door on the shuttle and exited.

The shuttles were ready for launch.

# | twenty-seven |

The armored vehicle came to a stop, the back door was flung open, and Benjamin Drake and Jimmy Something were unceremoniously thrown out onto the road.

"Welcome to Shangcorp, my friends. Enjoy your stay."

The Shangcorp Security officers slammed the door shut and sped off, leaving Drake and Jimmy standing in the middle of the road, with no town or settlement in sight.

"Well, that didn't go quite as planned," Drake said, dusting himself off.

"What do you mean? We're in Shangcorp. That was the plan, ya know?"

"I know, buddy, but that cost a lot more credits than we planned," Drake reminded Jimmy.

After the stand down at the border crossing, Jimmy and Drake had been stuffed into a Shangcorp armored vehicle. Once inside, one of the officers processed their entry and gave them all the clearance they needed to be able to stay in Shangcorp. He scanned their HIC's and ticked all the waivers for them. Even when the red rectangle filled the screen to warn him that they were wanted, the operator just accepted the warning and made it disappear. Next to the DDU operator was the driver, and behind them sat the team leader. Jimmy and Drake sat in a semi-circle with the rest of the team, facing him.

"You guys were early," he said, looking at Jimmy, then Drake and back to Jimmy again. "If we didn't show up when we did, you would be on your way to a dark room in a big Penta building right about now."

For once, Jimmy's instincts kicked in at the right time. "Sorry about that, but shit happens, ya know? So how much is this taxi ride gonna cost?"

"Well, if you'd shown up on time, the credits would have been enough to cover all expenses," he said, sweeping his head, implying his team. "But now there are more . . . expenses."

Drake caught on that the team leader was the contact had Jimmy called and bribed to get them safely across the border. Now the whole team was involved, and more palms needed greasing.

"I see, I see," Jimmy said, stroking his patchy stubble. "I guess we could double the original agreed amount?"

"Double *that,* and we become best friends," Jimmy's contact replied, smiling.

Drake gave him a small nod. To refuse the offer would be suicide.

"Let's do this," Jimmy said. He rolled up his sleeve.

The instant the transfer went through, the vehicle stopped, and the back door flew open, ejecting its newest occupants.

"We still have plenty left, ya know?" Jimmy said, once they were back on their feet and watching the armored vehicle disappear into the distance.

The terrain was still pretty barren, with no trees in sight to offer relief from the sun. The road was a long black line that bisected the landscape into two identical halves. Both looked equally void of any life or refuge.

"We need to get out of this heat," Drake said and started walking along the road, the same way the armored vehicle had gone.

Jimmy checked his HIC. "The closest settlement is about two hours away."

"Oh, that's not too bad. Haven't walked that far in maybe ever, but sounds okay."

"Um, sorry partner, but that's by hydro—"

"What?" Drake yelled. Jimmy flinched, and Drake immediately felt terrible.

"Sorry, I should've been clearer, ya know?" Jimmy mumbled.

"Well, yes, but," Drake tried not to get angry again, "let's just keep moving."

A few Hydrocomets whizzed past, but Drake knew they were all on Autodrive, and besides, they had deadlines to meet. Picking up two lost souls in the middle of nowhere was not going to get them their bonuses. Drake wondered if he would have stopped and helped them if he had been driving past. He knew the answer, so he just kept walking.

They had been walking nonstop for hours, and the sun was starting to sink closer to the horizon. The temperature was dropping fast, and Drake wondered how cold it would get out here. Jimmy was already rubbing his arms.

"You got something on you to make a fire?" Drake asked him.

Jimmy patted his pockets and pulled out a thumb-sized gas torch, guiltily handing it over. The only people who carried small gas torches were ones who smoked tobacco. People still used tobacco, despite it being classified as a chemical weapon and incurring high penalities.

"Thanks, buddy. Let's get warm," Drake said. There was no need to lecture Jimmy.

It took them a while in the sparse landscape to find enough sticks and dry plant matter. They decided to stop when the first stars came out. By then, they had a good-sized pile, and it was getting too dark to see anyway. Drake made a small heap and lit it up. The dry plants immediately burned out, but he quickly added some sticks to it. Jimmy brought over a good-sized piece of some dried plant and threw it on the fire. The flames doubled in size, and Drake and Jimmy stepped closer to the heat. They stood there, letting the heat from the fire warm them up, neither of them saying a word.

They were as free as they would ever be.

***

Lt. Wells knew she had screwed up. She had to come up with a plan quickly. She stood at the border crossing, watching Drake and Jimmy

Something getting hauled away to who knows where. Her orders were to return to base if Jimmy and Drake should enter Shangcorp, which they now clearly had. Headquarters would then revise their strategy and decide how to proceed. What that meant was that Captain Santo would bury the case in paperwork, and they would both be free. She knew that if she went back to HQ, it would be the end of the case. Even if the investigation was left open, she would lose all her momentum and would have to start over again. Also, Captain Santo would most likely already be gone.

Her team had their orders. They were happy to go back to HQ and their homes since this was just a job to them, and they did not care one way or the other if they returned home empty-handed. But Wells had unfinished business and had to get back to that border crossing and pick up the trail before it went cold. A trip back to HQ was out of the question.

She decided to risk a call to Santo to ask permission for a short personal leave. The mission was over for now, and she could not see any reason he would refuse. She seldom took time off and had plenty stockpiled.

The three circles became one, and Captain Santo appeared.

"Thank you for contacting me. Unfortunately, I'm on personal leave. Contact your nearest Penta security office, and they will gladly assist." The image disappeared.

Wells knew she had no more time to waste. Captain Santo was on the run, and she needed to start chasing, now.

# | twenty-eight |

The four gleaming white shuttles greeted Captain Santo and his crew as they arrived at the hangar. He always played his cards close to his chest and did not react like everyone else when they saw them. Unlike his crew, he did not utter gasps of awe or show excitement at seeing them. Sure, they were like nothing he had seen before, and quite a feat of engineering, but Captain Santo took pride in his stoic nature: a quality he believed all leaders should have. Only let your enemies see what you want them to see. And double that for your friends.

"Listen up. Jackson, here, has all the boarding itineraries. When you are signed off, board the shuttles and familiarize yourself with them. You are going to spend a month in there, so make sure you know how everything works and ask questions before we leave." Captain Santo dismissed the team and went looking for McKenna.

The Zuma crews were already loading all the cargo, which included weapons, food, clothing, and medical equipment, into the holds. His team was hustling to get into the shuttles and check them out. Although they were extremely professional, there was still a tangible excitement in the air. Not many people ever had the opportunity to travel to Mars, not to mention going in the world's fastest shuttles. Santo could not deny them that, as he was also feeling some excitement when looking at the shuttles.

"They truly are something, aren't they?" McKenna startled him.

"Jacob, I take it we are running on schedule," Santo said, forgoing any chitchat.

"Yes, of course. What do you expect from me?" McKenna replied, smiling.

"My team will be briefed an hour from now and will then be operations-ready," Santo said.

"Good, Raymond. They do look the part, don't they?" McKenna turned to face the shuttles. "Any word on your troublesome lieutenant?"

Santo took a deep breath. "The team gave up the chase when those idiots crossed a border into a Shangcorp territory. She and her team are now on their way back to headquarters and will receive new assignments. As I said, everything is under control."

McKenna turned his head to offer a smile to Captain Santo and then turned back to face the shuttles that were being prepped and loaded.

"I truly hope so, Raymond."

***

Lt. Wells had a choice to make: chase the two dimwits or stop Captain Santo. If she caught up to Drake and Jimmy Something, she would still have to convince them to help her in giving evidence against Santo. Without the ability to guarantee them immunity for their crimes, she had little to offer. Appealing to their sense of morality was most likely a long shot, at best. And even if she did catch up to them and convinced them to help her, Santo would be long gone.

Pursuing Santo was also not so easy. The man had officials all over Penta in his pocket. Tracking him down would be a time-consuming endeavor, and if he were on the run, with all his resources he would be impossible to catch.

So Wells decided to do the one thing she was good at, the job she excelled at—finding answers. She logged into the Mongoose's DDU and did a search on Captain Raymond Santo. She included every possible parameter, hoping to find just one small piece of information. The drive back to headquarters was going to take several hours, so she had some time on her hands. The rest of the team was already getting comfortable and falling asleep, except for the driver whose attention was on monitoring the DDU in front of him.

The results came back and showed Wells mostly what she was expecting—lots of mundane paperwork with Santo's name on, from holiday approvals to team allocations. He was, for the most part, an administrator, so this did not surprise Wells at all. He hardly worked cases, and when he did, he usually had the second in charge do all the paperwork. Lt. Wells didn't know what she was looking for, so she had no idea how to alter the search. She decided to work her way backward, hoping that somewhere he had screwed up and left her a small clue.

Two hours later, Lt. Wells found something. At first, she missed it, but her gut told her to dig into it a bit further. A few months back, a special unit had been assembled. Its main objective was riot control. There were already such teams, but bureaucrats always had to justify their positions and salaries, so Lt. Wells did not find it that suspicious that another squad was being assembled to do something redundant. Captain Santo had the same feeling, as he signed off on it. She was about to give up when she got that feeling in her gut again. The feeling she knew she had to trust.

A training facility, including accommodation, was set up for the new team with an awe-inspiring arsenal of weapons. The whole affair had the air of a special projects team to it. Everything on file showed them to be ordinary officers in training, but the facilities, arsenal, and training personnel attached to it was total overkill. Yet Captain Santo approved every request from the team for more resources. It seemed like they were gearing up for a small scale war, not a possible riot.

Wells sat up, closed her eyes, and let her mind run free with the realization that had started to form in the back of her head.

*What is the primary use of Bismuth?*

To produce fuel for the shuttles that go to Mars.

*What is on Mars?*

A healthy workforce, compromised of criminals. Minimal security personnel.

*What else?*

Untold amounts of minerals and metals.

*Who else has a connection to all this that would have an interest in mining Mars?*

Jacob McKenna and his Zuma Corporation.

*Where was the stolen Bismuth headed?*

Zuma.

"Santo is going to help McKenna take over Mars," Wells said to herself in the back of the Mongoose, between the rhythmic snoring of her team.

# | twenty-nine |

"It is quite something, isn't it?" Drake said.

"Never been out of the city, ya know? Most nights, you could hardly see any stars, what with all the lights and pollution, but this . . ."

Drake had to admit, even to a hardened hauler like himself who traveled out in the open all the time, it was still something to behold. The Milky Way stretched from horizon to horizon, and the stars were as bright as he had ever seen them.

"You see that bright one over there?" Drake said, pointing into the sky.

"Uh, I think so," Jimmy said unconvincingly.

"There, the brightest star of them all. Watch closely, and you'll see it doesn't flicker like the rest."

"Yeah, yeah, I got it now!" Jimmy yelled.

"That, my friend, is Mars," Drake said and kept staring at the bright speck in the sky.

"No fucking way," Jimmy exhaled.

"Yeah fucking way. The place where men go to die," Drake said, bringing Jimmy back to Earth.

"Not all men, ya know? Soon it will be just like Earth, but better! I've heard most of the planet is now livable, and soon they will be taking families there. They are going to build them houses and give them jobs, and it's going to be like humanity is starting over. Earth is going to be the place to die, ya know?"

Drake knew that Jimmy was half right. The long-term plan for Mars was to be a second Earth, and scientists and engineers had been work-ing at it for decades now. First, they sent probes and autonomous vehi-cles. Then they started to send humans on a six-month journey there. Over the years, it had become quite a significant outpost. But the popu-lation was growing too quickly, and the infrastructure could not handle it. Most of the people there were scientists and engineers: lots of peo-ple with brilliant ideas, but what Mars needed was more people who could do the heavy lifting. For a while, it looked like it might have been a failed experiment. Then Penta got the idea of sending criminals there to serve out their sentences as cheap laborers. They built bigger shut-tles and started to send the criminals over with a small group of security personnel.

The latest reports suggested that Penta had suspended sending criminals over and was getting ready to replace them with civilians. Penta did not own Mars; in fact, the first few shuttles were sent by Nikolatec and Citro, both huge companies dealing in energy and tech-nology (Nikolatec made most of the vehicles and Citro had a monopoly on HICs and ARPs), but once Penta sent their criminals there accom-panied by their security forces, it became a de facto Penta territory. No one else was sending shuttles, so Penta was slowly and very unofficially claiming more and more of Mars as their own.

Drake did not have a massive interest in Mars and hardly stayed up to date with its development. What he knew, he got from drunken conversations in bars.

"You really think Mars is all that great, Jimmy?"

"Oh yes!" Jimmy said. "It's the place where anyone can start over, ya know?"

"Who told you that nonsense? If you're a wanted man here, you'll still be a wanted man there. I know Penta doesn't own it, but they sure as hell run it as if they do." Drake knew he'd just pissed all over Jimmy's dream but he also knew he was right. Jimmy was building Mars up in his head as this magical place where all his problems would disappear, but instead, he'd just be walking straight into Penta-infested territory.

He'd be arrested on the spot. All he would be doing was saving Penta the credits to send him to Mars.

"I guess so, but where else am I going to go? We're marked anywhere but here. And here? If we so much as look at someone wrong here, they'll shoot us, ya know? This is Shangcorp, not Penta. They don't play nice."

"I know Jimmy, but at least we're free. We can figure this out," Drake said, but his words sounded empty.

"Thanks, partner, but we're not the same. We have different lives. You got sucked into this, but I live like this, ya know. All this running around, dealing with degenerates like me—it's what I do. It's all I know how to do. I can't go hauling or get a job in a factory making shit, ya know? Sooner or later, I'm going to do something that'll get me caught. It's happened before, and it'll happen again. Only here in Shangcorp, they tend to shoot first and usually forget about the questions altogether." Jimmy looked up again at Mars. He smiled. "But there, we all get a clean slate. We can begin over and be whatever we want to be."

Drake knew he had no argument left to convince Jimmy not to go. If going to Mars meant that he would have peace, then it was not Drake's place to stop him. Drake knew it would be suicide for Jimmy to go, but he guessed staying here would not be that much better. At least on Mars, he could do it on his own terms.

"Yeah, maybe you're right. What do I know, anyway? As you said, you know this life. I'm just an idiot that fell into it. I hope that you're right about Mars, buddy," Drake said to Jimmy, who was still staring at the bright unflickering light in the sky.

"Me too, partner," Jimmy replied. A tear slowly made its way down his cheek and dropped down to the floor.

*** 

In contrast to the stark white of the shuttles, the people entering them wore all black: black tactical boots, black ripstop pants with black nylon webbing belts, and black shirts—functional and low tech. Each shirt had a gold Z on the chest, McKenna's personal touch. Everything he owned had his golden emblem on it, including his army.

The teams divided into four smaller groups and embarked on the shuttles. Captain Santo made sure he was the first one to board, just as he would be the first one to disembark. Heroes were the authors of their histories.

"I'll open communications the moment we are in flight and out of launch protocol," Santo said to McKenna as he stepped into the shuttle and disappeared.

"I'm looking forward to it," McKenna replied to the backs of the other security personnel already filing through the door.

Once inside, the officers started filling up the personal cubicles. As if a single organism, they unpacked and stored their items in unison. Simultaneously, they emerged from their cubicles and sat down in the chairs in the common area. The chairs were located at tables and fixed into place. They served a dual purpose as dining and general recreational chairs but also had safety harnesses attached to them for use during takeoff. It was the latter purpose that they now fulfilled, as the security team strapped themselves down in anticipation of the launch.

Most of the people in the cabin had experienced a takeoff before, albeit for low altitude space flights around the globe. Still, nervous energy filled the cabin, and no one said a word. Some of it was due to their training and discipline, but also that they sat strapped to an experimental shuttle that was about to hurl them into space faster than any human had ever traveled. Santo was not one to mingle with his subordinates and preferred to keep his distance from them, but even he couldn't ignore the obvious.

"Connect me to all teams," Santo yelled at the Zuma operator at the shuttle's DDU.

"This is Captain Santo. For the remainder of the journey, until we reach the target, you are not required to keep to mission protocol. All teams are expected to stay professional and alert, but should consider the journey itself as off duty. At ease."

As if a switched had been flicked, all the tension in the four shuttles eased, and people started to talk and laugh. Santo was impressed; the training had made them into the ultimate killing machines, yet they knew how to switch it on and off. A sense of immense pride and satisfaction washed over him. The mission was a guaranteed success.

*** 

McKenna watched on as the last shuttle hatch closed.

"Standby . . . All clear," a voice bellowed over a speaker.

He knew from countless test runs and meetings that once the hatches closed, the mission operators would wait for the shuttle operators to confirm everyone was strapped in and ready for launch. Once they got the thumbs up from the shuttles, the mission operators would run one last scan of all the systems on board the shuttle before clearing them for takeoff.

"Base, this is shuttle one. Cargo secure and ready to fly," a voice announced over the speakers.

"Thank you, shuttle one. Please stand by," one of the engineers next to McKenna replied and started to run the scans on their DDU. After only a few minutes, a green message appeared on the screen, indicating all scans completed and passed.

"Sir," the engineer pointed to the microphone that was at the ready in front of McKenna.

McKenna cleared his throat and recited the lines he had been rehearsing for weeks: "Today we become gods among men! Shuttle one, you are clear to launch!"

The round opening at the back of the shuttle turned red, and a blue flame blasted out of it. Almost comically, the shuttle crept forward, slowly gaining speed until it suddenly accelerated at a tremendous rate and took off into the sky. McKenna stared at it for only a few seconds, as it rapidly disappeared into the atmosphere.

The next shuttle was already waiting and ready to go. The engineers knew McKenna had already had his moment, so they quickly lined up the next shuttle, ran the tests and scans, and sent them off. Within ten minutes, three more white shapes rapidly disappeared into the sky, leaving behind them the men and women who would soon take the same trip themselves.

***

*Today, we become gods among men! Shuttle one, you are clear to go!*

McKenna's voice filled the cabin.

They looked at each other nervously; a few even shouted out excitedly. Everything started to shake, and without any windows, it was impossible to know if they were already moving. That was abruptly put to rest as everyone was violently pinned to their seats, and no one could utter a word. The only visual cue they got was from the DDU in front of the Zuma operator. It showed the blue sky quickly darkening and turning black. Within moments of taking off, the screen turned black, and everyone felt relieved as they were unpinned from their seats.

"Whoa!" someone yelled, and suddenly the whole cabin was talking again. Everyone got out of their seats and crowded around the DDU, the only view of the outside.

"Mars, here we come!"

"Look at all the stars."

"That was intense!"

Everyone had something to say, and as the adrenaline slowly started to fade, people began to calm down, some still watching the DDU, others going to their cubicles. The fun part was over, for now, and they started to settle in for the month-long journey that lay ahead.

# | thirty |

The first few days back at work were filled with endless data entry and debriefings. Penta administration loved to drown people in mindless after-the-fact bullshit, making sure every angle of every incident was reported and double-checked. Lt. Lily Wells knew she had stumbled upon the most significant case of her career, and yet she was stuck behind a DDU, recounting the last few days chasing Jimmy and Drake.

She had to get back to chasing the leads before they went cold, but she had no real evidence, except for her gut. That was good enough for her, but she knew no one else would even give it a second look. Accusing a senior officer of anything, let alone treason, was a risky move. She would be as exposed as Santo would be. No corporation, and especially not one who specialized in the security business, wanted their top-ranking members embroiled in scandal. So to accuse someone, you had to be willing to bet your life on being right. Wells was ready to make that bet. Every inch of her told her that Santo and McKenna were going to try to take over Mars. Jimmy Something and Benjamin Drake were just a diversion.

Captain Santo knew that having the charge of murder hanging over them would outweigh the theft charge, and everyone would be focused on catching them and not the cargo. He'd made sure he left orders at HQ for half the team to keep looking for them and keep up the chase. That would ensure human resources were diverted to finding the killers and not the cargo. By the time someone decided to look into the shipment again, Mars would be a Zuma territory, and McKenna himself would be on Mars—or on the way.

Wells knew she had to go back to the Zuma territory where the cargo first went missing. If she was correct that McKenna was building shuttles, then they would take the Bismuth where it was needed for manufacturing. Even if Santo was aboard one of the shuttles and long gone, it was still the best place to start looking for answers and evidence.

Wells' Human Interface Console vibrated. She had been reassigned. Another homicide case. Of course, Santo had taken her off the Jimmy Something case as soon as he was able. Putting his best officer back on the team supposedly hadn't been his idea, but Wells suspected that it was his doing after all. It made it look like he had even less to do with the whole affair and that his best was now on the case. So when she failed, it would seem that he had done everything in his power. A second-rate team would then take over, more for appearances than anything, and she had another big case to distract her.

Lt. Wells knew she had to get to Zuma. But more importantly, she needed Penta's resources. Going it alone would be utterly futile. She'd only be treading water. So she decided to risk it. She would ask to be reassigned to chasing the lost cargo. Asking for reassignment was a rare and usually fruitless endeavor, and came close to insubordination. You were told what to do, so do it. Fortunately for Lieutenant Lily Wells, she had a reputation for closing cases through stubbornness, determination, and working harder than anyone else. She also had a habit of getting her way. She only hoped that her recent stint behind a desk had not tainted any clout she might have had.

Lt. Wells knocked on the door and waited. She heard a big sigh before a voice called, "Come in."

"Captain Sturgis, I'm Lieutenant Wells. We've never worked together before, but I have certainly heard of you, sir."

This was a lie. Captain Sturgis was Captain Santo's stand-in while he was on his apparent leave. Unlike Wells and Santo, Sturgis had not an ounce of ambition in his whole body. His slumped posture, big soft belly, and multiple chins testified to his fulfillment of his dream of sitting behind a desk all day, unperturbed and most likely eating or napping. Not the sort of person Wells would have had use for before her career came to a grinding halt. Now she needed all the help she could get.

"I would like to be reassigned. I believe finding the stolen cargo that Jimmy Something and Benjamin Drake were hauling would be crucial in finding them. I believe that without finding the cargo, we may never find them."

"What's wrong with your new assignment?" Sturgis grumbled, not in the least interested in getting involved in more paperwork.

"Nothing, sir. I think it's quite an interesting case, but my head is still in this whole Jimmy Something case, and I'm sure I can close the case if I can follow that stolen cargo."

Sturgis gave her a look that was either pensive or just blank, depending on your knowledge of him.

"Captain Santo told me explicitly to give you a case as far removed from the Something case as possible. Said something about you getting too close to the subjects."

"Captain Sturgis, I can assure you that—"

"Let me finish, Lieutenant. Truth be told, I've never been a big fan of Raymond Santo. He always seems to have a hidden agenda. So, tell you what, if you reckon you can get an arrest by chasing the cargo and make us both look good at the same time, well, I'd be a fool to stop you."

"Sir, you won't regret this, sir—" Wells started, but Captain Sturgis held his hand up.

"Not so fast, Lieutenant. I cannot in good faith let you chase a possible ghost if we still have an unsolved murder case in front of us. So catch the killer, and then I'll give you all the permission you need."

"Sir, I—" The situation was far from ideal, but she knew that there were no other options. "I mean, yes, sir. And thank you, sir."

***

For the next two weeks, Wells put everything she had into solving the murder case. It took way longer than she anticipated, but fortunately, all the time she had spent in exile behind a DDU had made her very good at multitasking. During the day, she focused all her energy on solving the murder case, and at night she worked on the Santo-McKenna case.

As with most cases, a lucky break cracked it. An anonymous tip led them to a house where they found the suspect, with the whole ordeal captured on his ARP. Not the smartest person around, but most criminals weren't. Wells rushed through all the administration and data entry work and closed the case as soon as humanly possible.

The next morning she was back in Captain Sturgis's office.

"You are tenacious; I'll give you that," Captain Sturgis said.

"Just doing my job, sir."

"So, I guess you are here to get permission to chase Captain Santo?" Sturgis crossed his arms over that soft belly again.

"Yes, sir. We got him. The case is closed. I have all the documentation here." Wells swiped her HIC to transfer it to Captain Sturgis's DDU. It pinged, but Captain Sturgis ignored it.

"You understand that by backing you on this, I'm also putting myself at risk?"

"Sir, I promise you, I am right about this."

The look in Wells' eyes confirmed everything Captain Sturgis was seeking.

"Well, whatever you need, is yours. Good luck, Lieutenant."

\*\*\*

Lieutenant Wells could not get to her desk fast enough. Now that she was back on the Bismuth case and had official permission to chase the suspects, she was confident that she would get Santo. Technically, Wells only had clearance to follow up on the stolen Bismuth, but she was not going to let that slow her down. She quickly opened up the required forms on her Penta DDU and put in a request for some tactical gear, including some pulse guns and a Badger. The Badger was a four-person armored vehicle that was much lighter, and it had a higher speed than its bigger brother, the Mongoose.

On the way to the armory, she stopped by the cafeteria and grabbed some white box meals to go. Like the Mongoose, the Badger had a single-serve heating unit. Wells was not planning on making any unnecessary stops.

The Badger was all fueled up and ready to go when Wells entered the garage. She loaded her gear, guns, and food and got in. Wells typed in the last known coordinates of the cargo in the Zuma territory, and a green line appeared on the floor in front of the Badger. She slowly drove forward, and the two massive doors opened up. Lieutenant Wells pressed the accelerator, ready to get to Zuma as quick as possible, but a red warning appeared on the screen. Wells let out a deep sigh as she quickly ticked all the waivers, clearing Penta Corporation of any liability for any accidents happening while she was in the Badger. A green message came up, and Wells did not even wait for it to disappear before she buried the accelerator into the floor and followed the green line toward Zuma.

All security personnel had to undergo driver training, but most times, they just used the Autodrive feature. Wells was no exception, as this usually gave her time to go over some evidence or leads on the way to her destination. But today, she needed to get there as quick as possible, and Autodrive could not be programmed to go any quicker than the speed limits. Not that manual mode would allow the user to go faster than the speed limit either, as Nikolatec, the biggest supplier of vehicles, always built in speed limiters. This precaution was more to do with liability than any concerns for the user's safety. But Wells had picked up enough tips and tricks from the creeps and idiots that she had arrested through the years to know how to override the speed limiter. So once she got out of town, she entered the override code, and the Badger picked up speed. Wells loved the sensation of going fast and often overrode the speed limiter, even if there was no rush. She usually got some grief when she returned the vehicles, as everything was recorded and sent to headquarters, but she hardly ever got into any trouble for it. As long as you get results, people tend to look the other way when you bend the rules.

The road was quiet with only a few haulers and vehicles on it, and Wells settled into a nice fast rhythm, counting down the kilometers to Zuma.

***

"All shuttles have cleared orbit and are now in flight mode for the journey to Mars, sir," the engineer informed Jacob McKenna.

The shuttles had three basic modes: primary was for takeoff and used the most fuel, secondary was for the journey to the destination and used minimal fuel, and the last was tertiary, which was for landing and used a moderate amount of fuel. The shuttles were fueled for a return trip, as there was no Polonium on Mars. One of McKenna's main priorities was to find Bismuth or, hopefully, even a better substance to manufacture Polonium with, on Mars. Once the shuttles went back to Earth and returned with the engineers and scientists, he would be out of Polonium and stuck on Mars. So, he made sure he had some of the Earth's best geologists working for him and ready to be on the second fleet.

"Great work, everyone. Keep me posted of the progress," McKenna said to the room.

He had about two months to wait for his turn to board a shuttle and go to Mars and three months in total before he got there. In the meantime, he had to make sure to get rid of all the traces of the Bismuth and Polonium, as well as the equipment that was used to make it. If anyone came around asking questions, he would plead ignorance and show them that he had nothing to hide. He would then show them the records and footage of the truck coming into his territory and leaving the same day again, after refueling. If the person looking for the truck then followed its trail, they would find that it had been sold, with the appropriate paperwork, to a hauling company a few settlements over and that it was already on its way with its first load. The new owner would testify that he had indeed bought it from Benjamin Drake and was planning on contacting the authorities as soon as he could, but he was scared of losing the truck that he purchased legitimately, albeit very cheaply. The focus would by now be far from McKenna, and he would reimburse the new owner of the truck, as agreed upon, for his little role in this play.

McKenna looked out at the empty hangar one last time and left for his quarters.

# | thirty-one |

After two days of driving, Lt. Wells decided to pull over at the next motel and spend the night. She still had at least a day's driving ahead of her and wanted to stay sharp. She used Autodrive on the highway and took frequent naps but was still happy when the first advertisements for motels started to pop up on her screen. Captain Sturgis had been more than happy to sign off on her using air transport to get to Zuma, but Lieutenant Wells wanted to have a vehicle. Although it added few more days to her journey, she needed the flexibility it offered. Wells had no game plan and didn't know when and where she would have to go. She needed to be able to adapt quickly and make decisions on the fly if she was going to be successful.

Wells picked a random motel on the screen, and the telemetry on the screen changed to reflect the change in destination. Soon she found herself in front of a typical no-questions-asked motel. She went to the front desk, scanned her HIC, and got the code for a room. Within an hour, she was clean, full, and asleep.

***

Lt. Wells was traveling well over the speed limit, and red warnings of speed infringements kept popping up on her screen. She just ignored them, knowing that Penta would dismiss them if she was successful in capturing Drake and Something. She was refreshed after a good night's rest. She was making short work of the journey and could see by the numbers on the screen that she was approaching the Zuma territory quite rapidly. The territory was not on a major road network, and she would have to veer off the highway soon to get to it. Her research showed that this specific Zuma territory contained some mines and a few shanty towns for the miners. Wells had expected that anyone working on getting Santo and McKenna to Mars would have no dirt under their nails and would be living in a cleaner environment than a mining township. She was looking for engineers and scientists, not roided up miners. Since it seemed that the Zuma territory she was traveling to did not have any ordinary towns in it, she searched the nearest settlements in the surrounding regions. A town called Spirig, in the adjacent Nestem territory, seemed to be the perfect fit. Lovely clean town, far removed from the dirty mines but close enough for an acceptable commute to work.

The green line on the road was still going straight, but a small curved red arrow in the corner told her a turn was coming up ahead. It would be the turn off for the Zuma territory, she realized. Quickly she typed in Spirig as the new destination, and the red arrow disappeared. A new ETA also appeared on the screen: less than an hour to go. Autodrive was still engaged, so she read and reread all her notes on the case, making sure there was nothing she was overlooking.

***

A chime from the DDU brought her back from her thoughts, and a disclaimer on the screen advised her that she was now entering a Nestem territory. She signed off on it, and the car kept following the green line. Signs for Spirig started appearing on her windscreen, advertising rooms to rent, places to eat, and also things to do in town. Wells touched the screen where a motel advertisement popped up and connected to the establishment immediately via her ARP.

After booking herself a room for the night and setting the Autodrive to find it, she searched for the nearest security office. Most companies and their territories—with Shangcorp being the most prominent exception—worked together for the greater good, but it was never a given or something to be assumed. Every town and every security station had their way of doing things, and Wells knew it was better to play nice and tell them she was here on official business than to step on some toes.

Once she found her accommodation—nothing special but better appointed than the motel—she made her way over to the nearest security office. The building, like most in Spirig, was uninspiring but very clean and well looked-after. The town was a reflection of Nestem's ubiquitous white box meals: dull, boring, and uninspiring but doing its job as required every time without fail.

"Hi. I am Lieutenant Lily Wells from Penta security," she said, her normal hard tone hidden under layers of diplomacy.

The officer behind the counter looked at her for a few seconds, as if he was waiting for her to continue. When she didn't, he said, "Uh, welcome Lieutenant. Is someone expecting you?"

The safer the town, Wells believed, the more incompetent the security forces were. If there was nothing for them to do, no undesirables to keep them on their toes, they tended to relax and became soft. It seemed Spirig was pretty safe.

"No, Officer . . ." Wells hesitated, although the badge on the shirt clearly said 'Brody.'

"Yes, ma'am. I mean, Brody ma'am."

"Officer Brody, I'm passing through town and was hoping to talk to somebody about a case I'm working on."

"Yes, of course. Let me see who we have on duty."

Brody came to life. Like most of her team, he needed clear and concise instructions or goals to be able to perform.

He searched on his DDU for a bit. "Sergeant Navarro is on duty. Should I get him?"

"If you don't mind," Wells replied, wondering if time always moved this slowly in Spirig.

Officer Brody made the call and sat back, looking at Wells. It appeared there were no other pressing matters in Spirig at the moment. After a minute or so, the two sliding doors behind Officer Brody slid open, and a tall, dark man in uniform walked in. It was clear to Wells that he spent more time getting ready for work in the mornings than she did. And it worked. Wells felt her cheeks warm.

"Lieutenant Wells? I'm Sergeant Marc Navarro. Welcome to Spirig." The smile was pretty good too.

"Uh, hi, yes, I'm Lieutenant Wells," she muttered. She immediately felt like an idiot for letting her emotions getting the better of her. She quickly regrouped. "I'm here as a courtesy to your office, as I am investigating a murder, and the suspects might have passed through here in the last few days."

"I see. Are the suspects both from Penta?" Sergeant Navarro fell seamlessly into work mode. Wells struggled not to fall out of work mode.

"Yes, both suspects are from Penta, committed the crime in Penta, and as far as we know, have no connection to Spirig or Nestem but for the fact they might have traveled through here."

Wells did not feel comfortable telling him that she was planning on interrogating people living in Spirig, as he would surely have some concerns about that. So far, she was telling him the truth, and if he checked it out, as any proper security officer would, he would find she was on the case of a shipment of stolen Bismuth and that there was a possibility they had come through Spirig. So her reason to be in Spirig for a day or two would hold up. What she would be doing in those two days, though, was trying to find an engineer or scientist who worked for Zuma and lived in Spirig and then interrogating them using whatever technique she deemed appropriate.

A longer time frame would have allowed her to observe her target for a few days and then slowly gain their trust so that they would give up the information willingly. Unfortunately, she did not have time on her side.

"As long as no one involved is from Spirig or any Nestem territory, I cannot see it being a problem. Also, if you wouldn't mind checking in with me daily so that we can keep things official?"

Wells had no problem with that, no problem at all.

***

The logical place to find someone commuting from Zuma to Spirig was on the highway she had used to get here. If this had been a Penta territory, she would have parked next to the road, observed the traffic and scanned the cars. As she examined them, she could just run a data check on her DDU and see who the owner was and where they worked. It would have taken her five minutes to find a suitable Zuma employee.

Unfortunately for Wells, she was far from Penta. Spirig seemed to be well funded and would surely have cameras recording and streaming every bit of the highway. Once they saw her Badger parked for some time next to the road, they would have some questions that she would rather avoid.

Wells decided to find a local eatery. Although she had enough food in the Badger, she needed information.

She stopped at the first one she found and went in. In typical Spirig fashion, everything was clean, functional, and boring as hell. Wells started to long for the color and chaos of home.

Behind the counter was the usual array of white box meals, but as it was a Nestem territory, there were also a small number of different colored boxes. The girl behind the counter picked up on Wells' curiosity.

"The green boxes contain pieces of real fruit. The red ones have real meat. The blue one's real fish and the yellow ones have cheese in." She smiled at Wells, seemingly very proud of the offerings they had.

"It's been a while since I had anything organic," she confessed to the girl. "Better give me a red, green, and yellow box."

"Great choice!" the girl's enthusiasm seemed genuine, and Wells immediately liked her.

After Wells swiped her HIC on the scanner (and seeing a considerable amount of credits deducted), she took her three boxes and sat down. She realized she was excited about her meal, something that hardly ever happened. White box meals were designed to provide everything the human body needed in one meal. There was nothing extra or wasteful about them. Like Spirig, they attracted no attention to themselves while getting the job done.

Wells opened the red box and was overwhelmed by the aroma that hit her. She took an even deeper breath, trying to get more of the smell. She hastily grabbed her cutlery and started devouring the meal. She also opened the green and yellow boxes and was treated to the same experience. Within minutes of starting, the whole euphoric experience was over.

The girl behind the counter was still smiling at her.

"Wow! If it wasn't for the price, I could get hooked on this," Wells admitted to her.

"Most people in town treat themselves to one colorful meal a month," she replied.

"Does everyone in town work for Nestem?" Wells started working.

"Almost," the girl replied, "but some work in the mines in the Zuma territory down the road."

"I can't imagine dirty miners sitting down here for a meal like this!" Wells said.

"No, neither can I!" The girl laughed. "The people who work at the mine and live in Spirig are mostly engineers and such." The girls smile never faded.

"That makes sense. I guess it doesn't take people too long to get to Spirig from the mines," Wells stated, hoping she would keep talking.

"Not at all. Our neighbor is an engineer there, and she's usually home just before seven."

Bingo.

Wells made some more small talk for a few minutes, thanked the girl for the food and the chat, and left the eatery. Once outside, she switched on her ARP and started to scan the cars in the parking lot. At the far end of the lot, she found a vehicle that came up as belonging to a Sara Gabriel. The photo that was displayed on her ARP matched the girl behind the counter at the eatery. Wells kept walking so as not to attract too much attention but saved the address of the vehicle's owner.

When she got back in her car, she entered Sara's address into the Badger's DDU, and the green line dutifully showed her the way.

# | thirty-two |

Karen Giles's commute to Spirig usually took her about forty minutes, and she was already twenty-five minutes in. Forty minutes was just about enough time to clear her conscience and justify her life decisions to herself. Most of the drive was usually spent in tears, but she forced herself to stop as she got closer to home. If Alex saw her red puffy eyes, it would make everything ten times worse. The kid had already been through enough and she was on the cusp of escaping it all; she just had to hang in there a few more years.

Alex had been accepted to the Nestem University just last week, and it was the happiest day either of them had had in forever. Alex, being Alex, worried about the tuition, but Karen showed her the credits she was putting away for her education. Karen had a good job working at the Zuma mines, and she made sure that Alex would be able to receive the best education credits could buy.

After Alex's dad had run off with all their savings, Karen decided to leave her secure job at the white box factory and went to work at the Zuma mines. The pay was much higher and the hours better, but there were always rumors about Jacob McKenna and the people and territories with whom he had dealings. Karen decided that working at Zuma would be a short-term fix to get them back on their feet. She could turn a blind eye for a year or two, take McKenna's credits, and then resume her normal life back in Spirig at the white box factory.

That was six years ago.

Jacob McKenna had an unusual (one might even say autocratic) way of leading. Like a dictator, he placed himself above all and left everyone else scrambling for a place on the pecking order. He didn't seem to care who was in charge of anything, as long as it got done. This lead most departments to naturally organize themselves and create some hierarchy, even if McKenna did not care or recognize it. Their fear for McKenna and the obscene amount of credits they were paid banded everyone together, and what should have been a disastrous situation actually worked.

The Brains got to work on McKenna's newest pet project: building the Polonium-fueled shuttles. Although the work was fascinating and fulfilling, and Karen truly loved it, there was a catch: all the workers, scientists, and engineers had to sign non-disclosure agreements. McKenna even had their ARPs modified to activate and stream back to the security offices if specific keywords were used, outside of the work areas, by the people working on the shuttles. In any other workplace this would have been illegal, but McKenna's attitude was simple: allow it or leave. This was just another strange and irrational request from McKenna, and most people didn't even blink an eye. The more you were exposed to crazy, the less crazy it seemed.

As the project went on, McKenna started to tighten security even more and allowed fewer and fewer people to work on it. Karen Giles realized that the longer she worked on this project, the more she was sucked into Zuma. Her chances of ever leaving were fading away.

Karen entered Spirig and switched off the Autodrive. Her house was not too far from the main entry into town, and she liked to drive the last bit herself. It gave her time to retake control. She rounded a few corners and stopped in front of her living unit. The only thing setting her gray unit apart from all the identical units around hers was the number on it. She wondered if she would even find her home if it weren't for the numbers on it.

*** 

Lieutenant Wells was too scared to park anywhere for too long and draw attention to herself, so she kept driving in random patterns through Spirig, stopping now and then, sometimes even getting out, while the green line on the road kept readjusting to try and get her back to the destination. When she thought the time was right, she finally followed the line. Her timing was perfect. Just as she rounded the last corner, she saw the waitress's hydrocar parked in front of a gray housing unit. Next to it, on Wells' side, a late model Nikolatec slowed down and turned into the parking spot. A woman in her late thirties, maybe early forties, got out. She wore a white lab coat with a big golden Z on the pocket. Bingo. Wells knew she had her mark.

She kept driving past the unit and turned back toward her accommodation. She'd deal with the engineer tomorrow. She had already scanned the car and had all the details she needed to do a thorough check on her.

But first, she had to make a very tricky call.

***

The hotel employee behind the counter stared at the two dirty and dusty men standing in front of him. He had already pushed the security button. The piles of dirt in front of him were demanding a room and claiming to have the credits to pay for it, but it would not be the first time that someone had tried to scam their way into the hotel. And besides, the New Shangcorp Hotel Group was not a charity; quite the opposite. It catered for the well-to-do businessmen and women who could afford the best. The vagrants in front of him did not fit the description at all.

"All right, let's go!" A big guy in a security uniform said as he approached the two dirtbags.

"No way! We have the credits, ya know. Just scan my HIC, and you'll see!" the smaller one yelled back.

The security guard ignored him and just stood there, arms folded, and nodded toward the door. He must have weighed more than the two of them combined and he looked capable of carrying them out if he had to. His relaxed posture indicated that he knew it too and was not too fussed by this confrontation.

"Listen, we'll go quietly if you would only do me a favor and scan my friends HIC. It's a long story how we ended up looking like this, but trust me, we do have the credits," the other one pleaded.

The security guard shrugged.

"Fine, but after I check your precious credit level, will you please leave?"

"Sure, if you still want us to, we'll leave," the bigger one of the two said.

The smaller guy walked over to the counter and held his arm out for the hotel employee to scan his HIC. The employee dusted off the guy's arm with a face of disgust, cleaning up his HIC as best he could. He scanned the HIC and looked at a DDU on the reception desk. He cleared his throat and scanned the small guy's HIC again.

"I'm so sorry, sir, but usually our guests dress a bit more . . . uh . . . differently. My apologies to you and your companion."

Jimmy's little chest was puffed out as much as possible, and nothing could wipe the smirk off his face.

"Easy mistake to make, ya know? Can you please send clean clothes and some food for the room?" Jimmy said, already heading toward the elevator.

"Of course, sir, it will be our pleasure," the hotel worker said to his back. He scanned Drake's HIC to authorize it to open the room door.

\*\*\*

For nearly three weeks, Jimmy and Drake had trekked across the desolate landscape. They got a few rides and stopped over at some small settlements, but nowhere felt safe enough to stay for too long. It became routine to find some food, a place to sleep, and then hike out again in the morning. Sometimes they stayed a few days but never too long. It was draining and exhausting work, but they knew that a more significant settlement or city would offer them the anonymity they were seeking.

Drake and Jimmy Something had been walking for hours in the semi-arid landscape, seeing mirage after mirage, getting close to the point of giving up. They were sticking close to a major road, knowing that it would lead somewhere, but no one stopped to offer them a ride. Drake had no problem with that. Not only did they look all weathered and dirty, but they were wanted and on the run. Couldn't blame anyone but themselves for being where they were.

Another mirage appeared. Drake ignored it and just kept walking. Jimmy was standing still, hands cupped over his eyes, peering at the latest illusion. Drake stopped too and turned toward him.

"Buddy, we've been over this a million times. Stop wishing everything you see is an oasis. Let's just keep moving until we walk into something solid, like an actual wall."

"Drake, I think this one is real, ya know!" Jimmy said excitedly, not for the first time.

Drake turned to face the same direction as Jimmy. He had to squint as well, as the sun was glaring right in their faces. He copied Jimmy's cupped hand system as well.

The landscape was pretty barren, with little to no vegetation around them, but sticking out of the ground in the distance, Drake could clearly make out rectangular shapes reaching into the sky. He closed his eyes and tried again.

"Let's go, buddy!" he yelled and slapped Jimmy on the back.

It took hours, but eventually they reached the outskirts of a city called Shamo. It was quite big, with huge buildings towering in the center of town. They wasted no time and started looking for the nearest hotel.

Standing outside the New Shangcorp Hotel, Jimmy was beaming ear to ear, but Drake said, "This is not the place for us, buddy. Let's keep looking."

"No, this is it, partner. This is where I want to go. Just look at it! All shiny and clean and shit. I have never even been to a hotel like this before, ya know. C'mon man, we have the credits now, ya know. What's the point in having credits if you're not going to use them?"

Jimmy had a point. They had spent the last few days cramped in a truck and then a car. Then they had to spend a night sleeping on the ground in the desert. They were hungry, tired, and filthy. This hotel would change all that.

"You sure? We don't exactly look like we belong here," Drake protested one more time.

"Drake, this is Shangcorp. No one cares where your credits came from, as long as you have credits! We can live like kings, and no one would ask any questions."

"What happened to 'They'll shoot you for just looking at them in Shangcorp?'" Drake reminded him.

"So maybe we shouldn't attract too much attention, but can we at least stay here for a couple of nights?" Jimmy pleaded.

Drake looked at the dirty face with the puppy dog eyes. Damn you, Jimmy, he thought.

***

When Drake came out of the shower, Jimmy was fast asleep on his bed. Drake decided to leave him be and went out unto the balcony. Night had fallen, and the city was a kaleidoscope of colors and sounds. It seemed like the perfect place to get lost. Drake liked that idea. He glanced back over his shoulder at Jimmy. Then the three circles appeared in front of him. He closed the door, as to not wake Jimmy and swiped his HIC to accept the call. The three circles merged.

"Oh, hi! I was just telling Jimmy that I was wondering how you were doing," Drake said, grinning.

"Hello, Mr. Drake, or can I call you Benjamin or Ben?" Lt. Wells asked.

"You may not," Drake said, "but you can lose the 'mister' and call me Drake, like everyone else."

"Thanks, Drake. As you can see, I'm not contacting you through official Penta channels. This is my own line."

Wells paused, and Drake assumed it was for dramatic effect. So far, he was not very impressed by her acting. Drake knew she was trying a new and revised strategy on him. Since they had gotten away and he had nothing to fear from her anymore, he decided to keep chatting.

"They kick you out for not catching us? Tough break, but can't say that I blame them, though."

"I'm still happily employed by Penta and still very much on the case. But I believe that there is a much bigger crime happening here and that you and Jimmy can help me."

Drake was slightly surprised and intrigued by her new strategy of asking for their help, and since Jimmy was still fast asleep and it was quite a beautiful night outside, he decided to keep entertaining Wells.

"Oh, I see. So, we have gone from Most Wanted to Help Wanted then?"

"No. You are still on the Most Wanted list, but I believe that you are involved in something that you are not completely aware of," Wells replied.

"Does this mean you believe Jimmy's version of events now, suddenly?"

"Maybe. I'm not sure yet. But I do think that you are more valuable as allies and not enemies."

"Mmmm. So far, it sounds like you need us, but to be honest, Lieutenant, what is in it for us? Why would we help you? From where I'm sitting, I think we are doing pretty well, considering. "

"You can call me Lily," Lt. Wells said. "As I told you, this is not an official call. What do you know about the cargo you hauled? Or the destination?"

Although she had said this was a personal call and not business, he couldn't help thinking that it was all business for the lieutenant all the time. Her job was to find and eradicate criminals, and the last time he checked, Penta had them listed as precisely that. Personal call my ass.

"Why did you call?" he asked, ready to pull the plug if her answer was not to his liking.

"To be frank, Drake, you are just small fry, and I'm looking at something much bigger." Wells knew she was on fragile ice but felt that Drake was about to walk away.

"What? Are we not good enough for you anymore? I thought we were the top spot on your naughty list. We do have feelings, you know."

"Drake, I think McKenna is planning something big. Something that will change history. And I need your help to stop him."

The lieutenant had an intensity that he had never seen in anyone before. Most people he met were on Autodrive, but Wells had a fire in her. She had just let two high profile criminals escape her grasp, but she did not look fazed by it at all. She also didn't look desperate in an all-is-lost kind of way but more in a time-is-running-out way.

Most importantly, she seemed sincere. Drake had to fight the urge not just to tell her what she wanted to hear.

"I just don't see how this is my problem, Lieutenant."

"Call me Lily, please," she tried again. "It definitely is not your problem, Drake. But if you help me, I will do everything in my power to get you off the Most Wanted list. And Jimmy, of course."

Drake could feel how he was being sucked in but felt hopeless in resisting.

"What is McKenna planning?"

Wells knew he was cracking, the moment he said that.

"Do you know what the cargo was? It was stolen Bismuth, Drake."

"Sure. From Penta, and that's why we are having this discussion. I'm more than a pretty face, Lieutenant."

"No, Drake, we are having this discussion because I believe McKenna is on his way to Mars and that he is planning on taking it over."

Drake was quiet for a second.

"That sounds a bit far-fetched, but believable, I guess," Drake replied, "but if I'm not mistaken, isn't Mars a Penta Colony?"

"Only a de facto colony. Penta doesn't own any of it. But if McKenna takes over, he will make it a Zuma colony and most likely keep the whole planet to himself. Do you think Penta or Shangcorp will just let that happen, without retaliating with force?"

"I see, but it now seems even more like a Penta problem and less and less like a Benjamin Drake problem. As much fun as this conversation was, Lieutenant, I think our time has run out."

"You are right. I don't give two fucks if you care that a world war is upon us. All I need from you is your help in exchange for getting you off the list so you can be a free man again." Wells knew she had to go hard now, as she was clearly out of time.

"Wow, Lieutenant!" Drake feigned shock. "Let's not hurt anyone's feelings more than we have to, okay?" Drake knew he was getting played, but couldn't help himself. "What do you need from me, anyway? All I did was haul something from point A to point B. Unfortunately for me, I think you are overestimating my value."

"I beg to differ, Drake."

# | thirty-three |

Lieutenant Wells felt so good about her talk with Drake that she decided to treat herself to another colored box breakfast from the same eatery she'd visited the day before.

"Wow, Penta must be paying pretty well!" Sergeant Marc Navarro was standing in front of her. "Mind if I join you?" he asked as he sat down.

Wells watched him as he smilingly opened his everyday white box meal and took a bite.

"Yep, still tastes the same as yesterday!" he said, scooping up another spoonful. "How's the investigation going?"

"Slow. I was on my way to your office after breakfast, but you saved me the trip," she lied.

"Glad I could make your day easier." He smiled at her as he kept on eating.

Wells started to wonder if this really was a chance meeting.

"Just got one or two people I need to talk to, and then I should be on my way."

Navarro shook his head as he chewed. "If you give me the names, I could help you locate them."

The offer was rational, but Wells couldn't shake the feeling that Navarro was not being wholly truthful.

"That's very generous, Sergeant, but as I said, I'm just passing through and don't want to cause any waves or problems in your beautiful town."

"No problem at all. Pop into the office when you're done, and we'll find those people you need to talk to and wrap this thing up nice and quick." Navarro's smile had lost its power.

"Sure thing. The quicker I can get going, the better!" Wells played along.

"Great," Navarro said as he got up. "See you a bit later then."

"Sure will," Wells replied.

She finished her colorful meal but wished she had instead saved her credits.

***

Lieutenant Wells had a problem: Karen Giles would not return home until much later in the day, and Sergeant Navarro was expecting her to go to his office and give him the names of the people she wanted to interview. The only name she had was Giles's, and she did not want him to know that. If he looked into her, he would see that she was a law-abiding citizen, and it would raise suspicion as to why Wells wanted to talk to her. If he were any good at his job, he would then keep tabs on Giles to make sure he didn't miss anything. She'd have to come up with two names of people in Spirig who would seem likely to have had contact with undesirables like Something and Drake, and she'd have to be quick about it.

Wells decided to make another call.

"Wow, Lieutenant, you are terrible at this playing hard to get game," Drake said, clearly just waking up.

Wells got straight to the point. "Sorry to bother you again so soon, Drake, but it seems I'm going to need your help sooner than I expected."

"I haven't even had time to talk to Jimmy about our chat last night."

"I'm sorry. I know I told you I'd give you some time to think it over, but I need help. I was sincere last night, Drake. I can't do this without your help."

Unlike Jimmy, who was still fast asleep, he had barely slept a wink. His whole life had been turned upside down. The only thing he knew how to do was hauling—not that it took a genius—but he was good at it, and besides, it was all he had. Since he'd missed that contract from Bob

Turner, met Jimmy, and got involved in all this crap, he knew that his previous life was gone. He had a fair amount of credits now, but how long would those last? He would also never be able to leave this Shangcorp territory, for fear of Penta capturing him.

Oh, and then there was his new sidekick.

"I haven't really made up my mind yet, Lieutenant."

"Lily, please. I know, but something has come up. I just need some information that I can get myself, but not in the time I have."

Drake knew if he said yes to this, the next step was full submission. If he gave in now, she had him.

"Off the record, what sort information do you need, Lieutenant?" Drake was not ready to be on a first name basis with the enemy just yet.

"Drake, everything is off the record. I told you, this is not official. You need to believe me on that." Her words meant nothing to him, but her eyes told him the truth.

"So off the record, then, what info do you need?"

"The Spirig security force needs two names that they can connect to you and Jimmy."

"Wait! What? You need me to help you to catch us?" Drake got ready to disconnect.

"No, no, no. Drake, I need to buy myself some time so that I can talk to a Zuma engineer here in Spirig. The Spirig security thinks I'm here chasing you guys, so I need to give them some names that have a connection to you guys. Someone you might have had a small dealing with or someone that might remember you," Wells tried to convince Drake.

"I don't know," Drake said.

This conversation made no sense to him at all. Like most haulers, Drake had a healthy dislike for all security. Whenever they showed up, trouble followed. It was best to avoid them at all times, if possible.

But that seemed impossible now.

"You need to believe me when I say it's just my cover. I'm here for the engineer, Drake. I can't pull this off without you guys."

Drake stared into Wells' eyes. Her words meant nothing but her eyes—

"Okay," Drake said. He gave her the names of the two hydro shops they went to in Spirig and prayed he hadn't just sealed their fates.

\*\*\*

"What time is it?" Jimmy asked as he strolled out of the bathroom.

"More like what day is it?" Drake shot back.

"How long was I out for?"

"About three days, buddy. Not sure what happened to you, but I couldn't wake you at all," Drake lied.

Jimmy's face froze in terror.

"You mean I was in a coma?"

"Not sure I'd use the word coma, but yeah, sort of." Drake could feel his face twitching, ready to burst out laughing.

"But-but I just went to sleep, ya know. Do you think someone drugged me? Do you think it was Penta?"

Drake couldn't do it anymore and started laughing. "Sorry, buddy, but you just looked so confused. You only slept in by a few hours. Not days. I was just pulling your leg."

"You mean . . . oh you bastard! Good one partner, good one. Phew, I tell ya, you had me good there, ya know!" Relief washed over Jimmy's face. "Man, I'm hungry!" he said, more at ease now.

"Yeah, I could eat," Drake replied. "But first, we need to have a chat."

He wasn't sure how Jimmy would feel about him talking with Lt. Wells, but he had no intention of hiding it from him either. Like it or not, they were in this together.

"You remember the lieutenant that was chasing us and almost got us at the border?" Drake asked.

"Sure, but she had no chance of catching us, ya know?"

"Sure . . . of course . . . Anyway, she contacted me last night. She seems hell-bent on getting our help." Drake left it there to see Jimmy's reaction.

"Well, if we help her, maybe she could help us, ya know?"

Drake was stunned. He had not anticipated this reaction from Jimmy. Drake had expected Jimmy to lose his cool and flip out, but

Jimmy did quite the opposite. Drake was speechless. He had no reply ready for this scenario.

"But if you think she can go to hell, then I'm with you partner."

"No, I'm not sure, to be honest, Jimmy." Drake had to regroup quickly. He was ready to try and convince Jimmy that it would be in their best interest to help Lt. Wells, but Jimmy's willingness to help her had put him on his back foot, and now he felt like the one who needed convincing.

"How about we go downstairs, grab some white box meals and talk this out?" he suggested, and Jimmy was all too glad to agree.

***

Lieutenant Lily Wells noted down the two places Drake had given her and set off to the Spirig security offices to hand them over to Sergeant Navarro. Wells was taking a huge gamble, but she decided not to go and check them out for herself first. Not only because she didn't have the time to, but more to see where she stood with Drake. If the names he gave her came up empty for Navarro, she would know that he was not going to play ball and that he would remain nothing more than a person of interest to her. If the names checked out, she would still have to tread carefully, but at least it would be a sign of trust.

The same officer from the previous day was staffing the front desk, and he sat up when Wells entered.

"Good morning, Lieutenant. Sergeant Navarro said to let you through when you arrive." The officer seemed happy to have something to do today.

"Thanks," Wells said as she walked past him straight to Navarro's office.

Penta was all about efficiency and numbers, so most people had cubicles, and those with offices got small, cramped rooms. Spirig, on the other hand, opted for huge rooms with barely anyone or anything in them. Sergeant Navarro had his own office, an enormous room that looked like the inside of an empty white box meal. It was sparse and only contained the necessities. The walls were bare, and everything was a shade of light gray or white.

Wells hated it.

"Good morning, Lieutenant." Navarro flashed his smile at her. The magic had worn off.

"Sergeant," Wells replied.

Navarro pointed to a chair at a desk that had nothing on it. It was impossible to know if it was his chair or the one facing his. They each sat down, waiting for the other to speak. Wells was in no rush, as Karen Giles would still be at work for the next few hours, but she knew if she spoke first, Navarro would feel he had the upper hand.

"I've got those two names I need your help with," she said, playing the damsel in distress.

"Let's see who we have here," Navarro said. He waited for Wells to swipe up on her HIC and transfer the files to his. His arm buzzed, and a faint ping sound emitted from it. He ignored his HIC and instead pressed a concealed button under his desk. A huge DDU screen, previously camouflaged by displaying an image that mimicked the wall around it, lit up on the wall next to them. Navarro swiped his HIC, and the files appeared on the screen. He continued to use his HIC as the input device and used it to open the files.

"Although we try our best to keep Spirig clean, we do still have a few defects," Navarro said, looking at the two faces on the screen. "Luckily for you, these two fit that description, which means we'll have ample footage on them."

Navarro used his HIC to access some more files on the DDU. He opened one from the date when Drake and Jimmy would have passed through. An image appeared on the DDU's screen that showed a rundown building with a sign that read Joe's Hydro Shop. Navarro pressed something on his HIC, and the image came to life. Cars and the occasional person went past. Navarro upped the speed of the playback, and all the cars sped by Joe's.

"There!" Wells yelled out as two people turned into the lot.

Navarro quickly got the playback speed back to normal. On the screen, Benjamin Drake and Jimmy Something could clearly be seen walking into the office of Joe's Hydro Shop. Navarro zoomed in as much as he could, and they could see them inside talking to a quite large woman. They both shook their heads and came out again. Navarro paused the clip. Their faces were unmistakable.

"I assume that these are your guys?" he asked.

"Yes, without a doubt. But it looks like they lucked out at Joe's."

It seemed Drake had given her excellent intel. Wells told herself not to get ahead of herself but knew that if Drake was on board, things would go much smoother.

Navarro let the footage continue. "Let's see if we can follow them."

Drake and Something kept walking for a few minutes until they came to another similar establishment. Wells was amazed at the quality and coverage of Spirig's surveillance cameras. On-screen, Jimmy and Drake walked into the premises and were greeted by a rather large man. The three talked and then went behind the building. Navarro had to make some adjustments on his HIC to keep track of them and only lost them for a few seconds before he got them on-screen again. Spirig's cameras saw everything. The large man pointed to an old hydrocar, and after some more talking, HICs were swiped—to seal the deal, most likely. The man walked back to his office, leaving Jimmy and Drake behind with the car. They had a quick chat, got in, and drove off.

"It appears your suspects were indeed in Spirig, Lieutenant. I can have the two witnesses in the office ready for questioning in thirty minutes," Navarro offered.

Wells knew precisely where this would lead. They would either confess to helping them or deny it, but either way, Navarro would track the vehicle that Jimmy and Drake had bought and eventually have the footage of them at the border. It might take him several days, but with all the surveillance Spirig had in place, it would happen. He would then see Wells and her team trying to get them before they crossed into Shangcorp. Which meant he would know she already knew where they had gone and that she had no real reason to be in Spirig.

"That's disappointing, to be honest," she said, looking deflated.

"I'm sorry," Navarro said, a bit insulted. "I'm a bit confused, but I think the footage I—Spirig—supplied is quite remarkable. In a short amount of time, we got everything you wanted."

Navarro leaned back in his chair and crossed his arms.

"I'd better explain," Wells started, using the most apologetic tone she could. "I was not one hundred percent honest with you as to my reason for being in Spirig. You see, I'm investigating an internal leak we had in this murder case and was hoping to see someone from Penta meeting up or helping those two in these videos. We lost the two suspects at the Shangcorp border. They have been two steps ahead of us this whole time, and I'm just retracing their steps with the hope of finding something."

Navarro studied her face. He must have activated his ARP the moment she set foot in his office and would be tracking all her vitals to see if she was lying. By keeping the story as truthful as possible, she would keep her vitals within reason. Wells was indeed investigating a leak, but she already knew who it was. And she had told him about the Shangcorp border, so even if he checked it out, she would be safe.

"Having an internal investigation is never fun, Lieutenant, but I wish you had told me this from the beginning. Trust is always hard-earned but easily lost."

Wells could not afford to be thrown out of town before she got to Giles. Drake might have helped her with the names, but Giles was crucial.

"I'm sorry, Sergeant. It is quite an embarrassment to me, as I was the lead on the case. My pride must have overridden my common sense."

Navarro's eyes moved ever so slightly up and to the right. Not only did he have his ARP on, but he must have had someone (Officer Brody perhaps?) listen in. The moment Wells had confessed to being untruthful, the person on the other end must have looked for the footage and found something. It took them minutes, not days or even hours, to find the incident at the border. The slight eye movement Wells spotted would have been the clip being played back to Navarro on his ARP. Not a full-screen image, but rather a small insert in the corner of his view. Up and to the right.

"I can only imagine the shame of being investigated by one's own company," Navarro said.

Wells squirmed in her seat, hoping she wasn't selling it too hard.

"But I appreciate your honesty and humility, Lieutenant. Let's start over, but this time no secrets, okay?"

"Thank you, Sergeant," Wells replied softly.

"You can call me Marc," he replied with his faded smile.

Wells smiled back at him, happy to be sitting in the driving seat.

# | thirty-four |

Life aboard the shuttle was settling into a predictable and comfortable pattern, one that would be repeated over and over again for the next few weeks. No one on board minded, as they all had the training and mental attitude to deal with it. Everyone was enjoying this small break before the chaos started.

Although the shuttle slowly spun on its axis, the gravity it generated was only a fraction of that felt on Earth. It was enough to allow people to walk, sit down, and have a relatively natural existence on the long journey. Muscle dystrophy was a real concern in the lower gravity environment, so everyone made sure they used the electromagnetic-resistance exercise equipment. Exercising kept them in fighting shape, but it was also a good time killer.

Other activities included card games, various board games, and just chatting among friends. Space on the shuttle was limited, but no one seemed to get in anyone's way. Most of the team had been on similar missions, albeit back on Earth and on a much smaller scale, and they knew how to deal with the downtime before all hell broke loose. No one was getting frustrated or irritated, and everyone was cruising along, trying to conserve energy.

Santo once more realized that he had picked the best of the best and that victory was all but guaranteed.

\*\*\*

Karen Giles was almost home and checked her appearance on the screen in front of her. Not too bad. Most of the redness and puffiness had disappeared from her eyes. Not that it mattered. Alex would not be home. She had asked to spend the night with a friend to prepare for a test or something. The car was still on Autodrive as it entered Spirig. Giles had no intention of driving and only did so on infrequent occasions. The car dutifully followed the green line on the road. She checked her image on the screen one more time and, making peace with what she saw, closed the screen.

The car rounded the last corner before her house, and she started to gather her belongings. A red inverted teardrop hovered seemingly in front of the carport, and the hydrocar came to a standstill right on top of it. Karen Giles powered down the vehicle and got out.

"Hi Karen, can we have a chat?" a woman's voice said behind her.

Karen Giles felt a hand squeeze her heart, and she got light-headed as adrenaline flooded her system. She clutched her bag and felt her whole body stiffen. Heart racing, she turned around. A woman, maybe late twenties or early thirties with shoulder-length brown hair, stood in front of her. Karen Giles noticed her muscular arms and wondered if McKenna had sent her. She couldn't think why he would do it though, but found it alarming that that was her first thought—McKenna sending someone to harass, or even worse, hurt her.

"Sorry, it seems I scared you. I'm so sorry. I didn't realize you didn't see me approach you."

"Who are you?" Giles asked, looking around to see if anyone else was coming to the party.

"I am Lieutenant Lily Wells from Penta Corporations security," she said, extending her hand. Giles ignored it.

"Why are you here, and how do you know my name?"

Lieutenant Wells dropped her arm and offered Giles a warm smile instead. Wells took a small step backward, increasing the distance between them and, by doing so, giving Giles some breathing space. Giles continued to hug her bag in front of her, her whole body tense.

"I'm here because I need your help, Karen. And to be honest, I think it is a conversation best had indoors."

"I'm not letting you in my house until I know what you want," Giles replied, her voice an octave higher than normal.

The adrenaline started to fade, and Giles was now in full flight mode, ready to get in her house and call the Spirig security force. Her eyes kept darting from Wells to her front door and back again. Everything told her to run for it, but she was frozen.

"I'm running out of time, so I'll be upfront with you and hope for the best. I am investigating the disappearance of a truck full of Bismuth, which I believe Jacob McKenna acquired with the intention of invading Mars."

The two women stood in silence, staring at each other. The sun had slipped down over the horizon, and the automated street lights came on. Spirig spared no expense, and the street lights were made to slowly brighten and mimic the colors of the sunset, prolonging twilight.

Giles finally broke the silence. "It's not safe to talk in my house. We can talk in your car."

***

Karen Giles sat in the passenger seat of Lieutenant Wells' car, still clutching her bag, trying to get her thoughts in order. She had been dreaming of something, something that was out of her control, happening that would force her to leave McKenna. She did not have the will to do it herself. She wondered if this woman was that something.

Wells spoke first. "Thank you for coming with me. I know it must be scary and overwhelming for you,"

"That's okay. It's just . . . I don't understand why you picked me."

"To be honest, it was luck. I was at a diner and was served by one of your neighbors."

"Sara," Giles said to herself.

"Yes, but it only came up in conversation that her neighbor worked at the mines, and I did the rest. She never told me anything about you. She'd most likely not even remember our conversation."

"I believe you. Sara is a good kid," Giles replied.

They drove in silence for a few minutes. Wells hoped that Navarro was not tracking her every move, and that he had not seen Giles getting into her car, with one of Spirig's multiple cameras.

"So Karen—I can call you Karen, right?" Wells asked, but she did not wait for an answer. She needed Giles to believe they were friends and that she wanted to help her. "You can call me Lily. Anyway, as I was saying, I was on a team tracking some people who stole something from my employer. We believe they handed over the stolen goods in a Zuma territory. They are still at large, last seen entering a Shangcorp territory. My employer wanted me to keep chasing these criminals, but something told me the real story was attached to the stolen goods, the Bismuth."

Giles appeared to be on the verge of tears.

"Karen, that's where you come in. I have a theory, and I need to run it past someone. Someone who can verify it or tell me if I'm wasting my time." Wells gave her a reassuring smile.

"Okay," Giles whispered back, actually keen to hear it.

Wells took another turn and switched on the Autodrive. She entered something into the DDU, and the green line appeared on the road. Giles wondered where they were going, but didn't dare to ask.

"It's just a random pattern that will circle back to your house. I promise."

Giles gave her a little nod, and Wells continued.

"Here goes. As far as I know, the only real use for Bismuth is to make Polonium, right? And the only real use for Polonium is to make rocket fuel, right? So it goes without saying that Mr. McKenna has built himself a shuttle and he is going somewhere. And the only place to go, really, is Mars. The moon is pretty much hollow by now, so there is no need to go there. Now the question is—assuming I'm right so far—what is he planning on doing on Mars?"

The hydrocar made another random turn and kept driving. Wells needed to give Giles some time to process and decide what her response was going to be, so she let the silence settle over them. Even if she was spot on, it did not mean that Giles was going to play ball. Giles could do the opposite and run to McKenna with the hope of a huge bonus or promotion. Karen Giles got out of her car, and when Wells saw her puffy red eyes, she knew she had chosen the right person. Happy employees don't cry in their cars on the drive back home.

Night had now completely fallen, but the lights still made everything look like dusk. Wells patiently waited for Giles.

She didn't look up, but finally, she spoke. "Mr. McKenna is not who I thought he was when I started working at Zuma. If he found out I was even talking to you, he would—" Giles got lost in her thoughts. Tears started to flow down her cheeks, but she didn't even try to hide them. She was used to this.

"Karen, I think we need each other." Wells knew she had hit pay dirt.

"You are right about the Polonium, I mean. Mr. McKenna needed it to propel his shuttles. I helped to build them."

"There is nothing illegal or wrong in what you have done, Karen. No one is going to be going after you; that I can promise you. Can you tell me what McKenna's goal is?" Wells was confident she knew the answer already.

"You were close. The shuttles were made to go to Mars, but he's not on them. The first fleet is the soldiers who will be taking over the planet, and the second fleet will be Mr. McKenna and his engineers and scientists. He never said it out loud, but it's pretty obvious what's happening."

"Are you telling me that McKenna is still here?"

Wells had not even considered that McKenna could still be on Earth. If she could stop him from going, she could stop this before it even happened.

"Yes. He comes and goes, but he's definitely still here." Giles briefly looked up from her lap.

"Karen, how would you like to help me put McKenna away in a dark hole?"

***

Wells drove back to Karen Giles's house. Giles was still a bit nervous about helping her, but she was definitely on board. Wells' immediate problem was time. She'd told Navarro that she was passing through and had already used up the two names Drake had given her. She had no reason to stay here any longer, and Navarro would get suspicious if she did.

Wells powered down the car.

"Now what?" Giles asked her.

"Ideally, you'll start gathering enough evidence for me to convince Penta to send in the troops. I'm talking schematics, minutes from meetings, or even any video footage." Wells knew Karen would be taking a considerable risk in getting her the data she needed, so she had to push her very gently toward helping her. "Once I have all the information, and Penta swoops in, you'll be rid of him forever, Karen. Alex can go to school, and you can get a nice quiet job at the Nestem factory."

"If I get caught, he'll kill me. And Alex." Tears started rolling down her cheeks again.

Wells knew there was every chance that Karen would get caught. She was not trained to do this sort of thing and could easily panic and do something stupid. Or McKenna could catch her red-handed and she'd spill the beans. Not that Wells was concerned for her safety. But if McKenna was aware of her investigation, she'd have no hope of getting close to him.

"I know I'm asking a lot of you, but I also know you want out, Karen. So let's help each other. What do you say?"

# | thirty-five |

Shamo was an actual oasis in the desert and had been attracting people for as long as there had been a written history. Hundreds and hundreds of years ago, it had become a place for people to give their animals water and gain some relief for themselves on their long journeys. People started to stay there permanently, and a small town began to take shape. The small town grew, and over the years it went through countless transformations. At one time, people had avoided it because of the risk of pirates. Another time, a warlord had taken over the area and demanded high tolls for passage through. Then it became a trading Mecca and flourished. When companies had started to buy cities and eventually whole countries, Shangcorp quickly snapped up Shamo.

Shamo had always had a diverse population, and they all contributed to make it a truly unique experience. Walking down a busy street, one would think it was a Penta-owned town one minute, and twenty steps later, an aromatic assault on the senses would snap you back into a Shangcorp reality. At every turn, something new popped up. It was an overwhelming experience, but the more they saw, the more Drake and Jimmy liked it.

"I have no idea what I just ate, but it was fucking awesome!" Jimmy yelled.

Drake had felt the need to get out of the hotel for a while and they'd decided to go for a walk. He was never any good at staying still for too long, and the hotel room was starting to close in on him.

"That was quite something, all right."

The brown gloop did not look very enticing, and Drake had refused it at first, but when he saw Jimmy's face light up, he tried some too. He quickly bought two more servings from the street vendor, and the two of them devoured them on the spot.

"I think I might get used to this place, ya know?"

"I know, right? It feels a lot like ho—" A commotion in front of them cut him off. Two Shangcorp security officers, dressed in red and yellow uniforms with full armor, were pushing people around. Everyone was yelling, and it was difficult to figure out what was going on. A crowd started to gather, and Drake and Jimmy moved closer.

"What's happening?" Drake asked the person next to him. They replied, but Drake did not understand the language. He activated his ARP and asked them again. This time the ARP system identified the language and translated it in real-time. It then played the translated audio back via his cochlear implant.

"The shop owner refused to pay them their fee, so they are threatening to burn his shop down," the man said indifferently.

"What fee?" Drake asked.

"Protection, tax, whatever they feel like calling it. You're not from Shamo, are you?" the stranger asked.

"No. Is it that obvious?" Drake smiled.

"Yes," the guy replied flatly and turned back to the action.

The shop owner seemed ready for a fight. He refused to comply with the security officer's commands. One pulled a pulse gun out, but still, the shop owner did not budge. The officer adjusted the pulse gun, aimed it at the shop owner, and shot him. The crowd took a step back as the shot rang out. As the shop owner collapsed, they all took three steps forward again. The officer must have turned the pulse gun all the way down, as the shop owner was lying on the ground unconscious, but unwounded and still breathing. The other officer walked into the shop, which was stocked with colorful cloths and fabrics, and started shooting at them.

Pieces of fabric flew into the air and slowly rained down to the ground. The shop owner woke up and propped himself up on his elbows. He watched the destruction happening in front of him and slowly sat up. His shoulders drooped down; the fight had gone out of him. The security officer stopped shooting, walked up to him, and said something. The other officer kicked the guy back down again, and the crowd parted as the officers walked through them. The moment they passed the crowd, people started to pelt them with rocks, shoes, and whatever they could find. They turned around and raised their pulse guns, and within seconds the crowd had disappeared, shots flying low over their heads. Drake and Jimmy ran into an alley.

"What the fuck?" Drake said.

"I know! This place is . . . AWESOME!" Jimmy let out a yelp.

Drake had never been one to toe the line, but here in Shamo, the line was made up day-to-day. It was the sort of town that attracted people like Jimmy, but also the place that ate them alive. Drake had a feeling that if they stayed too long, they would never be able to leave again.

"Damn it, Jimmy. I'm not sure if I'm ready for a place like this," Drake confessed.

"What do you mean? This place is perfect for us, ya know?" Jimmy laughed.

"Jimmy, you know I'm just a hauler. I'm no angel, but I am not a criminal. No offense," Drake said, "but I'm not sure I can stay here. What do you think will happen once a security officer scans us and sees who we are? How long before they figure out we're on the run. Most likely they'll try to get some credits out of us. I think it's time to move on, buddy."

"What do you mean, you're not a criminal? Penta has a bounty out on you, ya know? That shit makes you a criminal in everyone's eyes, guilty or not."

When would it sink in? He kept saying he was just a hauler, but the chances of him ever hauling again were slim to none. He thought of Lieutenant Wells and her offer.

"Let's go back to the hotel, buddy. I need to make a call."

\*\*\*

Lieutenant Lily Wells got back in her car. It was getting late, and she was in dire need of a good night's rest, but at least she had gotten the break she needed.

Karen Giles had invited her into her house, as she'd pointed out it might attract some attention from nosy neighbors if they sat in an out of town security car for a long time. Once in the house, a modestly furnished interior greeted them, but unlike the outside, there were personal touches everywhere. Photos of Giles and a girl, presumably Alex, were everywhere, as well as some paintings. There were also small knickknacks on the shelves. All in all, Wells thought it was quite homely, albeit in the Spirig minimalist way.

Wells walked from room to room, not being nosy, but scanning the areas with her ARP. Karen believed that McKenna was capable of planting listening devices in his employees' houses, but Wells found nothing.

"It seems clear," she told Karen, "but I can only scan for known devices. If he has some new technology Penta are not aware of, then I won't pick it up. But I think we're safe."

Wells walked over to a couch and sat down.

"Thank you, Lieutenant." Karen sat down across from Wells.

"Lily, please." People never seemed to be able to use first names once someone had been introduced to them with a rank. As long as she was in uniform, Karen Giles would not be able to see her as anything other than a security officer.

"So, what do you need me to do?" Karen asked.

What Lieutenant Wells needed more than anything was a new reason to be in Spirig. She needed to get Navarro off her back, but that would never happen as long as she stayed in town. It would take Karen at least a week to get her enough information to convince Penta to step in. Wells needed to be as close as possible to Karen, both so she could get the information from her, and also to step in if things got out of hand.

"I have used up my excuses to be in town with the local security force," Wells said, "so the first thing I need is a reason to stay here." She moved a bit closer to Karen. "And I was thinking, maybe I ran into an old school friend, and I decided to stay with her for a few days to catch up and delay the inevitable shit storm that's waiting for me back at HQ."

Karen Giles was scared, easily intimidated, and desperate, but she was not stupid. "But the first thing Navarro would do is to run checks on us and see that we didn't go to the same school. I don't think we are even in the same age group! Also, if he's any good at his job, wouldn't he keep watching you?"

Wells was quite impressed by Karen Giles. She asked all the questions Wells would have if their roles had been reversed.

"You're right, Karen. We'll keep it simple: a family friend. If he starts asking questions, I'll try to be vague. He might press me for a name and address, but I'll do my best to keep you out of it."

"Okay. I'll tell Alex to sleep on the couch and you—"

"No, Karen. Thanks, but I'll take the couch. I'm asking a lot of you as it is. Also, speaking of Alex, when will she be home? We need to make sure that she buys the whole family friend thing."

"She has a lot going on at school and with her friends. As long as we keep it vague, as you said, we should be fine."

Karen was a wreck. She had dreamed of getting away from McKenna forever, but now that it was a possibility, she was frozen with fear. She knew she had to do it. She knew this was the opportunity she'd been dreaming of. But now, faced with the reality, it was difficult for her to go through with it.

Wells had turned countless informers and broken many suspects. She could see the inner turmoil tearing Karen Giles apart. She knew she had to let it simmer a bit longer before she jumped in and made it all better. Her arm buzzed, and Benjamin Drake's name appeared on her HIC. She wasn't expecting a call from him and wondered if he had gotten cold feet. Did he want out?

"Karen, I need to take this. Mind if I use your room?" Wells asked. Karen nodded.

"Hey. We need to talk." Drake seemed to still be in the same hotel room but wasn't as relaxed as the last time they'd spoken.

"Hey Drake, what's going on?"

"Just enjoying the sights and taking in the local culture. Normal touristy stuff. So, how did you get along with the names I gave you?"

"Wow, no dinner or a movie first?"

"Maybe next time, when I'm not wanted for murder."

"Raincheck then? Navarro ran the names, and they came up just as you said. Thank you, Drake. You really helped me out there. I'm glad you decided to help."

"About that," Drake said. "Let's talk about how you're going to get rid of this pesky arrest warrant that is still out on us."

"All right, let's talk business. First off, there are no guarantees here. The more you help, the better your chances, but in the end, someone higher up than me makes the final call. I want to be clear on that since you've given me what I needed with the names, and I don't want to proceed with any false hope or empty promises. You've been straight with me, and I'm going to be straight with you."

Drake never knew how much he treasured his freedom, his ability to come and go as he pleased, until it was taken away from him. The first impressions of Shangcorp were heavenly, but the longer they stayed, the more he realized that someone was always watching, and he knew that he would be running his whole life, trying to get away from that all-seeing eye.

He kept going through all the events of the last few weeks in his head and playing out all the possible scenarios of what might happen next. The only option he had at the moment that didn't involve living in a cave was to help Wells and hopefully get the charges dropped, or at least downgraded. Jimmy was most likely screwed, as the evidence of him shooting people was pretty damming, but who knows? Maybe even he could get a better deal out of this.

One thing was sure: he had nothing to lose in helping Lieutenant Wells.

"Lieutenant, you drive a hard bargain, but we're in. What do you need?"

# | thirty-six |

The time had come to get the hell out of Shamo.

Drake and Jimmy had arrived dirty and starved, but now they were rested and dressed in the best clothes credits could buy. For Jimmy, that meant visible labels, bright colors, and lots of them. For Drake, it meant understated, good quality that would last a lifetime. Jimmy also bought himself the newest Human Interface Console—full color and seamless skin integration. Looking at his arm, one would never even know it had a screen on it. Once activated, his skin transformed into a beautiful high definition flexible display. Jimmy tried to convince Drake to get one too, but Drake decided to play it safe and wait to see what was going to happen next. He would need all the credits he had to get his life back, once the dust settled.

After all the running and hiding they'd had to do, the freedom to go out and shop and eat as they pleased was a welcome distraction. But Drake knew that that was it all it was—just a distraction. They were not free. Not yet. Shamo, and Shangcorp in general, was a very corrupt place and Drake knew that sooner or later some official would find out who they were. They would find out about the credits and Penta's interest in them, and the blackmail would begin. Once that started, there would be no end to it. Drake had no concrete plan, but he knew that Shamo was not it.

Jimmy was not as keen as Drake to move on.

"This place is perfect for us, ya know?" Jimmy protested.

"I know it seems like it, Jimmy, and maybe for you it is, but I'm not from this world. I might be in it now, but if there's a way for me to get out, I'll grab it. If you want to stay here, believe me, no hard feelings. But I need to get out now, before I can't."

"So you'd just leave me here? After everything we've gone through?"

"Jimmy, all I said was I need to go, and I won't hold it against you if you stay. My mind is made up. I'm going, but what you do is up to you."

Jimmy Something had never had a partner like Drake before. He knew if Drake left now, he would never see him again, and Drake would go on, help that lieutenant and haul again like this had never happened. But for Jimmy, there was no normal to go back to. This place, this situation—this was his normal. He might have bitten off more than he was used to chewing, but it was nothing he couldn't handle. Only this time, he had a partner. Maybe even a friend—a friend he did not want to lose.

"Nice try, partner, but you ain't getting rid of me that easily!" Jimmy smiled at him and started packing.

Drake looked at the scrawny guy across the room. He'd known the name Jimmy Something for years, albeit only by his reputation, but only in the last few weeks had he gotten to know him as a person. Jimmy's reputation was anything but stellar, and Drake had no illusions that it wasn't deserved. But the more time he spent with him, the more he realized most of it was just a screen, and he was starting to get a glimpse behind it.

"Suit yourself, buddy, but you know there are no guarantees that the lovely lieutenant will come through for us, right?"

"I know, but what am I going to do here all by myself, ya know?" Jimmy kept packing, not making eye contact.

Drake almost told him he felt the same.

\*\*\*

Drake knew the only way to survive was to stop going along with this invisible force driving them forward and to do the driving himself once more. He needed to take back control of his life and do things his way again. It was time to be Benjamin Drake. That meant a new truck.

It took them most of the morning to find a dealer who still had what Drake was looking for, but finally, they found it.

"You sure that's the one? I mean, the other ones were much nicer, ya know?"

"It's perfect. I mean, you need to see its potential, not what's in front of you. But yes, buddy, I'm sure."

The salesman had made a feeble attempt to try and sell him something bigger, better, and newer, but he seemed happy to be getting rid of the eyesore.

"Could we maybe just look at one more?" Jimmy pleaded. But Drake's mind was made up.

"Trust me, Jimmy, this is the one."

After changing credits and ticking a lot of boxes on a DDU, the salesman transferred the truck's codes to Drake's HIC, and after some small talk, went back to his office.

Drake felt a wave of nostalgia wash over him. It looked just like how his old Hydrostar had like years ago, back when he bought it from Bob Turner. Thinking of that name soured the memory, so he quickly went over to the Hydrostar and got in.

The inside was in a much better state than his old Hydrostar was when he bought it. This Hydrostar must have belonged to an old-timer, who had driven it since new, looking after it, and then had most likely retired or been elbowed out by younger guys in faster Hydrocomets. It was old and worn, but clean and solid. Drake entered the codes and the old Hydrostar came to life. The DDU, which was an upgrade from his old one, came on, and Drake started the process of entering the new driver's details. He also changed the DDU's input name to Yolanda. After about five minutes, everything was set up the way Drake liked it.

"Yolanda, run systems checks." Drake ordered.

Numbers and schematics appeared on the windscreen in front of him. Some things were highlighted in red and needed him to read them and make some adjustments. Others were green and needed no input. There were also some in yellow, which he could look at later.

"Seems there are a few things we'll have to replace soon, but nothing immediate. I'd say we're about ready to go."

"Only a few things?" Jimmy mumbled back.

Drake proceeded to tell the DDU their destination, and the familiar green line pointed the way.

*** 

Wells agreed with Drake that Shamo, or any Shangcorp territory, was not the best place for them to be. Shangcorp played by their own rules and did not adhere to the humanitarian or ethical codes the other territories abided by. If an official in Shangcorp learned of the interest Penta had in Jimmy and Drake, they would surely try to capture them and ransom them out to someone in Penta. Or they might just take their credits and shoot them. Shangcorp was a lot of things, but safe and fair was not one of them.

But finding a suitable destination was problematic. Wells wanted them as near as possible to help her bring down McKenna. Giving Navarro their names meant they would be in both the Spirig and Nestem security systems. If they entered any Nestem territory, the nearest security team would be notified. If they entered on foot, cameras would pick them up immediately, and they would have no chance. The best chance they had was to cross the border in a vehicle that was registered to someone else. It would take Penta much longer if they had to run facial recognition scans. A surveillance camera would need to get a clear picture of their faces to be able to run a scan—something that might not happen for a few days.

"Are you sure they'll come through for you?" Wells asked Drake.

"Yes, and do you know why? Because I'm paying them. Nice and simple. I've known these guys for a long time, and although they hate authority as much as the next hauler, it's their love of credits that I'm relying on," Drake replied.

"So much for the supposed brotherhood of haulers then." Wells smirked.

"Oh, the brotherhood is real. Without it, they wouldn't even listen to me, but the clincher is the credits. Trust me, for the right amount, a hauler will do anything."

"Anything? Well, I'll keep that in mind," Wells replied.

"Almost anything. So, have you decided where we are going yet?"

"Ever heard of a town called Spirig?"

\*\*\*

It was time for Drake to test the brotherhood.

"I hope this is not your one call you get to make before they ship you off to Mars, because that will just be too sad to bear," Lyle Miller said.

"Thanks for your heartfelt concern there, but no, I'm still a free man," Drake replied.

"How the hell did you pull that off?"

"Don't sound so surprised! I know a thing or two, okay?" Drake tried to sound offended.

"Luck then, I get it. So, I assume this is not a social call?"

"No, business. I need to register a truck, but for obvious reasons, I can't use my name. I was hoping you wouldn't mind registering it in your name—for a fee, of course."

Drake was relying heavily on the fact that haulers usually had it in for the security forces and authority in general. Hauling attracted a particular type of person, one who preferred to do their own thing and play by their own rules. They tended not to react well to being told what to do, so naturally they despised all authority. Drake hoped his running away from Penta security would be enough to entice Lyle to help him out. The cherry on top would be the credits.

"Mmmm," Lyle said, pondering the offering. "So what sort of fee are we talking here?"

Drake told him and made assurances that he would not be implicated in anything. If shit went down, he could claim that he'd bought the truck and had paid someone to deliver it to him. Pretty flimsy, but Drake simply upped the credits when he saw any doubt in Lyle's eyes.

"Fuck it. If it'll piss off Penta, why not?" Lyle finally agreed.

"And help me stay alive, of course," Drake said.

"Nah. Pretty much doing it for the credits and screwing over Penta. No hard feelings, hey?" Lyle replied.

# | thirty-seven |

Driving across the border into a Nestem territory, Drake had a moment of panic. Although the Hydrostar was registered in Lyle Miller's name, Drake was still paranoid that they could be stopped as they tried to cross the border. The windscreen filled with forms that needed ticking, and for the first time in a decade, Drake actually read each one before selecting the accept button. Sweat beaded up on his forehead.

"Relax, partner. We'll be fine." Jimmy said.

Drake accepted the last form and waited for the inevitable red message to fill the screen and order them to pull over, remain in the vehicle, and await the authorities. As the last form disappeared, there was a small pause before the confirmation message appeared on the screen. Drake could hear the clicking sound in his throat as he swallowed. The message on the screen was bright and unmistakable. And green.

"See, what did I tell you?" Jimmy slapped him on the back.

The Hydrostar followed the green line, unperturbed by all the human emotions going on in the cabin.

"Wow, for a moment there..." Drake shook his head.

"Nah, no chance, partner. No way we get caught now!" Jimmy's confidence seemed higher than usual.

Spirig was not far from the border, and Drake took over the controls from the Autodrive. His hands needed something to do besides shake.

"Let's see how long our lucky streak lasts," Drake said, wiping his hands one at a time on his pants before gripping the wheel again.

*\*\**

The speed limit in towns was usually lower than on the highways, and Spirig was no different. Drake slowed the Hydrostar and kept following the green line to their destination. Spirig was the complete opposite of the crazy chaos of Shamo: gray buildings and serenity replaced bold colors and noise, the sidewalks were clean, and everyone looked like they shopped at the same clothing store.

Drake knew that no place was perfect and that underneath Spirig's pristine exterior, there would be all sorts of secrets.

The green line guided them through the town. The buildings were becoming dirtier and more run-down as they continued. The road signs and advertisements that popped up on the windscreen tried to guide people away from this direction, enticing them to turn around to better eateries and accommodation, but this was precisely where they needed to go.

Soon there was little to associate this place with Spirig, just minutes down the road. Most buildings were run-down, and even the traffic on the streets was pretty beat up. This part of town, although still within Spirig's borders, was not called Spirig. On the screen, it showed as 246E. Not even a name, just a designator.

The green line turned a corner and terminated in a hovering red inverted teardrop. Drake parked the Hydrostar, ran the shutdown protocol, and got out.

A big smile greeted them.

"I have to admit, you have a set of balls on you, son," the big man greeted them.

"I've been told they're decently sized," Drake quipped back.

"I'm very curious, indeed, as to why you are standing in front of me again, big balls and all."

"Well, our circumstances have not changed much since we bought that hydrocar off you," Drake said, keeping an eye on the ever-present pulse gun hanging by his side. "Right now, we need a place to park our truck for a few days, and I thought, with you being such an astute businessman, that we could work out a deal."

The big man mulled it over for a few seconds.

"Ten thousand credits a day."

"That's a rip-off. You can—" Jimmy started, but Drake shot him a look that said *What the hell?*

Jimmy shut his mouth and pulled his shoulders up. *What did you expect from me?*

"Exactly what I was thinking," Drake said as he turned back to the big guy.

Having a place to park the Hydrostar for a few days, a place where it would not attract any attention, was crucial. No one would look twice at an old Hydrostar sitting in the back of a used car lot. Now they had a base to hide out in and be close to Lt. Wells.

"I'll take five days in advance," the big man said, and Drake rolled up his sleeve.

***

The last few days were very productive. Karen Giles had been going to work as usual, and every night she gave Lt. Wells the data she got from Zuma. Wells then had to sift through it to see what was useful and what was not. If she was to build a case and get Penta involved, it had to be airtight and accurate. Wells was going out on a limb here, and a misstep could be the end of her career. Especially since she had only just gotten back on track.

Karen was about to leave for work, but she stopped by Wells first. Wells was sitting in her Mongoose in Karen's garage, working on her official Penta DDU.

"For heaven's sake, Lily, when last did you sleep?" Since Lt. Wells had become Karen Giles's de facto roommate, she'd started to call her by her first name.

Every night when Karen got home, Wells started working on the new data, late into the night, sometimes till the next morning. She slept in the daytime when Karen was at work, to maximize her productivity. She had never been this tired in her life, but she knew that time was against her, and instead of focusing on her fatigue, she used that energy on her work—something she had always done.

"I know. I'll take a nap when you leave. I think we're getting close, Karen. Just a few more days. Be safe, okay?"

"I will. I can't wait for this to be over," Karen replied and headed out.

Lt. Wells was beyond tired, but the data Karen was bringing her was more than she could have hoped for. Karen was able to bring most of McKenna's business files home, which created a problem in itself, as Wells had so much to get through. But the information she found was pure gold. Wells had no doubt she would be able to get Penta to back her and stop McKenna from taking Mars. She just needed a few more days.

***

The light buzzing from her HIC woke her. Drake. Wells closed her eyes, struggling to wake up, but since her ARP was now active, the three circles merged into Drake's face in the dark anyway.

"Well, I'm glad one of us has the time for an afternoon nap!" Drake said.

"Fuck off, Drake. I worked all night."

"Not a morning person then? Or is that an afternoon person?"

"Very funny. I get it. Where are you?" Wells asked, now fully awake.

"Beautiful Spirig. Or rather, the not-so-beautiful Spirig. At least, not where we are."

"Great. So things went smoothly with Miller and the big guy from the junkyard?" Wells asked.

"Yep, smooth sailing. Not a hitch, as expected." *No need to tell her about the small panic attack at the border*, he thought.

"Time to get busy then," Wells said. "First, you and Jimmy need to keep a low profile and try to stay out of view as much as possible. This town, especially the part of town you're in, is littered with cameras. I'm sending you a map with the camera locations now. Use them to plot routes to use, so you don't get scanned."

Wells swiped her arm, and the files appeared on his HIC a split second later.

"Got it. Thanks for that. If we had to stay put in the Hydrostar for a few days. . ." Drake shook his head. "Let's just say I'm very grateful."

"No problem. Karen has designed a device for you to use on D-day. She is a very resourceful woman."

Her respect for Karen grew every day as she saw how much she was willing to do to ensure a better future for her and her daughter.

"Sounds like you're all over it, Lieutenant. So, when is D-day?"

Wells knew she had enough data to convince Penta to step in, but she didn't want to rush it and be proven wrong. Three more days and she would have enough, she felt. Then she would have to travel back to Penta headquarters and make sure she talked to the right person. Big organizations love red tape, and Penta had enough lazy officials to make it a very long process. It might even be days, if not weeks, before they took action. But she needed to keep Drake, Jimmy, and Karen positive that this would happen quickly and smoothly.

"I'm hoping within a week or two at the longest," she embellished.

Drake was hoping for a time frame involving hours, not weeks. The Hydrostar was well appointed and had all the creature comforts he needed. Hell, he loved living in the small cabin and had done so for most of his adult life. Only now there were two of them, and that changed everything. As Drake was talking with Lt. Wells, Jimmy was relieving himself of last night's white box meal at an arm's length away. The door to the cubicle was closed, but that did not stop every sound and nuance from coming through.

"Sure, sounds fine to me. The sooner, the better, though," Drake replied as Jimmy's struggles continued.

"Drake, I'm doing my best here, but you know there are no guarantees, right?"

Drake knew this, but what was the alternative? What better option did he have? There were not a lot of offers on the table, and only one included a chance of freedom. Even if it was a remote chance, he had to take it.

"I know Lieutenant. We've been through this. As long as you try your best to help us out, we'll do our best."

Wells no longer saw a criminal who had to be brought down at all costs. All she saw was Benjamin Drake.

She hoped that what she saw was real.

# | thirty-eight |

Nine days, seven hours, thirty-two minutes, and a handful of seconds to their arrival on Mars. Soon he would need to get the soldiers ready for deployment. So far, it had been a holiday for them, but in the next few days, they would need to switch on and get battle ready. He had the utmost confidence his team would be able to switch on when needed, and as usual, Captain Raymond Santo had no doubts or second guesses.

He stood up, and with one step, he was close enough to open his locker. Everything on the shuttle was cramped, but without being too claustrophobic. He put on his Zuma tracksuit, the uniform on the shuttles, and proceeded to the common area.

"Good morning, sir." A woman in the same tracksuit was already sitting at the table, eating her white box breakfast. She made no effort to get up and salute, as Santo had given orders for everyone to be at ease on the journey. Soon that would change.

"Morning," he replied, joining her with his own white box.

Most of the crew was up and about, being social, playing games on their HICs, and generally trying to stave off cabin fever. So far, everyone seemed to be coping with the monotony of space travel. On most other shuttle flights, which usually lasted twice the time of McKenna's shuttles, there would be a few people losing their minds. A clause in the contract signed by all people traveling to Mars on Penta shuttles stated that the security personnel on board had the prerogative to subdue, restrain, and, in most severe cases, terminate a passenger who did not comply with their commands. What this translated to in real life was any person who complained, got stir-crazy, or did anything a security officer didn't like, was shot and thrown out into space.

As most shuttles carried prisoners, this was not a big deal and was hardly ever mentioned back on Earth. But the reality was that the prisoners were used to being kept in small spaces and getting bored; it was the civilians who lost the plot and tried to get out halfway to Mars. Captain Santo knew that statistically he would have to detain and most likely terminate at least three people on the way to Mars. Except for one small incident, there had been no issue, and Santo's confidence in his crew grew more and more each day.

\*\*\*

When Karen arrived home, Wells knew that something was wrong. She was used to seeing Karen's eyes red and puffy from crying in her car on the way home, but today she was more distressed than usual.

"What happened?" Wells asked when Karen stepped into the house.

"He knows! He knows everything!" Karen cried and collapsed on the couch, head in her hands. "It's over!" she sobbed.

Wells had known something might go wrong. Karen had no training for this, and she was already under an enormous amount of stress. Wells kept pushing her to get more data, fearing that the end was near. She was right.

Wells sat down next to Karen and waited for her body language to acknowledge her presence.

"Tell me what happened, Karen." Wells rested a hand on her back.

"He saw me. It's all done. I need to leave tonight," Karen said, but she made no effort to get up.

"Just take a second. Take a breath, and tell me exactly what happened. Step by step. Recall your day for me."

Karen sat up straight and wiped her face. Wells gave her a tissue, and after she had wiped her tears away, Karen said, "I got to work this morning at exactly the same time I always do. Everything was normal. I went to my lab and started my work, as I always do, but as soon as I started, McKenna called me into his office.

"He was busy on a call, but he waved me in to sit down, so I did. He finished his call and came over to me and said, 'We have a problem. Someone is stealing our plans. I suspect it is a Penta spy, trying to get our technology, but I can't prove it. That's why I called you, Karen. I trust you, and I need you to find out which one of your colleges is stealing from me.'

"Then he put his hand on my shoulder, leaned in, and said, 'I'm right to pick you for this task, aren't I, Karen?' I said yes, but he would have seen on his ARP that I was lying. I just know it. He is onto me and just being his cruel self. I'm sorry, Lily, but I need to leave tonight."

Wells tried her best to stay calm and be a friend first, then a security officer.

"Do you think that maybe what he said was true? That he really trusts you and wants your help?"

"Maybe," Karen said, "but it doesn't matter. I'm done. This is as far as I can go, Lily. I can't do this anymore. Please. You must have enough data by now. Don't you?"

Karen was right. Wells had more than enough data by now, and she had been planning on going to Penta soon anyway. She was hoping to have left Spirig with Karen still going to work so as not to raise any suspicion.

"All right, Karen. I'll go tomorrow," Lt. Wells said.

"No, not you. Us." Giles's statement caught Wells by surprise.

"What do you mean? You still have to go to work, Karen. If you leave now, he'll know that it was you and come looking for you. You need to keep up appearances. I'll be as quick as possible, and if there is even the smallest chance of Penta not stepping in, I will come and get you myself, okay?"

"No, Lily. I did everything you asked of me. You need to get Alex and me out of here. Now."

Wells could not be slowed down by babysitting Karen and her daughter. She did care about them, but the mission had to come first. Always.

"Karen, I promise you, the best thing you can do is to keep up the act. My gut tells me that he is not onto you. But if you run away and disappear, you'll give him a reason to come after you. Please think this through."

Giles's shoulders slumped, her arms limply lying next to her thighs on the couch. Wells hated seeing her like this, but what choice did she have?

"Fine, Lily. We'll stay," Karen Giles said, but Wells doubted it.

*** 

Wells waited until Giles went to her bedroom to contact Drake. She informed him that she was going to go back to Penta headquarters in the next few days. It meant that they had to be ready to leave for Zuma on short notice.

"Do you think you can convince them?" Drake asked.

"I think so. The amount of data Karen gave me –"

"I mean Jimmy and me. Do you think our little part in all this will be enough to get off their shit list?"

"Is Jimmy with you now?"

"He's asleep. Why?" Drake replied.

"Drake, everything I have gathered about you shows that you did something illegal for profit. There is no denying that. But in the bigger scheme of things, it's a minor offense. I'm sure that your help and just the fact that you are willing to help will get you off. Worst case, a fine," Wells said.

"And Jimmy?"

"Drake, he killed people. Proving self-defense will be tricky. I think it will be possible, but Jimmy will still be arrested, and then we'll have to sort it out. Murder is less easy to erase."

Drake knew this, but it still hurt to hear it out loud.

"Well, let's just get through this first, and then we'll worry about the details, okay?" Drake said.

"I'll talk to you as soon as I have news."

***

A few feet behind Drake, Jimmy was lying on the bed in the sleeping unit, apparently asleep.

But he wasn't. Jimmy was wide awake, eyes shut, looking at Lt. Wells on his ARP. When Jimmy had taken control of Drake's old Hydrostar's DDU, he'd also snuck a transmitting code onto his ARP, allowing Jimmy to see everything Drake saw when his ARP was on. Just a precaution.

"I'll talk to you as soon as I have news."

Jimmy kept lying still, in case Drake was watching him through the translucent door. "I'd like to see you try and arrest me," he said quietly, fighting back the tears that were trying to humiliate him.

\*\*\*

Lieutenant Wells decided to stop by Sergeant Navarro's office before she left Spirig. She wanted to leave on good terms and make sure she could come back if needed, but also to see if he mentioned anything about Drake and Jimmy being back in town.

A new officer was staffing the desk. She looked about twelve to Wells, and her uniform was brand new. As she walked in, Wells noticed her swiping her arm, most likely to start recording on her ARP. All very by the book, and not very subtle.

The officer noted Wells' uniform. "Good morning, Lieutenant. How can we be of assistance?"

"I'm here to see Sergeant Navarro if he is available."

"I believe he just came back a few minutes ago. Please take a seat, and I'll see if I can reach him." Wells was impressed by the young officer, seeing a lot of herself in her. She sat down on the bench and waited.

"Lieutenant Wells! I thought you had left already." Navarro made his usual grandiose entrance.

"Not yet, but I am actually on my way out of town. I think my friend has had enough of me by now, and it's time I go and face my superiors."

"One can only run away from one's problems for so long. But I'm sure you will come out fine." The fake teeth appeared and almost blinded her.

"Thank you, Sergeant. I hope so. Anyway, I just wanted to thank you for your hospitality and cooperation in this sensitive case." Wells extended her hand.

"My pleasure. And if anything pops up, I'll let you know." Navarro shook her hand, but did not let go. "We still have Drake and Something as people of interest in our system, so if they or any known associates show up, we'll let you know."

*All this equipment and you have no idea they are back in town and have been for quite a few days,* Wells thought. *Money well spent.*

"Thank you; I appreciate that," she said, pulling her hand back. She decided just to rip the band-aid off, so she turned around and walked out.

Safely back in her Mongoose, she made a call to Drake.

"How are things in Hotel Hydrostar?" she said before Drake could get a word in.

"Oh, someone came prepared!" Drake smiled. "Always room for one more in the hotel, or I could just get rid of Jimmy. Just say the word. Please!"

"Thanks, but I prefer my own bed."

"Does this mean you are going back today?" Drake asked, sitting up.

Wells had the urge to go and visit Drake but knew that Navarro would be watching her leave town. She had not been face-to-face with him since the border ordeal and wanted to see him, look into his eyes, and make sure she wasn't making a huge mistake. But she would have to keep trusting her gut like she always had.

"Yes. Just spoke to Navarro, and I don't think he knows you are here, but still, be careful and use the camera maps I gave you, okay?"

Wells waited for her gut to tell her something, but it was silent.

"You all right? You zoned out there for a while."

"Yes, sorry, I'm all good. I need to go. Be careful."

"Don't worry about us. You just make sure you convince whoever you need to convince and get everyone what they want," Drake replied.

# | thirty-nine |

Lieutenant Wells stepped into her apartment and felt like an intruder. She had never really felt at home in her apartment. Most of her time was spent at work or in the field, and she hardly ever did anything but sleep here. There were no pictures on the walls or anything personal lying around. The only indication that someone used this space was a portable Penta Security DDU that sat on the kitchen counter. She knew that her work defined her, and she was fine with that. It gave her a sense of purpose and belonging. She identified more with Lt. Wells than she did with Lily Wells. Like the hero in an old comic book, her civilian clothes were the disguise, not the uniform.

Putting her bags down, she went to her bed and sat down on its edge. Tomorrow she was going to take all her evidence to Captain Sturgis, the officer who was looking after Captain Santo's affairs while he was on leave. She had one chance to convince him that Captain Santo was in bed with Jacob McKenna and that he was aiding him in seizing Mars. If Captain Sturgis did not bite, it was game over. Accusing a high ranking officer of treason was a considerable risk, but she knew she had the data to back it up. Convincing Sturgis to even look at the evidence would be the trickiest part. If she got this wrong, not only would Santo and McKenna get away with it, but she could end up being in a far worse position than desk duty. Maybe even in a detention cell.

\*\*\*

A huge multistory building of glass, steel, and concrete housed Penta's headquarters. It was a formidable building that towered over the surrounding structures. Penta's business was weapons and the people who used them. Most other territories used security personnel from Penta or sent their own people there for training. Penta also sold weapons to whoever wanted to buy them. Penta had the data on who bought what and how much of it, and this allowed them to be better equipped than anyone out there, except for Shangcorp—no one ever really knew what they were up to.

Penta was a gigantic war machine waiting to flex its muscles, and Lieutenant Wells was walking into the belly of the beast, hoping to awaken it.

Captain Sturgis was sitting behind his desk, staring at his DDU, when she let herself in.

"Do we have an appointment?" Sturgis asked.

"No, sir, but I have some critical information that I need to discuss in private, off the record."

"Did you find your targets, or do you have something new you would rather do?"

"Both," Wells said. "I found them, but I also found something else."

Captain Sturgis was back on his DDU, not taking the bait.

"Captain, I need to speak to you, off the record, please!" Wells raised her voice slightly. This got the captain's attention. He didn't seem too amused by her tone.

"Lieutenant, I hope your next sentence will justify your presence."

Wells was facing a dilemma. All the Penta offices were monitored 24/7 in a bid to prevent corruption. It was a great idea, except that there were thousands of recordings every minute, so Penta had to use highly complicated algorithms to filter out the casual conversations and track the flagged ones. So, by using smart coding, one could fool the algorithms into believing any conversation was harmless.

The problem was that the use of these codes and programs was a punishable offense unless a superior officer gave explicit consent. Just asking for permission could get you into trouble, so Wells knew if Captain Sturgis refused her request to speak off the record, she could end up in detention.

"Captain, I am requesting the rest of this conversation to be off the record," Wells said, for the third time.

Captain Sturgis pushed himself away from his desk and DDU. He crossed his arms and rested them on his belly. "Fine," he finally said.

Wells wasted no time and immediately switched her ARP to scrambled mode. She had to wait for Captain Sturgis to do the same, and only then would it be secure.

"So, tell me, how was your recent trip?" Captain Sturgis asked clearly. But what Lieutenant Wells heard via her ARP was *You have one shot at this Lieutenant, make it count.*

"It was lovely, thanks. Really enjoyable," Wells replied, but Captain Sturgis heard *Captain, I will be as brief as possible and will elaborate at your request.*

The captain gave her a long hard stare, then a small nod. Wells' lips moved, but different words continued to ring out in his ARP.

"Captain, when I was working on the Drake and Something murder case, I found it suspicious that no fuss was made over the fact that they were hauling stolen Bismuth. I was desk-bound at that stage and did some digging. I found out the Bismuth had been stolen from Penta, and I thought it was strange that it wasn't mentioned in the file. So I followed the trail, and time after time, one name kept popping up. I followed that name to see where it would lead.

"It led me to Jacob McKenna, CEO of Zuma Corporation, who was the final destination for the stolen Bismuth. It looks like McKenna going to Mars, which in itself is not illegal. But after digging more, I started to unravel something much bigger than a single private shuttle trip.

"The name that kept coming up in my research, sir, was Captain Raymond Santo. I have evidence that proves he's trained an elite squad of soldiers and that he has boarded on of four shuttles that are this moment heading to Mars with the intention to colonize it for Zuma. I have detailed proof, sir."

Wells wished she had some water to drink. Her tongue felt swollen, and she could hardly swallow. Captain Sturgis's expression had not changed throughout, and now he was staring at his folded hands, which were resting on his belly.

Finally, he spoke. "Do you understand the implications, Wells? This could start a war."

She did.

"But, if you are wrong, then *you* will face treason charges for falsely implicating a senior officer. Do you want to continue this conversation, Lieutenant?"

"Yes, sir," Wells replied without hesitation, "I do."

"Show me the data."

***

Lieutenant Wells sat patiently, but nervously, across from Captain Sturgis for about two hours. He didn't ask her any questions, but he did glance at her on occasion. She was bursting to say something or explain the data to him but knew she was ahead and needed to stay there. So she just sat there, watching a fat man read a DDU screen for two hours. Finally, he pushed himself back from his desk and folded his hands on his belly again.

"Glad to see you are back. How was the mission?" Captain Sturgiss said, but Wells' ARP unscrambled his words: "This is great work, Lieutenant."

Wells' confusion only lasted a split second.

"I cannot find any errors," he continued. "Everything checks out, which means we now have a problem on our hands."

"Thank you, sir. I believe Captain Santo is days away from landing on Mars."

"Hold on," Captain Sturgis stopped her. "I'm on your side, but there is no way that we are ready to act on this yet. I might be satisfied with the data, but you know I need to have all this verified first."

Wells had expected this. He was not a man of action, but a well-seasoned bureaucrat. There was no time for this. But Wells knew she was not in charge of this case anymore. The plans and data she'd gotten from Karen showed that Santo was not going to launch the assault until the shuttles returned to Earth, and McKenna was safely on his way. This was to ensure that once word reached Earth of the coup, McKenna would be untouchable. It meant they still had a few weeks to get to McKenna and stop this.

"Of course, sir. I understand that we need to do things by the book, but . . . if I may?"

"Lieutenant, this is bigger than anything either one of us has ever encountered. We have to do this right. Understand?"

By confiding in Sturgis, she had handed the reigns over to him. It was now his operation, until someone higher up the food chain decided they wanted to take over and get the glory.

"Yes, sir. But I do have a plan for how we can get to McKenna, unnoticed."

\*\*\*

Wells told Karen about her meeting with Sturgis, and when she finished, it was Karen's turn for an update.

"It seems I got a lucky break. Not to get too technical, but since I'm investigating the suspected data theft, I have been able to change the dates on the logs and cover my tracks. Now, it looks like the only person who accessed the data was me, while investigating it. I think I might be okay." Though tired, Karen sounded happier than she had in the last few days.

"Wow, that's great, right? Do you think McKenna will back off now?" Wells asked.

"I think so. The shuttles are supposed to start their return to Earth in a day or two, so he's a bit preoccupied."

"Stay safe and if anything happens, contact me."

# | forty |

"Ma'am, we have four unscheduled incoming shuttles," the operator shouted out.

The woman, standing behind another DDU operator at the far end of the room, acknowledged him with a nod. She gave the operator in front of her one last instruction and made her way over to the other operator. She glanced at the screens of the DDUs she passed on her way over, making sure everyone was on top of things. There were only twelve units and operators set up in three rows of four, and she wound her way in an S-like pattern to get to the operator who had called out to her. All the operators faced a giant DDU. The room was dark and crowded, with the only light sources being the smaller DDUs at each station.

The officer finally made it to the operator.

"Are you sure they're shuttles?"

There were no scheduled shuttles for at least another five months, so this had to be an error or natural phenomena like meteors. Errors and glitches happened daily—there were lots of floating things in space.

"No ma'am, but the heat signature is in the same range as that of a shuttle. But," the operator sounded unsure of himself, "they are traveling at twice the speed of a shuttle."

The DDU showed that the four shapes were clearly on their way to Mars, and with a projected impact in less than 24 hours. What made her doubt their being shuttles was not only the speed, but the impact zone was hundreds of kilometers away from the settlement.

"Keep track of them, but at that speed and size, they will most likely burn up and not make a huge mess." The operator nodded and made some notes on the DDU.

*** 

The numbers on the wall now read less than one day. Santo stretched out and grabbed his tracksuit for the last time. The next time he got dressed would be in full uniform.

On his way to the common area, he could feel the change in the atmosphere on board the shuttle. Everyone was a little tenser, and there was none of the usual banter and laughter. Captain Santo was quite impressed. He could not have picked and trained them any better. Without barking out orders, everyone was prepared and had put their game faces on. He made calls to the other three shuttles, and by all reports, the crew aboard all four shuttles were behaving the same way. Santo was overflowing with pride and confidence.

"Sir, we are now getting ready for phase three," the operator at the controls of the DDU said as Captain Santo approached him.

Phase one of the shuttles' flight plan was the lift-off and breaking of Earth's gravity. Phase two was the longest, as it was the flight to Mars. Phase three was the slowing down and landing on Mars. The landing zone was a few hundred kilometers away from the main settlement on Mars. McKenna knew that the shuttles would be spotted as soon as they entered Mars' space, so he decided to have them land a few hundred kilometers away in the hope they would be considered space junk or something not worth investigating. The shuttles all had biosphere tents in their cargo holds, and the first task for the crew was to set them up and get the oxygen concentrators up and running. The tents had been made as small as possible, and living in them were going to be cramped, but having them so small was a necessary design compromise to have them assemble or disassemble quickly, and cut down on the weight and packable size. Every day the crew were to pack up, refill their oxygen tanks at the concentrators and move toward the settlement. Then they would reassemble the tents, get the concentrators running, and repeat the next day. This slow movement toward the target site ensured that they would not easily be picked up by any scanners. No one on Mars was looking for a group of beings trekking across the surface. Most of the sensors and scanners were looking skyward, and the ones that weren't were more concerned with detecting storms. A slow-moving group of elite soldiers was not going to pop up on anyone's screen.

Captain Santo looked at the telemetry on the DDU screens. Everything seemed to be well under control.

*** 

The Martian operator couldn't help checking in regularly on the four objects that he'd spotted earlier in the day. Something in the way they were traveling bothered him. Mars was pelted with meteors every week, but these four blips on his screen felt different. His job was to look out for any big pieces of space junk coming their way and notify his superior if their projected impact zone was within a hundred-kilometer radius of the settlement. They, in turn, then informed the security team, who used a pulse cannon to track them and shoot if necessary. So far, this had only happened twice, and both times the meteors were dispatched with ease. But they were tiny in comparison to the four anomalies that he kept checking. The range of their impact zone was well outside the danger area, and he should have given up on them by now.

And he was about to, when they all did something a meteor never does; they all slowed down in unison.

# | forty-one |

The alarm was about to go off, but he didn't need it. Many years following orders and being a very strict disciplinarian had taught him excellent body control. If he needed to be up at a particular time, then he woke up at that time, no alarms required.

He got up, and for the first time in weeks, reached for his uniform. It was not his usual Penta uniform, but the black and gold detailed uniform that McKenna had designed for them. Santo didn't mind it, as a uniform was a uniform to him. As long as the armor did its job, he was happy with it.

After getting dressed, he took one more look in the mirror and stepped out of his living unit.

"Attention on deck!" a voice yelled.

In front of Captain Santo, the whole crew stood assembled, in uniform, and ready to go. Displayed on three DDU screens behind them were livestreams from the other shuttles with exact copies of what Santo saw.

"At ease," he ordered. "Seeing you all right now confirms my trust and confidence that this mission will succeed, and future generations will know us as the conquerors of Mars!"

The crews on all four shuttles let out war cries with fists in the air. Santo let them go on, allowing them to work themselves into a frenzy and get their blood pumping. They would need to draw on this raw energy when the fighting started.

***

The objects were now minutes away from impact, and still decelerating, like they were landing, not crashing. The operator decided to have one last try at his supervisor.

"Ma'am, they're slowing down. They look like shuttles. They're . . . well, the best word for it is 'landing.'"

The supervisor scrutinized the telemetry.

"I need to be sure. Are there any shuttles scheduled that might have gotten thrown off course?"

"No, ma'am," he said, somewhat insulted, "I have checked twice and had another operator confirm. There are no shuttles scheduled for another five months."

The supervisor sighed, her eyes still fixed on the DDU. If this was an unscheduled landing, it could have some serious implications. If this were indeed a landing, they would need to intercept or at least try to make contact with whoever was flying them.

"Well, if no one sent a shuttle, then it can't be one, now can it? If the impact is within tolerance, then abandon your tracking and mark it as space debris."

The operator watched as his supervisor left. He worried that a big mistake had just been made.

***

The shuttle shook violently, and Santo tugged on his harness to make sure it was tight. It was difficult to make out the numbers on the DDU mounted in the front of the shuttle, as he could not keep his head still, but what he could make out were numbers in reassuring shades of yellow and green. No red. The shuttle had no windows, and the operator had the DDU set to show the telemetry, not the video feed from outside that they were used to, so there was no way to know how long this was going to last.

Santo strained his neck to look around at the rest of the crew. Some had their eyes closed, but most stared ahead, riding it out. Lift-off had been a bit shaky and unstable, but this felt like the whole shuttle was being torn apart. For the first time, the captain started to wonder about the integrity of the shuttle and scanned the surfaces around him for any cracks or fractures, but saw nothing. He hoped the outside was the same.

A high pitched shriek filled the cabin. Red numbers started to flash on the DDU, visible to everyone in the shuttle. The operator struggled to control his shaking arms and hands and punched some buttons.

"Report!" Santo's voice bellowed through the shuttle, as a sudden quietness filled the air. Most of the red on the DDU disappeared, and the shaking was all gone. No one dared say anything yet.

"Sir, landing in five, four, three. . ." The operator pressed some more buttons, and everyone felt a little thump.

***

There was no impact or seismic abnormality. The four blips slowed and then simply stopped on the surface of Mars, intact, according to the data.

The operator was certain it was a landing.

"Ma'am, the objects have. . ." He hesitated to use the word *landing* again. ". . . stopped. They are about a hundred and eighty kilometers from the settlement. All movement has ceased."

The supervisor came over and had another long look. The system was not designed to track small movements on land. The dots were barely visible now.

"If there is no change in an hour, log it and move on," she said.

"Yes, ma'am."

If the objects didn't move again, they would most likely never be seen again. No one ever went outside of the habitable hundred-kilometer zone. To do so was suicide. Most Martians did not have the suits or equipment to wander out of the zone. Only the security teams had suits, and even they only had a few. There were also a few for the scientists, but they were too busy making sure everyone stayed alive to wander out looking for crashed objects.

"C'mon. Please move. Just a little," the operator urged the dots on his screen.

# | forty-two |

The sun was down, and although the street lights came on, there was still lots of darkness around. It was in these dark hollows that Drake and Jimmy operated. At first, they'd needed the cameras map, but now they were able to find their way around without it. Jimmy's nose for the less desirable aspects of life led them directly to all the establishments in Spirig that were not on the travel brochures. They still had to be careful, as the seedier the place, the higher the risk of surveillance by the authorities. However, these establishments knew their clients valued their privacy and used every trick in the book to minimize the risk to their clientele.

Soon Drake and Jimmy had the freedom to go out every night for a drink, and escape the seemingly shrinking Hydrostar. If it weren't for the map provided by Lieutenant Wells, Drake would have turned himself in to the authorities. Having to share a space designed for one with someone like Jimmy was tantamount to inhumane torture. Drake made a mental note, every time they got off the Hydrostar, to thank the lieutenant.

"You reckon we're close to getting the call?" Jimmy asked Drake again. It had become his opening line every night they went out.

"At least one day closer, Jimmy," Drake took a long sip of his expensive beer.

Jimmy and Drake had become regulars at the bar, but that did not stop the owner from charging them double for every drink. It seemed a fair deal to Drake to ensure their anonymity.

"Yeah, yeah, I know, I know. Just busting to do something, ya know?"

Drake felt the same. Not that he looked forward to what they had to do, but more the aftermath. If Lt. Wells held up her part of the bargain, he would be as close as possible to being a free man.

Although they mostly kept to themselves, they still got wind of the general chatter, and it seemed the big topic was the rumored launch from the neighboring Zuma territory. It had happened so quickly that it caught everyone by surprise. As no one had been anticipating a launch, it had left everyone with the capability to track one scrambling. By the time everyone realized what had happened, the shuttles were well out of range.

Because of the speed the vehicles traveled, people assumed they were just exploration drones, not shuttles, and McKenna did nothing to confirm or deny these claims. As a mining company, it made sense for Zuma to explore nearby asteroids as they had done in the past, so it was not that strange. Sending four at the same time was a bit excessive, and McKenna's competitors started to wonder if he had hit on something big. Soon the talk was more about what the possible find could be and less about the possibilities of them being shuttles.

Most of the haulers in the bar were readying themselves for when the supposed drones would return, bringing the opportunity for some lucrative contracts. Not so long ago, Drake would have been keeping a close eye on the developments himself, hoping to get a big fat haul. Except that he and everyone else would have been greatly disappointed once the truth came out.

"You still think your lady friend is good for her word?" Jimmy asked, pulling Drake away from the conversation at the next table.

"Of course. I mean, I have to. What other choice is there?" Drake took a quick sip and tried to act casual.

"So, she reckons she is getting us both off scot-free if we do this for her?"

"Why are you asking me this now? You know the deal. We help her, and she will do her best to help us. Not the best deal, but it's all we have." Drake finished his beer and stood up. "Another one?" he asked, to be polite. He left before Jimmy could answer.

When he returned, Jimmy was still giving him that same look.

"Buddy, you know what I know, okay?" Drake wondered where this change had come from.

"Sure. Just making sure, ya know?" Jimmy said. He finally broke eye contact to look at the girl gyrating on the stage.

\*\*\*

Unpacking the shuttles and setting up the tents took a bit longer than planned, but Santo knew that with practice, they would get better at it. Once the small nomadic base was set up, the plan was to settle in for three days, get used to the environment and acclimatize. Then the shuttles would return to Earth. Once the shuttles started their return voyage, the invading forces would begin their nomadic journey toward the Mars base.

Unlike the shuttles, the tents had no private cubicles. Instead, they were just a big room for everyone to sleep in and get set up in their suits. There was another tent used as the mess hall. Everyone had to share from now on. Santo was not exempt from this, and he put his gear down on an inflatable mattress that appeared unoccupied. From now on, their days would consist of sleeping, packing up, or setting up, and walking—no more downtime or farting around.

The tent began to fill up with other team members, and soon all the sleeping mats were filled, and people started to fall asleep. Santo closed his eyes and made a mental note of when to wake up the next morning.

\*\*\*

The first night went down without a hitch; the condensers worked flawlessly, and everyone got a good night's rest. They were camped right next to the shuttles, as per the plan, to ensure they could evacuate to the shuttles should there be a malfunction.

Santo woke up just as the whole tent started to stir. Some people jumped up immediately and began packing up their personal items, and getting into their enviro-suits, some took a more leisurely approach, taking their time waking up. It was still early with time to spare, so Santo gave them the benefit of the doubt and started with his routine.

The condensers only worked in a closed environment. The moment the tents got taken down, the condensers became redundant. It meant that everyone had to be in their enviro-suits before the pack up began. The e-suits, as everyone called them, supplied oxygen as well as food and water through tubes. It also protected the wearer from cuts and smaller penetrations. The insulation kept body temperatures in a healthy range. Solar absorbing material was also used that charged the batteries to keep the suit functioning for up to twenty hours.

Once the tents and everything else was packed up, they were loaded onto hand-carts. The carts had the same abrasion-resistant solar absorbing material over the tops, which charged the batteries for the condensers. Ceramic bearings were used on the carts, and with Mars's gravity being only a third of Earth's, they were easy to pull along.

Once he had his suit on, Santo walked over to the nearest officer and requested a check. Everyone had to get a second person to check their suits for any faults or abnormalities, and if everything was fine, then the suit could be activated. Santo was not crazy over this added safety feature, but had not been able to convince McKenna to scrap it. Once the officer was happy, he entered his personnel code on the suit's DDU, which mimicked the wearer's HIC and was mounted on the arm of the suit in the same spot an HIC would be.

Once everyone's suits were activated, the appointed team member switched off the condenser. Everyone checked their e-suits' telemetry and gave the thumbs up if everything was green. The team leader then gave the order to start packing up.

Although Santo had to share the tent with the team, he did not participate in the packing up. Not out of vanity, although that most certainly played a part, but to oversee and supervise the whole operation. Captain Santo hardly ever got his hands dirty, but he was always embedded in the team, standing right next to his men and women. The team knew this and respected him for that. He had a reputation for al-

ways being in the field with his teams, unlike most captains who preferred to lead from the safety of a Mobile Operations Mongoose.

The e-suits made packing up a little more complicated, but the
teams had practiced in them for countless hours before departure, and
coupled with the low gravity they now experienced, it went much
faster than anticipated. Santo was delighted with this little bonus. If
they could pack up and set up a bit faster, they could walk a bit longer
each day and reach their goal earlier.

Once everything was on the carts, the team leaders gave the command, and the trek across the Martian landscape began. Leaving the
shuttles behind, the invaders started their first long walk on the dusty
red plains.

# | forty-three |

The small dots on the DDU remained motionless. The operator went over the recordings for the last 48 hours twice to make sure, but he could not detect anything. No signals, no movement, no nothing. He knew if he got caught wasting time observing them, his supervisor would be furious and most likely reprimand him. It was time to face the facts: he had no more reason to try and convince her to keep tabs on them. They had landed on the surface and had since been dormant. No sign of life or movement. It was time to let it go.

The operator closed the screen and reluctantly logged it.

***

Drake came to life when the three circles merged into Lieutenant Wells' face.

"Oh, hey! I started to think you forgot about us."

"Drake, I have some good news." Drake could see she was bursting to tell him something.

"Spit it out!"

"Penta is on board! Still got a few hoops to jump through, but they are in!" Wells could barely sit still.

"You mean, *you* are in?" Drake corrected her little slip.

"Yes, you know what I mean." Her enthusiasm did not fade a bit.

She told him about her meeting with Captain Sturgis and how he wanted to make sure that everything was done by the books. She also told Drake that she had told Sturgis about the plan and that he was reluctant at first, but conceded that it would be a huge benefit having Drake and Jimmy on board.

Drake could feel the tension leave his body when she told him this. If the captain refused to use Jimmy and him, they would not have any chance of a pardon. At least now they were helping Penta and had an opportunity to prove their worth.

"That is damn good news, Lieutenant."

"It is still no guarantee, Drake. I need you to know that. I'm just trying to be truthful here, but you know there are no guarantees on this trip."

"I know, I know. But at least now we have a shot, right?"

"Yes, that is true."

"So, what now? When do we go?" Drake asked.

"I have a meeting with the captain tomorrow morning to go over a few more things. I'll let you know the moment we are done."

Drake was dying to get on the road but knew there was no point in pushing it since she was now at the mercy of the Penta hierarchy and not calling all the shots anymore.

"Good luck. Let me know as soon as humanly possible, please. The Hydrostar is much smaller than I remembered."

"Will do. And say hi to Jimmy from me." Lt. Wells signed off.

Drake sat, grin on his face, staring at the wall in front of him partly because they might be on the road tomorrow, and partly because of the smile the lieutenant had given him just before she disconnected.

\*\*\*

Lieutenant Wells was sitting outside Captain Sturgis's office when he arrived. He shook his head, the slightest hint of a smile on his lips, and walked past her into his office.

"Come on in already!" he bellowed out to Wells, who was still waiting outside.

When she walked in, he was still shaking his head. "You are one persistent pain in the ass, you know?"

"Just want to make sure we get Captain Santo, Sir."

Sturgis switched on his DDU and moved around in his seat to get comfortable.

"I will be taking charge of this operation from here on. Is that a problem for you?" Wells knew it was go-time.

"No, sir!" she replied.

"Good. Anything you decide to do, you run past me first, understood?"

"I thought you were running the operation, sir?"

"Yes, but I'm not a field man, Lieutenant. My expertise lies here." He motioned across his office. "Best we each do what we're good at."

"Sir, I just want to be clear, so there is no confusion at all. Are you saying I'm the team leader on this?" Wells tried to swallow, but couldn't.

"Yes, Lieutenant. Your work so far has been exemplary, and I see no reason to give the reins over to someone else now. Do you?"

"No, sir, of course not. When would you like us to be operational?" she asked, falling straight into her comfort zone.

"As soon as you have a team assembled, Lieutenant. I expect daily reports, starting now. Good luck."

Wells did not hesitate a second longer. After thanking the captain briefly, she ran to her desk. She already knew who she wanted on her team. She started to get all the logistics in order.

***

The finger was already past the first knuckle but struggled on. It was putting tremendous strain on the walls of the nose, but so far, they seemed to cope. It twisted left to right, trying to gain some more traction. It seemed to work, and it was now well on its way to the second knuckle.

Drake had been watching Jimmy pick at his nose for the last hour, and there seemed to be no end in sight. Drake wondered if he would actually be able to get a whole finger up there. At this rate, it seemed to be the goal.

Three circles suddenly blocked his front-row view, and a much better picture took its place.

"Give it to me straight, Lieutenant; are we going?"

"Hello, Drake. Yes, everything was approved, and we are operational," Wells replied. Drake noticed that she was a bit more reserved than usual.

"So what do we do?" Drake asked.

"As you know, Captain Sturgis has approved your involvement in the operation," Wells recapped, "which means we will proceed as planned. You can depart at dawn. We will be in range by then and will be monitoring all your movements."

Drake was ready to leave right there and then, but he knew for him to stand any chance at all of getting out of this a free man, he would have to follow orders like a good soldier.

"Sounds great, Lieutenant. We'll leave first thing in the morning. I can't wait to get this over with," Drake said, realizing how much was riding on this.

"Stick to the plan, Drake, and you will do great. Stay out of harm's way and let us do our work, okay? No heroics. Just do your part." Wells dropped the Penta veil for a split second. "Please, Drake, stick to plan, all right?"

"Yes, ma'am!" Drake saluted her.

"Funny. I'll check in tomorrow after dawn." She disconnected before Drake could get another word in.

Wells' face was replaced by Jimmy's, who thankfully had stopped searching for his brain.

"And?" he shouted at Drake, who was two feet away.

"And," Drake replied, "you'd better pack your bags and get ready for a road trip, buddy."

# | forty-four |

Jacob McKenna had not been sleeping for weeks. His doctor gave him medicine, but it had only worked for the first few nights. The insomnia was tiring and annoying, but nothing compared to the paranoia that had taken hold of him. Not only was he convinced that there was a spy in his midst, but Santo was not reporting back as frequently as he was supposed to. Up until two days ago, he had received daily updates, brief, but regular at least. McKenna knew that the flight was a success, and they had already done their first tests of the equipment, but he felt powerless at being so far away. McKenna knew once he was on board a shuttle that he would feel better, but that was still weeks away. He just wished Santo would report more frequently.

As his paranoia over Santo and the lack of communication increased, his fears over a spy in his midst started to wane slightly. He'd picked an engineer called Giles to investigate, as she seemed the least capable of doing anything as drastic as spying. She was as thorough as he thought she would be, and she presented him with more information than he cared for, and soon he was quite sure that there was no leak. His paranoia did not dissipate completely, so he left her alone to continue the search. Better safe than sorry, he thought.

Jacob McKenna decided to check with engineering to make sure all the communication systems were operating at a hundred percent. As he walked to engineering, he checked his HIC but saw no new updates from Santo. A feeling and a thought he didn't want to accept started to creep into his mind.

\*\*\*

"You need to get me out of here now! And Alex. Something is wrong!"

Lieutenant Wells had just fallen asleep when her arm buzzed, and the three circles started dancing in the dark. It might have only been a few minutes of sleep, but she still needed a few seconds to come fully awake and process Karen Giles's latest meltdown.

"Karen, what is going on? We are packing up tomorrow. I told you that we are on our way." Wells knew she was doing a poor job of hiding her frustration.

"Santo is not sending the shuttles back," Karen said.

"What do you mean?" Wells asked.

"Last night, just before we left work, McKenna came storming into engineering and yelled at us, accusing everyone of working against him and helping Santo. He was rambling on, and we had to do our best to talk him down. Eventually, he calmed down a little bit, and I'm paraphrasing here, but he said that Santo had killed all communications, and McKenna thinks that he did not return the shuttles on the day he was supposed to.

"McKenna thought that there must have been an issue with the communication link, so he had us run multiple tests to check all the systems and make sure that the line of communications was still open and working. All tests came back positive, as in no problems or issues, so we tried sending different messages on different channels. It takes about fifteen minutes for a message to travel there, and then after the receiver replies, another fifteen back to Earth. So we had to wait a few minutes for all the messages to go through all the channels, but one by one, we started to get the same reply."

Giles took a sip of tea, and Wells had to fight the urge to yell at her to continue.

"The message we got back was an automated one, saying that the receiver had blocked all incoming messages." Giles waited for Wells to respond, but seeing that she did not grasp the meaning of this, she jumped back in. "Lily, this means Santo deliberately blocked McKenna from communicating with him. All the telemetry shows that they have started the trek, but they've locked McKenna out. Santo is going to take Mars by himself, Lily!"

Wells needed a minute to process these new developments. Was McKenna just being overly paranoid and jumping the gun? Could there be an issue, and the plan was still going ahead?

Karen read her like a book. "I checked it myself. The data logs show that the communication hardware is still up and running, but it has been taken offline. We tried to reengage it, but couldn't."

"This changes things, but not the plan. Stay at home today. Is Alex there?" Wells asked, her mind running at full speed.

"Yes. I'll keep her here and lock everything. I'm scared, Lily."

"I know you are, but the safest place for you right now is your house. It's almost over, Karen."

"Please hurry!"

***

Jacob McKenna was livid. After all the engineers left, he went back to his office and poured himself a traditional whiskey. It had cost him an obscene amount of credits, but tonight he was drinking it all.

*That lowlife, that backstabbing piece of shit. Who does he think he is? Doesn't he realize I can build ten more shuttles filled with troops and annihilate him? He is nothing but a degenerate that got greedy. I will destroy him.*

But the truth was Jacob McKenna was bankrupt. He had huge outstanding debts, and most of his mines had run dry. Shangcorp had been squeezing him out of the game for the last decade. He had been able to hang on until now, draining his vaults, but time had run out.

That's why he had to get to Mars. He had to get away from his debts and start over. Once he controlled Mars, he could mine it hollow and not only pay off his debts but start buying back more mines on Earth, and soon Zuma Corp would be the new dominant corporation on Earth. Screw Penta and Shangcorp—soon, Zuma Corp would be the only superpower.

But now that bastard Santo had screwed up everything. There were no more credits to build more shuttles, and soon there wouldn't be any credits to pay for anything.

Jacob McKenna's whole body was contracting, every muscle in his body trying to pull itself free. His body was vibrating with energy, and he could feel the enormous pressure in his jaw from him clenching down. He became aware of a sharp pain in his hand. Blood was running down his closed fist, shards of crystal protruding from between his fingers.

McKenna walked over to a cabinet in the wall, grabbed the napkin that was under the remaining crystal tumblers, and wrapped his hand in it. He took a tumbler and poured himself another whiskey, blood soaking the white cloth.

***

A red message flashed on the DDU. Usually, the operator would act on it immediately, but there was no operator. Nor were there any operators monitoring the DDUs on the other shuttles. Instead, all the Zuma employed operators who had to fly the shuttles back and pick up Jacob McKenna and the engineers and scientist, were lying next to each other on the Martian soil. Each one had an identical pulse burn above the right ear, which had killed them instantly.

COMMUNICATION OFFLINE.

Captain Raymond Santo watched the red message flash in front of him.

"That will be all," he said to the security officer who was standing beside him. Since their departure from Earth, Santo had had members of his team shadowing the Zuma operators on each shuttle. They'd had to learn everything they could about operating the shuttles. As the shuttles were pretty autonomous, it was not a big ask. The biggest hurdle was getting the passwords and codes from them, but his team was the best of the best and it proved to be no problem at all. The operators had thought they were all on the same side.

It was no longer Jacob McKenna's mission.

***

The shadow moved quickly and swiftly through the house. It had never been here before, but it knew what it was doing. Without setting off any alarms, it found the two people it had come for and sedated them. They would not know what happened to them until they woke up much later. The shadow stuffed them into the back of the hydrocar it found in the garage and drove back to its hideout. There it put them into a much tighter cargo hold where they would be asleep in for most of their journey. Then the shadow disappeared again.

# | forty-five |

The green line guided Drake and Jimmy out of the junkyard and toward their destination.

When Drake had woken up that morning, he was surprised to find Jimmy already up and dressed. Jimmy was usually a late sleeper, but Drake assumed it must have been the excitement of getting this all behind them that woke him so early.

"This is it, partner. Today we will learn our fates," Drake said once they left the last building of Spirig behind.

Jimmy was quieter than usual, staring out the window. They drove in silence for a few minutes. Then Drake said, "Jimmy, buddy, you okay?"

"We're partners, right?" he replied.

"You know we are. What's gotten into you?" Drake was genuinely worried now. Zuma Corp was only a short drive away, and they would be there in just a few minutes. Now was not the time for life-changing heart-to-hearts.

"If you had to choose between the lieutenant and me, you'd pick me, right?" Jimmy asked.

Drake swerved the Hydrostar off the road, kicking up rocks and dust. It took a few seconds for the big truck to come to a halt.

"Buddy, we are minutes away from either getting killed or getting out of this. You better tell me whatever it is you need to tell me right now before we go any further."

Drake waited for Jimmy to spill the beans, but Jimmy just stared straight ahead out the window, not making eye contact. If the Hydrostar stayed put on the side of the road for too long, an emergency crew was sure to be notified. Drake had to push Jimmy.

"Either talk to me or get out. I can't do this with you only half-assing it," Drake said, one eye on the clock.

"I'm just nervous, I guess," Jimmy finally said. "I just wished . . ."

Drake had no choice but to keep moving. If an emergency crew got called out, they would track them, log the incident, and make it impossible to shake them.

Once back on the road, he tried again.

"What, Jimmy? What do you wish?"

"Nothing, man. This, all this, ya know? Just that we get out alive, I guess," Jimmy said without conviction.

For a split second, Drake considered stunning him with his pulse gun and dealing with him later, but he couldn't bring himself to do it. He just had to hope Jimmy would snap out of it soon.

"I need you here, man. We only have one shot at this. Okay?" Drake tried to motivate him.

"I know, I know," Jimmy replied. He gave Drake an empty smile that made him regret not stunning him.

\*\*\*

Jumping in the Mongoose, Lieutenant Wells felt the adrenaline buzzing in her veins and making her skin tingle. Her team still had a few hours to get to Zuma, but she knew Drake and Jimmy would be there in a few minutes. She gave the officer behind the wheel the go-ahead to drive and opened her HIC to make a call.

"Hey," Drake said.

"Hi, Drake. Just wanted to check in one last time. You okay?" she asked.

"Sure, just nerves, right Jimmy?" Jimmy looked even more nervous.

"Well, try your best not to be, all right? If McKenna thinks something is wrong, there's no telling what he might do."

"Easier said than done, Officer. Some of us lack the training for this, you know?" Drake said, although he was a bit more at ease.

"I know, and I think what you guys are doing is very brave." Wells immediately regretted using the word brave and hoped she didn't sound patronizing.

"Hear that, Jimmy? She called me brave." Drake said, elbowing Jimmy in the ribs. Jimmy smiled weakly, again. "Well, I tried," Drake said to no one in particular.

"Now, remember to have your ARP recording the moment you make contact. If he has a scanner or something similar running and asks you to stop it, do it. No point in risking this, but try to get a livestream. It would make it a lot easier for my team. If you have to switch it off, only switch it back on when you need us to move in. Got that?" Wells hoped he would follow orders and not see them as suggestions.

"Ma'am, yes, ma'am," Drake replied.

Wells was happy to see him more relaxed now. She did, however, wonder why Jimmy was so miserable. Surely he was the more experienced criminal here. Maybe even the only one? Shouldn't he be the one chatting and wisecracking?

"I'll see you guys soon." Wells cut the connection.

She really wished Jimmy hadn't looked so nervous, because it made her nervous too.

*** 

Shortly after leaving Spirig, the Hydrostar crossed the Zuma border, and Drake had to accept all the on-screen waivers. He switched on the Autodrive to do this, but once he'd finished, he retook control of the big truck. The Zuma compound where they first met McKenna was now very close, and it was time to put their game faces on.

Jimmy was still pretty sullen. Drake wished he could see inside his head to know what was going on. Why, of all days, did he have to be in a mood today? Drake wondered if there was something more to it, but a sign showing the turn off they needed to take popped up on the screen. The compound would soon be visible.

"Well, buddy, here we go. I'll do the talking, and you can just keep sulking in the background, okay?"

"Just nerves, ya know?" Jimmy mumbled.

Drake decided to ignore him and concentrate on the job at hand. Why fucking now, Jimmy?

Drake steered the Hydrostar around a tight hairpin curve and the Zuma buildings they'd left behind just a few weeks ago rose in front of them. Two security guards stood in front of the gate. As the Hydrostar approached, they took a few steps forward. Drake slowed the Hydrostar down and brought it to a stop just short of them. One took a few steps back. The other came over to Drake's window.

"Name and appointment code?" the security officer barked at him, his arm held up to Drake's face to accept the requested information on his HIC.

"Hey, buddy. Not sure if you were here a few weeks ago, but my partner and I did a pretty big job for your boss, and we're back to have a chat with him. Can you let him know we're here, pretty please?"

The security officer did not flinch and kept his arm in Drake's face.

"Name and appointment code, or fuck off," Drake's new friend repeated.

Drake decided to try a new approach.

"Hey, let's keep it friendly, okay?" Drake tried. "My name is Benjamin Drake. I don't have an appointment code, but I'll guarantee you that if you tell Mr. McKenna that we are here, he will give you one." Drake watched the security officer just stand there. Was this guy one of Penta's new androids he'd heard about?

"Are you one of us?" Drake asked the guard and pinched his arm, just next to the HIC. The guard snapped his arm back, and his colleague raised his pulse gun.

"What the fuck are you doing?" the officer yelled, very human-like.

"Just checking something," Drake said. "How about that call to Mr. McKenna?"

The security officer walked over to his partner. They had a bit of a chat, and then he went into a small cubicle next to the gate.

***

"Sir, we have Benjamin Drake here, and he says he wants to see you. He has no appointment code and he is traveling with Jimmy Something. They are both on Penta's wanted list, sir. Do you want me to engage?"

What did those two idiots want now? More credits? Most likely spent it all on drugs and women in Shangcorp somewhere and thought they could come back for some more. McKenna had no time to deal with this, but his curiosity got the better of him.

"Send them in and get a squad ready to meet them in the warehouse."

McKenna made his way to the warehouse and decided he would give them one minute before killing them.

***

The gate swung open. The second security officer stepped aside, gun still pointing at them.

Drake assumed it meant they could go in, so he put the Hydrostar in drive and passed through the gate. He made sure to give the guard a single finger salute on the way through.

"We're in!" Drake slapped Jimmy on the chest.

Jimmy looked like he was about to vomit.

# | forty-six |

The three circles just kept on dancing, never touching or merging.

This was her third attempt at contacting Karen Giles and Lieutenant Wells was getting more worried at every failed attempt. Had she gotten cold feet? Was all the stress just too much for her? It did not really affect the mission, but Wells was still a little disappointed that she hadn't even told her. They had, after all, become friends through all this. Maybe she felt ashamed? Heaven knows, Wells did put enough pressure on her.

Lt. Wells hoped that she was at least somewhere safe and not locked up in some basement under Jacob McKenna's liar.

\*\*\*

The warehouse felt smaller than Drake remembered it. The shuttles were now gone, but he struggled to imagine four of them crammed in here. McKenna stood in the center of the building with three guards either side of him. A few more guards were scattered around, watching them. McKenna had certainly stepped up his security. Drake shut down the Hydrostar. Sweat was running down Jimmy's temples. Drake should have stunned him when he had the chance.

"Right, buddy, let's get rid of those damn wanted labels," Drake said. He jumped out before Jimmy could unnerve him even more.

As his feet hit the ground, all the guards lifted their pulse rifles at his head.

"Wow! What sort of a welcome is this?" Drake said, hands above his head.

Behind him, he could hear Jimmy getting out as well.

Jacob McKenna stepped forward, and the guards matched him, staying one step behind him at all times.

"Mr. Drake. I don't usually entertain unannounced visitors, but considering our previous favorable encounter, I broke my own rule. Please don't make me regret it." McKenna stopped in front of Drake.

"I'll try my best, but no promises," Drake smiled. The pulse rifles were still aimed squarely at his head.

McKenna stared at Drake, and he realized it was still his turn.

"So, Mr. McKenna, we heard through the not-so-reliable criminal grapevine that Captain Santo has gotten a bit ambitious and decided to not return your shuttles to you."

It appeared that McKenna was not in a very talkative mood.

"So, Jimmy and I thought we would offer you our services in procuring you some more of that Bismuth you need to get off this planet. Assuming that you are going after Captain Santo, that is."

McKenna took another step toward Drake.

"How do I know that you two are not in bed with Santo and just trying to get more credits out of me?" McKenna asked.

"I can assure you, Mr. McKenna, that the only person I want to share a bed with is you." Tough crowd.

McKenna nodded toward the closest guard. He stepped in front of McKenna and got really close to Drake, his pulse rifle almost touching Drake's nose.

"Please escort these gentlemen out," McKenna said.

If he called out to McKenna now, he might get shot, so Drake just smiled at the guard, inches away from him. He remembered that his ARP was still on and that McKenna didn't say anything, which meant he had never scanned for active ARPs. This meant that Lieutenant Wells would be watching this play out. She could not risk communicating with him, so he was flying solo, but at least she was aware of the situation.

Watching McKenna walk away, Drake hoped that he had done enough.

*** 

When Drake was driving past the gate and graciously giving the guard the one-finger salute, his other hand had pressed the button on the small box mounted under his seat. The device, which Lt. Wells got from Karen Giles, could capture the local security footage and also broadcast to it. Within a few minutes, it would have recorded enough footage to play back a loop on all of McKenna's DDUs showing scenes of no activity at all. All he had to do was get the Hydrostar inside the warehouse and keep it there until Wells' team could show up unnoticed. As long as he was there, the box would show that there was no one approaching or raise the alarm. But if he was escorted out, the device would fall out of range, and Lt. Wells and the Penta team would arrive to meet a small but capable security team, ready to fight.

*** 

"Crap. Drake is not going to stay in there long enough. We need to prepare for contact on arrival," Wells told her team as she watched McKenna walk away from Drake.

They were still minutes away and needed more time. If Drake left the warehouse with the Hydrostar, the signal to McKenna's DDUs would fade, and he would see them approach. This would give him ample time to either escape or bunker down and defend his position. Either way, without Drake's Hydrostar in there, the mission would most likely fail. McKenna was rich and paranoid and surely had some kind of escape plan in place if things went south.

Wells watched the minutes count down on the Mongoose's DDU with a growing feeling of doom and got ready to risk contacting Drake. Then Jimmy appeared on the screen, holding a pulse gun to Karen Giles's head.

*** 

"Okay, buddy, let's get rid of those damn wanted labels," Drake said and jumped out.

Jimmy opened his own door and got out as well, but didn't follow Drake. Instead, he stayed put next to the Hydrostar. His heart was beating in his ears, and his palms were clammy, but he knew he had to do this.

Drake and McKenna started to talk, and all the guards' focus was on Drake. Jimmy slowly and silently moved to the side of the Hydrostar to access the cargo hold underneath. He opened the latch and retrieved his bargaining tool.

As McKenna was walking away, Jimmy Something calmly walked past Drake and stopped a few feet in front of him. The guards backed up, commanding him to stop, and McKenna turned to see what the commotion was.

"I caught your spy. She's the one who stole your data."

Comprehension dawned on McKenna's face. "It was you? Who exactly are you working for? Santo? Penta? Is it Shangcorp?"

"I want safe passage to Shamo and one million credits." Jimmy tried to get the focus back on him.

Benjamin Drake was watching, mouth ajar, as the knife was going into his back. He knew Jimmy was a criminal and should not have been surprised, but he thought he had gotten to know Jimmy, and he even thought they had become friends.

"Did you hear me?" Jimmy shouted, his eyes turning red with rage and tears.

McKenna stopped. "Yes, Mr. Something, I heard you. Please hand over Giles. I will get you to Shamo, with some credits to last you a while."

"I said one million," Jimmy pushed the pulse gun harder against Giles's head. She seemed to have been paralyzed and offered no resistance.

"I heard you, Mr. Something, but unfortunately, I do not have one million credits to give you," McKenna said in a slow and measured tone. "You see, Captain Santo's little stunt has cost me everything I had. So if you don't mind, HAND OVER THE FUCKING ENGINEER!"

McKenna's outburst got them all by surprise. Veins were pulsating on McKenna's temples. Drake knew that things were about to go south for all of them and willed Wells to hurry up and come rescue them.

*** 

The Mongoose came flying around the corner. It fishtailed, but the operator got control again and straightened it out. It barrelled down toward the two guards standing at the gate of the Zuma Corp warehouse, with no intention of slowing down. The guards waved their arms and, seeing that the vehicle was not slowing, tried to get ready to shoot. It all happened so quickly that the Mongoose was already on top of them by the time they had it in their sights.

The occupants of the Mongoose barely registered the bumps as it drove over the guards and broke through the gate, stopping short of the entrance to the warehouse. Bursting in with the Mongoose might put Drake, Jimmy, and Karen at risk, and a more calculated approach was needed.

"Drake, Something, and Giles are considered friendly until I say otherwise, understood?" Wells briefed the team as they quickly gathered around her. Although Jimmy had a gun to Giles's head at the moment, she had to give him the benefit of the doubt, although her gut told her not to.

They only had minutes to get in and get the job done. The device Karen Giles gave Wells was projecting a short loop of what happened seconds before Drake and Jimmy arrived. If one of the security guards monitoring the DDUs paid close enough attention, they would figure it out and most likely send more guards to check out the gate and warehouse. Time was not on their side.

The team quickly split up into two groups: Wells' group, team Alpha, went straight for the open door of the warehouse, and the second group, team Bravo, flanked it, looking for a secondary entrance. Keeping an eye on Drake's feed via her ARP, it seemed that McKenna and Jimmy were at an impasse. As long as no one did anything stupid, it should give them enough time to enter the building and take charge of the situation.

Jimmy still had the gun pointed at Karen's head, and Wells made a mental note to give him one shot at lowering it before she would do it for him. Permanently. Team Alpha reached their goal, and they took cover positions, giving team Bravo a chance to secure entry as well. Within seconds Wells got the message that Bravo had located an entry. Wells gave the command and both teams entered the building, pulse rifles set to kill.

# | forty-seven |

The convoy made slow progress over the Martian soil. Everything was going better than planned, which filled the team, and especially Santo, with confidence and boosted the morale even higher. It was a surreal experience, one which Santo had to remind himself of occasionally, that they were actually walking on another planet, thousands of kilometers from home.

Santo did still call Earth home, as he had no intention of staying on this desolate rock for any longer than he had to. The team knew the plan, and it was for this reason they had signed up. Once the fighting was done and Mars was under their control, he would open up communications with Earth's Big Five.

The Big Five—Shangcorp, Penta, Nikolatec, Citro, and Nestem—had a very fragile peace treaty. They were all still trying to establish themselves as the dominant corporation, and without going to war and annexing land, it was close to impossible. With the Moon and Mars had declared terra nullius, it was even more difficult. But if another player, a smaller nonthreatening company, slipped through the cracks and stole Mars from underneath their noses and claimed it, they would come running to buy it from them.

This was the plan all along. Years ago, Santo had come across McKenna in a case he was working and realized the degree of the man's megalomania. A seed was planted, and Santo kept an eye on McKenna's progress, watching him buying up smaller companies and expanding his own empire. He was still nowhere near the Big Five, but his ambition would not slow down.

Over time his expansion slowed down, as other companies got wise to his growth and stopped him where they could. Santo knew that this would make McKenna desperate, and that's when he had decided to set his plan in motion.

Santo's ambition propelled him through the ranks at Penta Corp at a faster than average pace, but once he became captain, it slowed down. The old dinosaurs occupying the top jobs clung to them and their power for as long as possible, and the number of captains and competition grew every year. He knew he had to find an alternative path.

Convincing McKenna to go along with his plan was a piece of cake. The man was so desperate to expand his legacy that he never questioned Santo's motives or why he chose him to partner up with. Santo would supply the fuel and the soldiers; McKenna would supply the vessels and fund the project. The profits from the Mars mining would then be split fifty-fifty. Or at least, that was what Santo told McKenna.

Santo watched the red dust being kicked up by the boots in front of him and slowly settling down again, and it put him in a calm meditative state. A rare smile appeared on the captain's face.

*** 

Jacob McKenna and his security team had their backs to the open door. If they were to turn around, they would see what Benjamin Drake was desperately trying not to stare at and alert them to. Lt. Wells and team Alpha had entered the building and silently took down the Zuma Security personnel stationed on their side of the warehouse.

Hidden from both McKenna and Drake was team Bravo who had also dispatched of their targets silently and now moved in on the group in the middle of the warehouse.

Wells raised a bent arm with a closed fist in the air, and team Alpha stopped and crouched. She didn't need to worry about team Bravo, as they would stay put until contact was made.

According to her intel, there were only six Zuma guards left now in the immediate vicinity, but there was one threat that she had not prepared for: Jimmy Something. Having pulled Karen out from god knows where and having a gun to her head really made things more complicated, but Wells knew the best thing was to stick to the plan, and eliminate everyone but McKenna. Then she would improvise and try to diffuse the Something situation. You have one chance, Jimmy, she warned him mentally.

With hand signals, Wells directed her team members to their positions. She stayed crouched behind a thick column and watched her team get into place. Everyone was ready and awaiting her command.

*\*\*\**

Drake watched as the Penta security officers entered the warehouse and silently killed the Zuma officers. He knew shit was about to go down and, most likely, Jimmy too.

"Jimmy, what the fuck, man?" Drake yelled out, making sure the attention was on him now. The Zuma guards refocused their guns on him. "This is not quite what we talked about, now is it, buddy?"

Jimmy's knuckles were white with tension, and his eyes filled with fear.

"I heard you and your girlfriend talking, ya know. She's not getting me out. I-I have to do it myself," Jimmy stammered, tears rolling down his cheeks.

"What the hell are you talking about?"

McKenna seemed to have calmed down for the time being and was watching the drama unfold in front of him.

"I heard her. She said there was nothing she could do for me."

"How? Doesn't matter. You are wrong, though. She is going to help us, but I don't think whatever this is that you're doing now is going to help." Drake was getting nervous that Wells and her team might be jumping in soon, sending pulses everywhere.

"You don't get it, ya know?" Jimmy said with a tremor in his voice, his emotions getting the better of him. "Doesn't matter what happens here. You're going back home, and I'm still screwed. She was right.

They'll never just let me go." Jimmy turned his attention back to McKenna. "I'll settle for safe passage and whatever credits you got."

"Jimmy. . ." Drake didn't actually know what to say.

McKenna moved toward Karen Giles. "Watching you die will bring me some sort of satisfaction, I guess," he sneered.

"Hey, that's not cool, man. I thought you might just fire her or something, ya know?' Jimmy protested, clearly not having thought his plans through, again.

"What I do with her is none of your business. Hand her over, and I'll give you what you asked for." McKenna reached for Karen.

"Wait, wait, wait," Jimmy said, stepping back and pulling Giles with him. "Um, I need a minute, ya know? I'm not sure—"

One Zuma guard dropped to the floor, and before his body hit the ground, the other five followed him, leaving McKenna standing all alone in front of Drake, Jimmy, and Karen Giles.

***

Jimmy's so-called plan was collapsing and Wells knew this was when he would be most unpredictable. She jumped up and fired her pulse gun at the head of the security officer in front of her. The rest of her team stepped out of the shadows and took down the other five guards. They came forward, half of them focused on McKenna and the other on Jimmy. Well trained and experienced, they also kept a cautious eye on Drake.

"Jimmy, this is your only chance." She walked toward him. "Drop that gun right now and let Karen go. I'm not giving you a second chance or a countdown. Do it now!"

She steadied herself. Jimmy was holding Karen Giles close to his body, but he had obviously never done this before and had his whole head exposed. Wells had no doubt whatsoever that she could take him out without harming Karen. Jimmy was suspended in time, making no movements or apparently any decisions, so Wells squeezed the trigger.

***

Drake knew his friend's life was about to end. He saw the tendons on Wells' gun hand flex.

Without deciding to, without even thinking about it, Drake jumped in front of Jimmy. At the same moment, the pulse gun let out its electric blue projectile.

*** 

Time didn't slow down or go into slow motion, but Wells saw everything clearly as Drake jumped in front of Jimmy, as the projectile hit Drake in the neck, as he hit the ground like a sack of rocks. Jimmy still had Giles in his grasp, but he was now standing next to her. Wells aimed again and fired a second shot. This time no one jumped in front of it, and Jimmy joined Drake on the floor. Her team rushed to secure the scene. Someone grabbed Giles and escorted her away. McKenna was also taken away, in restraints.

Minutes since they had entered the warehouse, it was all done.

# | forty-eight |

"You are indeed one of the best, Lieutenant Wells," Captain Sturgis said. He stood up from his desk and walked over to her, hand extended. Wells grabbed it and shook it.

"Thank you, sir. Just doing my job."

"Well, you did it very well." He motioned for her to sit down. "Now, let me hear what happened, directly from the source, so to speak."

Wells started her debrief, picking up just days after her first meeting with Captain Sturgis. She had been banking on Jimmy and Drake causing some chaos, but she had not even considered that Jimmy would kidnap Karen Giles and her daughter. Despite his criminal activities in the past, she had not thought he would resort to violence. She was quite surprised that he could pull it off right under Drake's nose, but it did not change her plans at all, although she had used a bit more caution. Their primary aim was to get McKenna alive, and the secondary was to protect Drake and Jimmy. Giles and her daughter were somewhere in between. Shooting Jimmy had been deliberate. Drake less so. Once Karen and Alex were safe, Jacob McKenna, the owner of Zuma Corporation, was arrested on undisclosed charges. He was currently in interrogation.

"Which brings us up to date," Wells concluded.

"I must admit that I am not a fan of your unorthodox methods, Lieutenant, but your results speak for themselves. Congratulations. Your reputation is well earned."

"Thank you, sir," Wells said, feeling drained after having to relive it all again.

*** 

Three floors below the basement parking of the Penta headquarters building, Jacob McKenna was sitting naked in an empty room on the floor. There was no one with him, but a hidden voice said, "Jacob McKenna, you are in a private holding room in an undisclosed location. We need you to tell us everything about your involvement with Captain Raymond Santo and your plans to occupy Mars. We will be recording this room and will contact you again once we are satisfied with your report. Until then, there will be no contact, food, or water. If you die before we get our information, we will simply use data extraction to retrieve it from your Human Interface Console and your Augmented Reality Projector. The choice is yours. Goodbye."

The room went silent.

Usually, people lasted hours, if not days, before talking. Some did die down here, never saying a word. Penta had enough resources to get away with it. But Jacob McKenna's will to survive was even more stronger than his ego; he started talking immediately.

Wells sat next to one of the two beds in the small room, watching the DDU above it.

"All the vitals are in range," the nurse had said. "He should fully recover."

Back at the warehouse, when she saw the fear in Jimmy's eyes, she had activated stun mode. She had put Jimmy in that position after making sure he heard the conversation with Drake. She had wanted him to be unpredictable, and she got what she wanted. He did not deserve to die because of her actions. She had also put Karen Giles in the middle of all this, and right then, he had a gun to her head. So she had two people in the middle of a complex operation that she had put there but needed urgently out of the way. So she decided to shoot Jimmy with a stun-pulse and eliminate him from the equation.

What she did not expect was for Drake to put his own life on the line for Jimmy Something. Even a stun-pulse could be fatal, especially if it hit you in the head or neck. The moment she hit him, she feared the worst, but she still had to deal with Jimmy. Once he was down as well, she ran over to Drake, a sense of regret filling her.

She still carried that regret sitting in the small room but felt it fading when Drake started to stir, and a smile appeared on his bruised face.

"Hey Lieutenant," he said, eyes still closed.

"Pretty confident, aren't you, Drake?" she replied.

His face was sore and bruised from the pulse projectile, and hitting the hard floor hadn't done him any favors either. He strained to open his eyes.

"When you're right this many times, it's hard not to be."

Wells wanted to do something to him, but she was unsure what.

"You knew my gun was set on stun, didn't you?"

"Maybe. Let's say I took a calculated risk."

"Calculated or lucky?" Wells asked, knowing it was the latter.

"I'll have to look up the difference once my HIC has been replaced," Drake said, lifting his arm up. "Seems they aren't pulse resistant."

"I'll get Penta to issue you a new HIC. One that was actually made this century. You can thank me later."

Drake's head was pounding, and all he wanted to do was sleep, but he tried his best to stay awake.

"So, how's McKenna doing?"

"I've never seen anyone confess so quickly or so thoroughly before in my life!"

Drake laughed, but the pain in his head doubled, and he resorted to a chuckle.

"Are they really necessary?" Drake nodded toward Jimmy, who was asleep, and cuffed to his own bed.

"It's just formality. We're almost done confirming all the data. Captain Sturgis had assured me this morning that you will both walk out of here free men. Poor, but free."

"Poor?" Drake asked, but immediately realized the obvious answer.

"Yes. As Penta citizens, you're not allowed to keep gains from illegal activity. You didn't really expect to walk out of here free and keep all those credits, did you?" Wells asked incredulously.

"Nah, what do you take me for?" Drake said, trying to look hurt. He'd never even considered losing the credits.

"And the Hydrostar . . ." she whispered, feeling really low for kicking him when he was down.

"Maybe you should just arrest me! What the hell am I going to do now? No credits. No truck. Fuck . . ."

Jimmy moved but stayed asleep. His vitals were stable, and Wells knew he would wake up soon too. He'd be pissed at having the cuffs on, but he'd get over it.

"We've notified the Mars settlement of Santo's plans. Penta is working day and night to come up with a way to save as many lives as possible. It looks like a full surrender for the Mars colonists might be the best course of action for now. They are vastly outnumbered and outgunned. Penta have employed Karen and her team from Zuma, and they are already working on building a fleet of fast shuttles to send an army to deal with Santo."

Drake stared at the ceiling, not saying anything. Lt. Wells knew what he was thinking.

"You did not know what Santo and McKenna were planning. None of this or any bloodshed from this is your fault. You were just the unlucky idiot who Bob Turner decided to sacrifice."

Drake knew that she spoke the truth, but still couldn't let it go. If war broke out, he had to take some responsibility. Accidentally or not, he was linked to this. The crushing weight of guilt sat heavy on his chest.

"I know. If anyone is to blame, it's this dickhead over here," Drake said, motioning toward Jimmy, hoping Wells bought the act.

Apart from being an accomplice to starting a war, he now had to start his life from scratch again, with no credits to his name or even a shitty Hydrostar. He wondered if Penta would go after Bob Turner too. He hoped they would.

His eyelids drooped and the warm blanket of sleep wrapped him up again. He wanted to get rid of the weight on his chest, so he happily gave in.

"Drake," Wells whispered, half-trying to not wake him. She stood up from her chair and moved closer to him. He was fast asleep. "Thanks for everything. I mean it."

She leaned over, kissed his forehead, and left the small room, ready to get started on her next mission.

CPSIA information can be obtained
at www.ICGtesting.com
Printed in the USA
LVHW031325241220
675070LV00007B/340